Saving EMILEE

"Violence is a dark contrast to what so many of us still believe in – love.

Robi Ludwig

To you, my readers.
The ones that still believe in me
Even when I sometimes stop believing in myself.

Table
Of Contents

Chapter ONE

EMILEE

THEY SAY WE are the writers of our own destinies. But I'm here to tell you that if that's the case, then I didn't pay enough attention in my literature class in high school. The story that I've been putting together for the last nineteen years was obviously written by some emo kid on a drunken bender after breaking into daddy's liquor cabinet and swallowing a bottle of mommy's anxiety pills. You can't make this stuff up. This isn't one of Shakespeare's greatest tragedies. There is nothing even remotely poetic about the life I lead.

Who am I?

Well, I can tell you with certainty that I'm not the same girl I was even ten years ago. Back then, I was a happy-go-lucky kid with a loving mother living in a happy home. It was just the two of us, but it was perfect. We didn't have much, her being a single mother and working two jobs. But what we had was filled with happiness, laughter, and love. We had a simple life, just the two of us, and didn't need anything more than this tiny home.

Then she fell in love, and everything started to change.

So, who am I now? I'm an introvert – not by choice mind you. I've been forced into solitude by society and their inclination to judge others on their imperfections – or what they perceive as imperfections. Their uncanny ability to point out the flaws of anything that goes against the perfect standards of what you're expected to be, how you're expected to look or dress. Because of the perfect societal *Karens* of the world, I have chosen to stay in hiding. But lately, I want to come out. I want to be seen. I want to admit that I'm not the only woman in the world that suffers as I have for most of my life. And I want to be free of it all.

Sitting on the edge of my bed, I shake away my wayward thoughts and focus on the task at hand. I tie my sneakers and make sure to double knot the laces, so they don't come undone while I'm working on my feet all day. I don't have to be at work for another hour – thirty minutes of which will be spent walking there – but I'm anxious to get out of the house. It's eerily quiet these days and I'd rather not stick around any longer than necessary. These rickety old four walls used to be filled with sounds of love and happiness but now resemble more of an empty tomb that no longer feels like a home but more like a prison.

My stomach rumbles loudly as I stand and reach for my favorite cardigan. I ignore it, reaching for the bottle of water on my nightstand instead, knowing that I'll fix myself a sandwich when I get to work. Ralph doesn't mind as long as I'm not ignoring the customers to fulfill my own needs. I never do of course. I depend too much on the extra tips considering I only make the basic waitress wages which isn't much, unfortunately.

I had hoped that I would have a better job by now but there isn't much to choose from in this small town. Independence is a town practically dwelling in the stone ages. Okay, maybe not that far back, but still. I used to watch the movie *Pleasantville* with Amber, who used to be my best friend in high school, and we'd make jokes about how Independence reminded us so much of the town in the movie. Everyone walking around with their plastic smiles and living their perfect little lives while ignoring the world changing all around them.

One last stop into my bathroom, I gaze at my reflection in the mirror and cringe slightly at the face staring back at me. My hair is pulled up into a tight ponytail and my pale complexion shines brightly in the florescent lighting – an artificial glow from an overuse of concealer beneath my eyes. An unfortunate side effect of malnutrition and lack of sleep. Malnutrition because I only eat once a day, and only on days that I work at the diner. Lack of sleep because I hate being in this house and have nowhere else to go. Sadly, neither of which I'll be able to remedy as long as I continue to live in this house. Don't get me wrong, I love this house. I grew up here. I've literally lived in the same house for my entire life. But it isn't the same since my mother died.

Running my fingers through my ponytail, I take in the rest of my appearance in the mirror. My Freedom Diner shirt hangs loosely on my frame. My cardigan feels heavy on my shoulders but hangs nearly to my fingers on each arm. It's springtime but it's already humid outside. Even in my bedroom, the air is hot and stale. My little window unit is just about worn out after having been used for five years already but I can't afford to replace it. I hate having to wear the sweater, but I don't need any questions from the customers if they notice the marks on my arms. Not that I should expect them to, I'm practically invisible to anyone that lives in this little town.

Walking out of my bedroom, I step into the quiet hallway. The air in the rest of the house is sticky and hot, you can practically cut through the humidity with a butter knife. There isn't air conditioning in any other part of the house besides my bedroom and even with the open windows, the breeze is minimal. Not that it matters since I primarily hide out in my room when I'm home, aside from when I'm cooking dinner. Thankfully, I only have to cook for one, so it doesn't take long before I'm able to close myself up in my room and curl up in front of the somewhat cool air conditioning.

Walking down the hallway to the front of the house, I run my fingertips along the cracked and peeling paint. The faded paint is littered with darker splotches of various shapes and sizes – the ghostly shadows of the past – telling the story of a time where pictures once hung proudly. Pictures that depicted a life full of love, vacations and time well spent with my mother. The story of my childhood once adorned the walls and flat surfaces throughout the house in full color only to disappear without a trace. I came home from working at the diner several months ago and they were all gone. A distant memory desperate to be forgotten. Even the photos that I took in high school while learning photography, along with my camera and laptop. Everything was taken from me, the last of my happiest memories.

Stepping out onto the porch, there's a slight reprieve from the horrid temperature inside the house. It's several degrees cooler outside, but still humid. The tickling sensation of sweat dripping down my back started almost instantly once I stepped out of my bedroom and I know it will only worsen as the day goes on. I've learned to ignore it as much as possible over the last several months.

Careful to avoid the loose boards on the porch, I turn my gaze to the wooden swing laying cracked and aged against the railing like a neglected trophy. Ivy and honeysuckle have already started creeping through the porch railings and overtaking the wooden atrocity that was meant to be the perfect place to sit and read while sipping on a mason jar of sweet tea on cool afternoons. "Probably no sense in daydreaming about that swing now." I say to myself as I tiptoe down the porch steps, keeping my feet as close to the sides as possible for fear of falling through one of the rotten boards. "It's probably as decrepit as the porch itself at this point. I'd end up breaking my neck the first time I sit on it and the seat finally breaks."

Thanks to the abundant amount of rain we've had lately, the grass is already taller than my ankles, tickling the sliver of skin between my sock and the hem of my jeans. I know I'll need to make time to mow it down soon. I'll just add that to my never-ending list of things I need to do. Several of my neighbors are already out mowing their own lawns as I walk down the street. Not even one of them bothers to look up or acknowledge my presence. It's like I don't exist unless I'm at work, and even then, they shout their orders at me like I'm a stranger, not even bothering to make eye contact. Everyone in this timeless town treats me like an outsider even though I've lived here since I was born nineteen years ago. I grew up with all their children, went to school with them, even played on the same softball team as several of them.

I don't even feel guilty when I don't bother to wave at anyone I pass. It doesn't matter anymore if they see me or not. I'm done waiting around for someone to notice me. I tried when I was younger to get them to see me, to reach out and offer help when I needed it. I've come to terms with being invisible knowing that it's only myself that'll be able to get me out of this town. I just have to keep my head down and my arms covered.

Following my normal everyday path to work, I pause for several minutes at the edge of the city park. There are no children playing today, it's early enough in the day that most of them are still in school. I watch as birds flit gracefully from branch to branch on the budding trees, inhaling the sweet scents of spring. The sun shines brightly through the branches, igniting the small buds with multicolored flames like twinkling lights at Christmas time.

This is honestly my favorite time of the year in this timeless town. When all the trees and flowers start to bud and bloom, igniting my senses with the sweetest fragrances. I only wish I still had my camera; I could immortalize the images rather than have to rely on my imagination to recall them later. Unfortunately, not only was my camera taken from me, but I don't even have a phone anymore. Just another piece of my past that I'll have to fight tooth and nail to get back. If only I had a better job, I could replace everything and start living my life again in peace.

I thought I had it all figured out. My mother saw my interest in photography when I was a freshman in high school. She worked hard to help me achieve my dreams, not only waiting tables at Freedom Diner – the same diner I work at now – but she was also a receptionist at the small doctor's office in town. I had dreams of graduating and going away to college. I wanted to be a nature photographer, traveling the world, and viewing the sites through the lens of a camera. And I would have, if only she hadn't gotten sick. When she died, everything changed.

Not that I mind working at Freedom Diner. Ralph is a great boss, and he takes care of his waitresses. He inherited the diner from his parents when they passed away a few years ago, but I remember eating there when I was a kid. On the days my mom was waiting tables, I would walk to the diner after school, and she'd let me sit in one of the booths toward the back of the diner and work on my homework. Mrs. Jacobs, Ralph's mother, would bring me a slice of pie and a jar of sweet tea. "To give you enough energy to get through all that schoolwork," she would tell me with a smile. She was like the grandmother that I never had.

The Jacobs family had run the diner in our little town for over fifty years. Ralph was a dishwasher for a long time before finally learning the ropes and the menu. I was happy that he kept it open after his parents' passing. This town might not be much, but the diner is the best place to eat in the entire county as far as I know. Of course, I've never been outside of Independence, so I don't know what else is available. But remember that I'm invisible. I'm really good at disappearing – in plain sight – and listening to the customers talking over their meals. To hear most of them talk, they'd probably starve to death if it weren't for Ralph's cooking. Especially the meatloaf. It's his grandmother's recipe, and everyone loves it.

Honestly, I worry about what's going to happen to the diner when Ralph is ready to let it go. He doesn't have any kids, he never married. He says he's been married to the diner for most of his life and couldn't make the time for anything, or anyone else. Unfortunately, that means there's no one for him to pass the apron to when he's gone. He doesn't have much staff either. He cooks and does dishes, by hand mind you, and his minimal wait staff does the rest of the cleaning and taking care of the customers. It's a lot of time on your feet for minimal pay but I can't picture myself doing anything else in this town.

Then, there's Amber. She's a waitress at Freedom Diner too. She was my best friend growing up, even though she's a couple years older than me. She graduated from high school when I was just a sophomore and we stopped hanging out as much. She didn't go to college, and she isn't married. She doesn't stay with anyone long enough to consider a long-term relationship. She's been working at the diner longer than I have, I didn't start there until my mom got sick and I dropped out of school to help her out around the house.

It still haunts me to this day how she was getting so much better. Even the doctor said it was looking good. Then I came home one afternoon from the diner to find her in her bed. I thought she was taking a nap, she'd always been so tired since she first found out she was sick and started her treatment. It wasn't anything new to find her napping in the middle of the day. But she didn't move when I walked into the room. She didn't wake up when I placed my hand on her shoulder. She was gone, my worst fears realized when I came home to find out that I truly was alone. They said she had been dead for several hours which means that she passed away shortly after I had left her that morning to go to work. My poor mother had spent the entire day alone in her bed, no one there to hold her hand as she took her last breaths.

Knowing that I'm almost to the diner, my fingers twist together nervously as I take several calming breaths to clear my thoughts. Amber should already be there, having worked the morning shift. She usually has something snarky to say to me when I get there because I'll be several minutes early, whereas she's always running late. It shouldn't bother me as much as it does, but it hurts when she pops off at me for no reason. She was always so sweet to me when I was younger, watching over me like the big sister that I could have had in another life.

It's horrible sometimes, the way things change as you get older. People that you thought you could count on to have your back tend to show their true self when you least expect it. The ones that should have taken care of you when you needed it the most, even if just a shoulder to cry on when everything fell apart, are the ones that turned their backs instead. They're the ones that hurt the most to watch walking away from you when all you want to do is run up to them and throw your arms around them, hold them close forever.

One of these days, I'll be the one walking away. I'll be the one that gets out of this town and never looks back.

Chapter Two

LANDON

CHECKING MY WRISTWATCH for the time, a groan builds in my chest before I turn my attention back to the computer screen. I have a meeting with a lawyer this afternoon and the plotter is taking forever to spit out my latest blueprint. As much as I need to leave if I'm going to make it across town in time for my meeting, I'm determined to check this print before I get it over to my foreman. I may own the company, Strong Designs, but I'm still the primary architect and I wouldn't have it any other way.

My father was an architect, as well as his father before him. I followed in both their footsteps when I decided to go to school and get my degree in architecture and minoring in engineering. Both my father and grandfather worked as architects here in the city. I took it a step further and started my own design company. Not only do I get to design the buildings going up around the city, and surrounding areas, but I have a construction crew that does the majority of the work. That allows us to continue working when the weather gets too cold to break ground for new construction. We were able to expand our services to offering reconstruction and remodels as well.

I didn't grow up in the city, however. I grew up in a small town about forty-five miles outside of the city called Independence. It's a boring little nowhere town. Granted, it's a great place to raise a family, which is what my grandparents did with me. They took me in when I was eight years old after my parents were killed in a car accident. I'll be honest, I believe that my grandmother was a saint to have put up with me during my teenage years. Looking back, I know I gave her a hard time. Especially after my grandfather died and it was just the two of us.

I wasn't a rebellious teen, at least I don't think I was. But I wasn't an easy one either. More than once, I snuck out of my second story window to go to parties. I even hooked up with cheerleaders under the bleachers after football games. Yeah, I was probably a glutton for punishment, only I never got caught. I knowingly took advantage of my grandmother's heavy sleeping and hearing loss more than I should have. But I was a good student too – I got good grades and graduated with honors. I went to college on a scholarship without having to put my grandmother or myself in debt. I worked my ass off for five years and graduated with my degree.

It didn't take me long working for someone else in the design field to know that I wouldn't be able to follow orders forever. I'm just not wired that way. I began planning and researching and finally opened my design and construction company four years ago. Since opening, we've become one of the top design houses in the state and I've had to increase my workforce so we could take on more jobs over a larger expanse on the map. It's a great feeling though when I can drive through the city streets and see so many buildings in the metro area that I designed myself.

A buzz sounds behind me on my desk pulling me from my thoughts and preventing me from slamming my fists against the top of the plotter in frustration. Walking over to my desk, I push the button. "Yes?"

"You're going to be late," my assistant Melodee replies into the small intercom device. "You told me to remind you so you could leave on time."

"Thank you, Melodee." My reply to her is short. It isn't her fault that the plotter has taken all the patience I have to spare for the day. I think it's time for an upgrade. I bought this machine new when I opened Strong Designs four years ago, but it's been used enough for ten years' worth of blueprints. If I had known four years ago what I know today, then I would have paid for a more expensive machine with a longer warranty. Making a mental note to research new plotters, I concede that the print won't be done before I have no choice but to leave. Grabbing my suit jacket from the back of my desk chair, I check to make sure my keys are still in my pocket and walk out of the office.

"I'll be back in an hour, Melodee," I call over my shoulder as I push the button to call the elevator car.

"Okay, Mr. Strong. Anything you need me to do while you're out?"

"No. I'm trying to print a blueprint, but I'll check on it when I return. I'll need to set up a meeting with the foreman so we can go over it together, but I want to double check the design first." I don't wait for her to say anything else as the elevator opens and I immediately step into the car. Thankfully, there is no one else in the elevator so I don't have to worry about pleasantries.

Taking the elevator down to the parking garage below the building, I pull my cell phone from my inner jacket pocket and check my emails. I have an email from the lawyer confirming our appointment this afternoon. I only wish I knew what the meeting was about. His original email to me requesting the meeting was vague and didn't specify what the reasoning was for contacting me.

It's a bright and sunny spring day today and everyone is out in droves. The streets are overcrowded with downtown lunch traffic, and it takes me an extra fifteen minutes to get to the lawyer's office. Stepping into the office, I'm immediately greeted by the receptionist with a pleasant smile. Her bright red hair is pulled up into a tight bun on top of her head, her lips overly painted with an odd shade of burgundy that clashes with her eyes and hair color. It makes me wonder if she put her makeup on in the dark this morning before coming to work.

"Landon Strong. I have an appointment with Mr. Nichols," I calmly state as I approach her desk. The nameplate in front of her blotter says her name is Rebecca and I smile to myself. She looks like a Rebecca. I bet she doesn't even shorten it to anything like Becky or Becca either. She probably insists that people call her Rebecca just because she's better than everyone and deserves to be addressed properly.

I know.

I know.

I shouldn't make snap judgments about people that I don't know. I swear, I never used to be so cynical. Having grown up in Independence, I got used to other people doing the same thing to newcomers when they happened to step foot into their precious town. It made me this way. I'll add it to the list of attributes that I need to work on. If my grandmother were here right now, she would probably slap me on the back of the head for being so judgmental of the beautiful young woman working the reception desk.

Trying to look at her with a different set of eyes, I wonder if she would be the type of person to go out for a night on the town. Maybe a nice dinner and dancing – vertical or horizontal doesn't matter to me. It's been months since I've had a beautiful woman under me.

No.

I just can't picture it. I've never been a fan of red hair to be honest. And that shade of lipstick is off-putting.

"Mr. Nichols has been expecting you," she replies with a forced smile. I don't miss how her eyes travel over my face, down my chest to my abs and stopping just above my waist where her view is cut off by the highbacked desk. She gets a wicked gleam in her eyes as I cross my arms over my chest impatiently. I've never been to this office before, never had a reason to meet with a lawyer before thankfully. I may have been a hellion growing up, but I didn't get into trouble. As her gaze wanders back up to my face, I lift my brows in question hoping that she gets the hint. I have nothing more that I want to say to her while I'm here. "Second door on the left," she finally relents.

Without a word, I turn away from the reception desk and walk toward the hallway. Pausing long enough to knock twice on the door that I hope belongs to Mr. Nichols, I open the door to a greying man in a three-piece suit sitting behind a huge mahogany desk. This guy obviously does well in whatever type of law he practices if he can afford such a monstrous desk as that. This isn't a bad location for an office either, so I know he pays a pretty penny for rent here.

"Ah," I watch silently, still standing in front of the now open door, as he stands behind his desk and extends his hand in my direction. "Mr. Strong. I was beginning to wonder if we were going to need to reschedule."

"My apologies." Walking forward the few steps it takes to get to his desk, I reach out and take his hand in mine in a tight squeeze. "The traffic was terrible."

"Yes, I suppose it would be for a Friday at this time." Releasing my hand, he sits behind his desk, and I take the seat across from him. The chair is vintage but doesn't make a single squeak or creak as I sink into the buttery soft leather. Again, I wonder to myself what kind of law this man practices to afford such niceties as these. "I hope you don't mind," he begins as he extends a hand toward his desk phone. "I'd like to have Rebecca join us for this meeting. She can take notes."

Just as I thought, she doesn't bother shortening her name. "No problem." He doesn't say anything into the phone as I would have expected, just pushes a button, and sits back patiently in his chair. Seconds later, his receptionist walks into the room, a tablet clutched against her chest. I watch warily as she saunters across the room, her gaze eating me up wantonly while she walks around to the side of the desk and takes the chair closest to Mr. Nichols. Her skirt is short enough to show the delicate curve of her ass as she crosses one leg over the other.

Suspicion burns through me as I watch how he looks at her when she sits next to him. I can't help but wonder if there's some sort of office romance situation taking place behind the scenes here. Not that it's any of my business but judging by the amount of grey hair he has, and the laugh lines carved deeply around his eyes, etched into his thick overly tanned skin, he has to be at least fifteen years her senior. "Thank you, Rebecca," Mr. Nichols says to her as she lowers the tablet to her lap. She returns his smile and I notice how his hand goes briefly to her thigh in a gentle caress. She doesn't move or otherwise dodge his touch which only confirms my suspicions that they are more familiar with each other than just a boss and employee. It doesn't go unnoticed that he is wearing a wedding band on his left hand. Judging by the fact that she isn't, I would assume this is an interoffice affair of some sort. A shiver runs down my spine at the thought.

"So," I begin in hopes of moving this along. I don't want to be here and have to witness their obvious display of familiarity any longer than necessary. "What is this meeting about?"

"Of course," Mr. Nichols says before clearing his throat and moving his chair closer to his desk. "I know you're a busy man." I watch as he fumbles through his desk drawer before pulling out a folder, several papers enclosed and held together by a large silver paperclip. He removes the paperclip and clears his throat again before he begins to read. "The last will and testament of Beverly Strong…"

I don't hear anything else that he says for several minutes. My grandmother had a will? I didn't realize that she would have anything left to will to anyone, much less anything that would need to be delivered to me by a lawyer. I have a trust fund that was left by my parents when they passed away. I wasn't able to touch it until I turned twenty-one and used part of it to start my business four years ago. I still have a huge chunk of it left but I don't touch it. My grandfather left me some money when he died six years ago that I added to my trust account.

"...five hundred thousand dollars as well as the house an all her personal effects left at the property in Independence." My attention is brought back to the lawyer as he continues to read. "You are the only remaining relative and therefore next of kin to the deceased. There will be no question about the delivery of the estate. Funds will be transferred into the account of your choosing by the close of business Monday. Do you have any questions?"

"No." Honestly, I'm not sure what I would even ask at this point. I knew that my grandfather had left her with enough so she would be taken care of over the years. But I had no idea that it was that much money. I'm not even worried about it. They can put it into the trust account with the rest of it. I'll most likely never touch it. I make enough from my business to keep me going and living comfortably for years to come. But it is nice to know that I'll have more to leave to my own family if I ever find someone that I'm ready to settle down with. Not that I've had much time to look in that department.

But the house.

What am I supposed to do with the house? "Do I have to keep the house?" I ask Mr. Nichols once he's finished putting the papers back into the folder.

I watch as he cocks his head to the side, his brows furrowing in confusion. "No. I don't suppose you do. There's nothing stopping you from putting it on the market."

"Very well. Do I need to sign anything?" I'm suddenly anxious to get out of this office. I have no intention of ever moving back to Independence so there's no reason for me to keep the house. I already pay someone for regular maintenance and upkeep on it, I have for the last several years since my grandfather passed away. I didn't want my grandmother to have to worry about making any repairs on the house herself. And I'd rather not use it as rental property. I've seen first-hand what people do to rentals and I don't want to be responsible for the maintenance when they tear it up.

"No. I'll have Rebecca contact the bank and begin the process of transferring everything. I'm assuming you'd like it put into your trust account?"

"Please."

"Then that's all we need for now. I'll be in touch if anything else comes up."

Standing, I reach out to shake his hand again. "Thank you." Nodding once at his receptionist, I show myself out the door. I'm ready to finish my work on that blueprint if it ever printed and call it a day. I'll start making plans this weekend on what to do with the house.

Chapter THREE

EMILEE

WEEKENDS ARE A LITTLE more hectic at the diner, but thankfully Ralph has extra help so Amber and I won't be running our legs off. Today is a typical Saturday. Breakfast and lunch on weekends are the busiest times requiring both Amber and I to work at the same time. We'll both leave just before the dinner crowd when a couple of high schoolers will come in to take over for us.

"Order up," Ralph calls from the pickup window. Knowing it's mine, I wander over to the window silently to pick up the plates and deliver them to my table in the back corner. "What's wrong with you?"

Lowering my brows, I glare at Ralph curiously. As hard as I try to hide my discomfort, he doesn't miss anything. I refuse to tell him, though, that I'm not feeling well. I haven't eaten anything all day because we've been busy, and I haven't had a chance to slow down long enough to make myself anything. I've been chugging water most of the day just to keep the full feeling in my stomach from distracting me from being able to do my job. "I don't know what you mean," I answer sheepishly, forcing a smile that I hope looks genuine and hoping that he'll drop it.

He gives me a one-sided shoulder shrug before turning back to the grill. The subject successfully dropped, I resume balancing my plates on my forearm and turn to carry them to my table where a family of three waits patiently for their meals. Gritting my teeth against the tremors moving through my body, I set the plates down on the table before straightening my posture and fisting my hands at my sides. "Can I get you anything else?"

"No." The response is short and to the point and not unlike what I would have expected. Even though I grew up in this town, no one pays much attention to me. God forbid they should show me the same courtesy they do to any other neighborly face in the town. I don't wait for anything further from the family as they cut into their food. Nodding my head once, I turn away from the table.

A few steps away from the table, I stop and face the front window of the diner. The weather is nice and clear today, the sun shining brightly against the hillside in the distance beyond the town limits. The view here has always been remarkable. The trees are blooming, bright with colorful buds that give the hills beyond the town an effect similar to a water painting. Standing in place for several minutes, I save the view to memory. I only wish I still had access to a camera. I would give anything to be able to burn the colors of the distant hillside to film to be cherished and admired forever.

Shaking my head, I turn away from the window and walk back to the counter where Amber is already rolling silverware. My dreams are far off memories, washed away with the death of my mother. I'll never have the opportunity to follow my dreams of being a photographer. Not only do I no longer have any equipment, but I'm just as stuck in this small town as the next person.

People don't generally leave Independence. Sure, they seem happy. They sit with their family and friends and enjoy Ralph's cooking. They socialize with each other and are friendly with neighboring tables. Talking with each other and sharing gossip like whispering schoolgirls. I don't have any doubt that they spend time whispering about me when I'm not close enough to hear their conversations. I see the way they all look at me as I approach to take their orders. I watch as their whispers and giggles fade the closer I get to their tables. They don't hide their gazes as they take in the sweater that I wear all year, even in the heat and humidity. I'm the odd duck – the outcast if you will.

It shouldn't bother me. I know what I am, and what I'm not. I'm an introvert – always happy hiding behind the lens of a camera. If only I still had one, maybe then I'd feel complete again. I haven't felt complete since my mother passed away. What I'm not is outgoing, attractive, fun. I don't spend my weekends hanging out with friends – not that I have any to speak of. I don't date – not that I wouldn't want to, but my options are limited. How can I bring myself to go on a date with someone that lives in the same timeless town as I do? Someone that knows everything about everyone. And how can I open up enough to someone that might tell the rest of the town my secrets? Not to mention, I don't like being touched – how could I ever allow anyone to get close to me?

God, I wish I could get out of this town.

"Emilee, can you grab me another pack of napkins?" Amber asks from the other end of the counter. She's still rolling silverware and I know I should help her. Not that we're running short on silverware, but it's better than standing around and daydreaming about getting out of a town that I'll never be able to escape.

"Yeah," I respond. Bending over, holding the groan that wants to escape my throat at the action, I grab another unopened pack of napkins from beneath the counter. Giving my hands something to do, I tear into the package as I walk over to where Amber is standing, patiently waiting for me to hand her the napkins. "Here you go." Setting the package down on the counter in front of her, I grab a few pieces of the silverware from the tray and help her roll it all up.

"You should come out with me tonight," Amber says quietly without lifting her eyes away from her chore. "There's a party on the other side of town. It's been a while since you've gone to a party with me."

My hands freeze, the silverware pinched between two fingers on one hand and the napkin in the other. "I don't think that's a good idea," I whisper, a slight tremor in my voice. Closing my eyes, I reign in my emotions, not willing to give away my feelings against going out. It's not that I don't want to hang out with Amber, we used to be close friends. We were thick as thieves in high school before she graduated. We used to do everything together. To be honest, I miss the carefree and innocent camaraderie that we used to have together.

"Oh, come on!" She looks up at me now, the excitement evident in her gaze at the prospect of me going to the party with her tonight. "It's been forever since we hung out together. It'll be fun!" She's practically bouncing on the balls of her feet.

I really don't want to let her down. But she'll never understand. To her, I'm probably just the depressed co-worker slash ex best friend that shut down after my mother passed away. That isn't it at all, though. I really would like to be able to hang out after work. Maybe make some new friends. But at what cost? She couldn't possibly understand what it's like for me at home now. The responsibilities that I've taken on since losing my mom.

Not to mention what happened the last time I did go to one of the parties that she likes to attend on the weekends. It was a few years ago, I was still a junior and she had already graduated and was still living at home with her parents. There was a boy there, Jason, he was a senior and Amber knew I'd had a crush on him all year. His family had moved here at the beginning of the year, so he was new in school and was still getting over that awkward new-kid stage.

Amber had convinced me to go talk to him. She'd managed to get a few drinks into me at that point and my inhibitions were nonexistent. I wasn't the only one that'd had a few too many drinks that night. When I went up to Jason, he smiled that charming smile that turned me into instant goo. Flashing his mega-watt white teeth at me with that perfect dimple on his left cheek, he threw an arm around my waist and pulled me into his hard body as if he had been waiting for me forever. He even ignored the snickering from the other guys standing around him when they saw him lean in and kiss my forehead.

That was all it took. The guy that I'd been crushing on all year paid me attention, showed me a little affection, and I was a goner. I'd have followed him anywhere. And it so happens that I did. Regardless of how much either of us had drank that night, I should have known better than to get into his truck with him. But I did it anyway because I was so elated at the attention he was showering me with. He drove us away from the party, parked us outside of town on a deserted country road. One thing led to another, and I was giving him my virginity in the bed of his pickup while laying on a tattered blanket that he had stashed behind the driver's seat.

It wasn't until it was over that I realized that he hadn't even asked me my name. I had just assumed that he knew it from school. Not that we hung out in the same crowds, but he could have heard it in passing at some point. He took me home immediately after and never talked to me again. My heart was shattered when I went to school the following Monday and he treated me as if I didn't exist. He laughed alongside his friends when they whispered and shot accusatory glances in my direction.

It was then that I decided I had no desire to date anyone in Independence. I'd rather be single and become the town spinster than deal with the politics and idiocies of a small town.

"Hey," Amber pulls me from my thoughts and places a hand on my forearm. "Earth to Emilee." She pulls her hand back as if she's been burned the instant I jerk my arm away from her touch. "Sorry."

Shaking my head, I clear thoughts of Jason from my mind. The past is the last thing I should be dwelling in. I have enough going on in my present to keep me focused on finding a way out of here. "Thank you for the invitation, Amber. But I need to get home after work here. I have things that I need to do." Of course, I don't tell her what those things are that keep me home every evening after work. The things that keep me from being able to go out and meet people and make friends. Things that make me afraid of getting too close to anyone.

"Your loss then." Amber huffs out a breath and turns to walk away. She makes a trip around the dining room, checking on her tables to make sure everyone is still enjoying their meals. It's only then that I look around and realize that all my tables are empty.

Grabbing an empty container, I walk around and clear the plates and empty glasses from my tables, pocketing my few dollars in tips in my apron, and head to the kitchen to clean up.

Chapter Four

Emilee

A SHELL. AN EMPTY, soulless shell is all I've become in my life of nineteen years. There is no meaning, no reasoning for my days to draw on from one to the next with no hope of a happily ever after in sight. There is no laughter, no smiling, no reason for being other than working at this miserable diner every day for pennies on the dollar. I can't even remember the last time I was happy.

Then there's Amber. Waltzing into the diner at ten minutes past the start of her shift, singing to herself lightly without a care in the world. She's the vision of carefree with her high ponytail shining in bright red – courtesy of Clairol – and her bright pink fingernails. She wears her shirt loosely tied around her waist with the top three buttons undone, her skirt pulled higher to show more leg. To look at her, you'd think we slung cocktails at the local watering hole rather than delivering Ralph's famous meatloaf to the town locals.

The same locals that hide in the shadows, safely protected in their own homes and dead-end jobs, while ignoring the ever-changing world around them.

In another life – or another place – I could have been like Amber. I could have had a carefree existence as I travelled the globe, viewing the wonders of the world through a lens. I had a happy childhood even if it was just me and my mom for so long. My mother worked hard at two jobs just to make sure I had everything I needed as I was growing up. She was eager to help me attain my dreams; supporting me in my love of photography and encouraging me to make it into a career. Everything was great until she got cancer and died my senior year of high school. I never finished school after skipping the last semester of my senior year to help take care of her, and now I work at the local diner just to make ends meet. My goals have always stretched further than the horizon and remain vastly unattainable.

We had talked frequently about me returning to school for my GED and then continuing to college to pursue a career in photography. She was getting better and better each day that passed and felt there was no reason for me to continue putting my life on hold. At least, that's what we thought.

I miss her optimism.

I miss her ability to find the silver lining in everything that could possibly have gone wrong.

I miss our life together.

It was a great life – until it wasn't.

"About time you showed up," I mumble under my breath as Amber reaches for her apron behind the counter.

"Sorry I'm late," Amber calls out in her sing-song voice as she ties the apron behind her back and shoves a pencil into her tight ponytail. "You wouldn't believe the day I've had so far."

I tune her out automatically as I rip my apron from around my waist and toss it beneath the counter. I'm anxious to get out of here and get home. As much as I'm sure Amber is eager to brag about her latest conquest, I just don't have the desire – or the time – to listen to it.

"Not so fast, Emi," Ralph calls from the kitchen. "You know you have to put these dishes away before you leave."

"Ah, come on!" I exclaim. "You know I have to be out of here at a certain time. It's not my fault Amber was late, and I had to care for her tables."

"Not my problem. Rules are rules." Ralph is standing on the other side of the window with a scowl on his face, and his hands on his hips. He's not a bad guy but he runs a tight ship around here. He's had the diner since his parents passed a few years ago and has carried on their tradition with the menu and the short staff. But he's right, rules are rules.

I toss a glare at Amber as she ambles out to the dining room to flirt with the few guests that are left finishing their dinners. Ralph doesn't say anything else to me as I put away the clean dishes and wipe down the counters again before finally jogging through the door to walk home.

My feet are aching in my tennis shoes while I walk as quickly as I can through town. At a normal pace, I can make it between my house and the diner within thirty minutes. I'm already late getting home and don't want to take any more time, so I calculate in my head how long it'll take me if I cut through a few yards and alleys. Picking up the pace, I cut diagonally through the parking lot of the dollar store, barely dodging a car as it backs out of its space without looking.

Twenty minutes. It takes me twenty minutes to get to my porch steps from the diner and my legs feel like overcooked spaghetti noodles. Reaching out, I grab the wobbly banister and pull myself up the three steps to the porch. Standing in front of the door, I take several deep breaths to calm my racing heart. It was a brisk walk but with the way my body reacts, you'd think I just ran a full marathon.

There's a window on the door, nearly blacked out with years of filth. Through the gaps in the curtain, I can see a faint light on the inside and my heart plummets to the soles of my feet. I don't remember leaving any lights on when I left the house earlier this afternoon. Bracing myself for what I already know I'll find inside, I open the door slowly.

"Where have you been?" Closing the door softly, I freeze in place and close my eyes. I'm still facing the door, my hand on the knob, Charlie's harsh words sending a chill down my spine. I had hoped that he wouldn't be home yet. That he would have still been out with his friends or sitting at the bar drowning his worthless existence in a whiskey. At least, that's what he does most nights.

"I've been at work. You know I had to work this afternoon." Taking a deep breath, I ready myself to turn and face him sitting in his recliner chair. As I turn around, I take in the disaster of the house around him. No matter how much I try to keep it picked up, all it takes is one bad day for Charlie and it's destroyed again. He obviously had a rough day judging by the number of broken dishes and paper strewn throughout the living room and attached kitchen. Not that I expect anything less – he has more rough days than not.

ff my feet
before having to work again around the house. Obviously, I was
mistaken.

"I was waiting for you. You know I expect dinner when I get
home from work."

"I'm sorry." Stepping away from the door, I begin to walk into
the kitchen. I don't stop to pick up any of the trash on the floor, I
don't take my sweater or my shoes off. I go straight to the
refrigerator to pull out the fixings for tonight's dinner.

"Don't walk away from me when I'm talking to you." I listen to
the sound of the recliner snapping back into place, the hard
footsteps of Charlie's work boots on the hard wood floor as he
stalks toward me. I don't even have a chance to brace myself before
I'm shoved against the kitchen counter. I barely have a second to
brace my hands against the bite of the hard edge against my hip
before my ponytail is grabbed and yanked backward. Losing my
balance, I stumble and fall to the floor, the shock reverberating
through my body as I land on my side with a loud thud, my head
knocking hard against the cheap linoleum. Charlie just barely steps
out of the way, so I don't fall into him. My hands immediately
move up to cover my face, knowing what comes next. I don't need
marks on my face that anyone at work will be able to see. I don't
need anyone to be brought into the hell that is my life.

"I'm going to the bar." Charlie steps around me, leaving me
sitting on the floor with my hands over my face. "I expect this
house to be cleaned and dinner ready when I get back."

I don't move. I barely breathe. I stay lying on the floor in the
middle of the kitchen as I listen to his footsteps get further and
further away. I wait until the front door slams shut and I hear his

30

truck pulling out of the garage before I finally get up and begin working on the house. Only when the trash is picked up, the broken dishes thrown away, do I finally take off my sweater and hang it on the hook by the front door. I wince against the pain as I pull my arms out of the sleeves, releasing a final calming breath before moving into the kitchen to start on Charlie's dinner.

I could have gotten away from all of this years ago if only people would have listened to me when I said there was trouble in my home. No one believed me though. No one would listen to me.

I've spent so much time talking to people that I thought were my friends, even my coworkers. They just smile and nod and pretend to pay attention to me. I told them that I wasn't happy, but they responded with words like "I understand. I know how you feel. I feel unhappy myself sometimes." But they couldn't possibly understand the thoughts and feelings that were going through my head. They don't even listen.

Even now, they don't see it. No one notices or pays attention to the fact that I have long sleeves on all day, instead of my waitressing uniform, to hide the bruises running down the length of my arms. No one sees how I have to take in my pants, so they aren't falling off my hips because I can't eat. They don't see the skin that hangs from my bones beneath my baggy clothes from losing too much weight too fast. They don't even notice how I've had to add extra layers to my makeup to cover the dark circles beneath my eyes from the lack of sleep.

I can see it. I see the signs of the trouble I have at home every time I look at my reflection in a mirror. But no one else sees it. Or they choose to ignore it and look the other way. Everyone in this town knows Charlie, he grew up here. He's always been popular in town and never goes long without a job. He was the captain of the football team in our little high school before he graduated. They don't see the terrible drunk that he became when he got older. They only see the championships that he won for the football team. No one believes that he's a has-been.

After cooking a simple dinner of hamburgers and fried potatoes, I leave a plate for Charlie in the microwave and take a shower. I rush through it and go straight to bed. Knowing that my night will be plagued with never-ending nightmares, I double check the locks on my bedroom door before laying down and forcing myself to go to sleep. Tomorrow is another day, hopefully a better one.

If I'm lucky, Charlie will drink himself to death before I have to deal with him again.

Chapter FIVE

LANDON

I HATE THIS FUCKING TOWN. I swore when I finally got out of it that I would never come back. If it wasn't for the estate that I'm trying to close, I wouldn't be here at all. My grandmother left me everything and I have no intention of keeping any of it. I know she had hopes that I would come back here and live out my life in the town that she loved so much. I have no intention of staying here any longer than I have to. As soon as I get her house cleaned out, it's going on the market.

Everything looks the same as the day I finally rolled out of this town. The shops are the same. Even the Independence Day decorations that stay on the light polls all year are the same faded silver, blue, and red tinsel flags and clumps of spider-like appendages that I'm sure once looked like fireworks. They never change even after all these years, like the entire town is stuck inside of a time capsule. It's been nearly ten years since I've stepped foot here and the lights lining the street are exactly the same as when I was growing up.

I had hoped to get here early this morning so I could get started on the house, but I got tied up in a meeting. I snuck out as soon as I was able to but that means that I skipped both breakfast and lunch. My rumbling stomach reminds me that I need to eat and thankfully, I see the diner up ahead. The building itself hasn't aged well, similar to everything else in this town. I can already see the peeling white paint beneath the ripped and battered awning from a few blocks away. I can only hope that the food is as good as I can remember when I grew up here. My grandfather had a secret affair with their meatloaf occasionally and used to drag me along with him after a long day of work. We'd whisper secrets across the table to each other; him telling me how the diner's meatloaf was even better than my grandmother's, and me nodding my silent agreement while my cheeks were puffed out like a chipmunk full of the buttery meat mixture and mashed potatoes. My mouth is already watering just thinking about it as I park my car against the curb.

Stepping out of my car, I immediately regret rushing here straight from the office. The humidity is causing my dress shirt and suit jacket to cling to my body in uncomfortable ways. I take the time to strip out of the jacket and lose the tie, tossing them both in the backseat of my car, before stepping inside the diner. The sign on the hostess stand says to seat myself, so I wander to the booth in the back corner. I don't even bother to grab a menu, knowing that that probably hasn't changed over the years either.

I'm greeted immediately by a short waitress as she brings me a glass of ice water which I graciously accept. I take a sip right away while she goes over the day's specials. I'm so thankful for the cooling relief of the water that I don't even listen to her as she goes through the list of daily specials. Setting my water glass on the table, I wipe my hand on the napkin and look at the waitress. I want to at least pretend that I heard everything she said, no sense in being rude. She has nothing to do with my reason for hating this town.

I'm immediately struck mute as I gaze into her azure blue eyes. Eyes that I could disappear into without a second thought. I've never seen anyone's eyes so strikingly blue before and I'm instantly hypnotized by her stare. "I'm sorry," my eyes trace down her face and stop on her nametag. "Emi. I don't mean to stare. It's already been such a long day."

"No worries," she smiles but I can tell that it's fake, probably the same smile she gives to all the regular customers as she struggles to just get through her day. I inwardly cringe at the fake smile, immediately wishing that I could see what a genuine smile looks like spread across her angelic face and wondering what could cause her to look so tortured. I have no idea why, but I'm willing to slay her dragons just to get a real smile out of her. I want more than anything to see her eyes dance with glee. "Do you know what you want?"

"Meatloaf," I state plainly. "Do you still have meatloaf on the menu?"

"We do. It's the best in town."

A chuckle slips past my lips at her declaration. Of course, it would be the best in town considering there are no other diners or restaurants for miles. "I'll have that." I force myself to look away from her and reach for my water glass again. My thirst is quenched and I'm already feeling cooler from the blast of air conditioning in

35

the diner. But I don't want to seem stalkerish by keeping my eyes on her too long. She already seems uncomfortable, and I don't want to add to that.

"Would you like anything else to drink?" she asks, her notepad still held in her hand.

"Water is fine. Just keep it coming. It's hot out there today." She doesn't say anything else, just nods her head once and walks away. I watch as she leaves and notice that she has a small limp to her gait. I wonder if she's in pain, maybe that's why she isn't able to offer a real smile.

She really is stunning. If I had to guess, I'd say she was just over five feet tall. Her hair is a beautiful shade of auburn that catches the light through the windows behind her, creating a halo around her head. Her ponytail is loose in the back, but even pulled up, her hair reaches her middle back. I wonder how long it would be if she were to let it down. It looks soft as silk, and I can imagine what it would feel like threading my fingers through the loose tresses. She's wearing dark blue jeans and a long-sleeved sweater despite the heat and humidity outside. I'm curious if she's in here long enough to catch a chill from the air conditioning.

When she returns with another glass of water, I take a minute to really look at her. She has more makeup on her face than I'm sure she needs – I know she's a natural beauty beneath all that war paint. I want to take her in my arms and wash that makeup off her face so I can see the perfect smoothness of her skin, the natural blush of her cheeks. I imagine a smattering of adorable freckles covering her nose.

"Thank you," I say as I take a sip of the new glass of water. She grabs the empty one from the table and ambles slowly away without saying another word.

Again, I watch as she limps away from me. She's a mystery that I'm anxious to solve. I want to know why she seems so tortured. Is she as trapped in this small-town as I thought I would be before I was able to finally get away? I hear the cook call out an order and I'm still watching her as she walks to the order window to pick up a plate.

I finally look away long enough to see him glaring at me. Obviously, he's overprotective of the wait staff and I just got caught staring at Emi's ass. I should feel guilty about that, but I don't.

After taking the last bite of my delicious meatloaf, I pick up my glass of water to wash it down. I haven't been able to take my eyes off of Emi since she walked back to the counter. She looks lost in thought, and I want to know what she's thinking about.

She keeps turning her gaze over her shoulder and looking at the clock on the wall. All the while she's wiping the counter in large circles over the same spot as I continue to watch her, and I'm surprised she hasn't rubbed a hole through the Formica yet.

Her eyes are practically glossed over as she continues to move robotically, her hand fisted tightly in the rag she's currently using to polish the counter to a mirror finish. She has the look of someone who's haunted, and I want to know about her demons. I want to take them from her and carry her burden for her so she can relax. I'm immediately taken aback by the sudden need to take care of her, protect her from whatever plagues her thoughts. I don't even know her, aside from the name she wears on her nametag, and I'm suddenly wishing I could whisk her away from this timeless town and show her a life in the city. I can already imagine the way the night lights would gleam off the blue of her eyes, making them sparkle like the deepest waters of the ocean.

But first, I need to get to my grandmother's house and start the process of cleaning it out. Today, I'm going through her belongings and picking out what little bit there might be that I'll want to hold on to. I'll most likely only hang on to the sentimental memorabilia like family photos. Anything else will be donated.

I have a crew coming tomorrow to meet me at the house to start clearing out the furniture and whatever clothing is able to be donated. The realtor will be meeting me again the day after to do a walkthrough and take pictures to put it on the market. It probably won't sell fast, nothing in this town ever does. I don't have any desire to hold on to it for too long though, so I'll be selling it at a low price. Maybe someone will pick it up as an investment property. Or perhaps a young couple looking for a nice starter home, something the old Craftsman cottage would be perfect for.

I wait for several minutes, silently praying that Emi will look up from whatever daydream has monopolized her attention. But she doesn't look up, and I need to get to the house if I'm going to get through everything today before needing to go back home to my apartment in the city. Grabbing a pencil from the suggestion box on the table, I scribble a short note on a napkin and toss it on the table along with a fifty-dollar bill from my wallet. It's way more than enough to cover my lunch and leave Emi with a decent tip.

Pulling into the driveway of the house ten minutes later, I can't hold back my smile. The house looks great considering my grandmother has been living alone for the last ten years since I left for the city. Obviously, the maintenance man that I've been paying for the last several years has taken good care of it. He was well worth the money, that's for sure.

My grandmother took me in when my parents died in a car accident when I was eight. They were on an anniversary date in the city when they ran off the road after hitting a patch of black ice on the way home. To be honest, I don't have many memories of my parents. If it weren't for the photos that are still hanging on my grandmother's walls, I probably wouldn't even remember what they looked like.

I open the trunk of the car and pull the empty boxes out before walking up to the door of the house. I'll take the photos, but they'll probably end up in storage. I work so much that my home is really nothing more than a place to rest my head every night, not somewhere that I've ever felt the need to hang pictures and photographs on the walls.

As soon as I open the front door, I'm immediately assaulted by the heat and humidity from inside the closed-up house. I should have had Ed, the maintenance man, come open the windows before I got here.

Stepping into the living room, my eyes are drawn to the photos hanging on the wall over the mantel. They're a series of gorgeous black and white portraits of the historical Independence Main Street. The same Independence Day decorations that hang year-round are sparkling brightly, even with the lack of color, giving life to the photos. I'm immediately drawn to how there's so much more character in these pictures than is actually in the town itself and am amazed at the way the photographer was able to capture so much feeling in something as ordinary as a small town's walking district.

I remember the day my grandmother brought the photos home. She was so proud of her purchase that day when she visited the local library that she had to call me and tell me all about them. She didn't know who the photographer was that took the pictures, but knew they had to be taken by someone that loved her small town as much as she did in order to have been able to catch so much of its beauty. Of course, the photographer would have to be local in order for their photos to be featured at the library. They only sold paintings, drawings, and photographs of local artists to raise funds to keep the library doors open. Everything they sold was donated to them for that purpose.

I make a last-minute decision to keep the three photos. I don't know where I would display them, but I can't bring myself to get rid of something that my grandmother thought so highly of.

I'm wandering around removing pictures from the walls for hours before exhaustion begins to creep in. The silence and monotony of the task has done nothing to alleviate the thoughts of Emi at the diner earlier today. I've watched her in my mind walk away from me over and over again. Constantly wondering what caused the slight limp to her walk, the emptiness in her eyes as she would cautiously meet my gaze at the table each time she came back.

I wonder what she's doing tonight. Maybe hanging out with friends. Or perhaps her boyfriend. There's no way a woman as beautiful as her is alone. I should push thoughts of her out of my mind knowing that I'm not going to compete with someone else for her affection. I'm only returning to this small town for this house, there's no way I can get involved with a local anyway.

Once the boxes are back in my car, I pull away from the house and decide to drive home. The city is only a forty-five-minute drive from town. There is no reason for me to stay the night here, I already know that I'll be more comfortable in my own bed than I would in any second-rate motel this town has to offer.

After returning to my apartment and making a quick sandwich to assuage my hunger, I decide to have a quick shower to wash off the dust from the house before going to bed. Tomorrow is going to be another long day. I have one more meeting to attend in the morning before going back to my grandmother's house to meet with the donation crew.

The hot spray of the shower does nothing to ease my thoughts of the haunted gaze of my blue-eyed angel. Closing my eyes, I imagine her laying on my sheets with her hair fanned out over my pillows. Next thing I know, my hand is wrapped around my aching cock. A growl rumbles deep in my chest as I imagine prowling toward her, her legs spread open in invitation, on my bed. I imagine her watching me as I approach her, her eyes focused on the movement of my hand as I stroke my cock slowly up and down. I watch as she licks her lips in temptation, her pupils dilating with lust and desire. I can picture her rising to her knees as I approach, the tight pebbles of her nipples getting harder in the cool breeze of the air conditioning. I imagine her reaching for me as I stop at the edge of the bed, my knees pressing against the mattress as she reaches out and wraps her small hand around my girth.

"Open," I would demand of her as I bite back a groan at the feeling of her hand wrapped around me. I imagine her lips wrapping around the purple head, her tongue lapping at the salty precum beading at the tip before swiping around the ridge. Closing my eyes, I imagine her taking me deeper into her mouth, my rounded head bumping against the back of her throat and her swallowing around me as she fights her gag reflex.

"Fuck!" I shout through clenched teeth, my free hand pressing against the tile of the shower wall. My eyes are closed tightly as I feel my balls draw up and my climax shoots out of me in thick ropes against the shower floor. I take several steadying breaths, my other hand pressing against the shower wall as I feel my legs weakening beneath me. I let the warm spray of the shower wash over my head as the endorphins flow through my blood.

My mind is made up as I crawl into bed and pull the sheet up to my waist. Tomorrow, I'll have lunch at the diner again before meeting the moving crew. I want to see Emi again. I need to know her better and see why she's so haunted.

"Shit," I think to myself. "I didn't even tell her my name."

Chapter
SIX

EMILEE

I COME TO WAKE slowly, same as I do most mornings with the sun shining brightly through the blinds on my bedroom window. A wave of nausea rushes through me before I have a chance to sit up in the bed and I squeeze my eyes shut against the feeling, willing my stomach to calm itself. The last thing I need to do right now is dry heave my way to the bathroom. There's nothing in my stomach to throw up anyway, I only had a chance to grab a few slices of bread yesterday at work. Reaching for my nightstand, I grab a few stale crackers to hopefully settle my stomach so I can move from my position on the bed. I'll get to work early today and hopefully be able to make myself a sandwich before we get too busy.

Keeping my eyes closed and relaxing back into my pillow, I slowly sip the bottle of water I left on my nightstand last night and think about the man that came into the diner yesterday. The way he was dressed, he had to have been from out of town, there are no jobs here that would require him to have been wearing a suit. Well, half of a suit at least. He wasn't wearing a tie, or a jacket and his top two buttons were undone casually. His dark hair was long enough for me to imagine running my fingers through it, the way he had it styled in a messy undercut. He had a neatly trimmed beard that was short but not short enough to be scratchy and rough. It looked soft and I wonder what it would feel like scraping against my thighs or my neck.

Who am I kidding? I can't allow myself to get caught up in the fantasy of him rushing in on his white horse to whisk me away from all my troubles. I'm old enough to know there's no such thing as fairy tales or white knights. If I expect to get out of this dismal town and my troubles, I have to soldier on and do it myself.

Finally, my stomach begins to settle, and I slowly sit up, swinging my legs off the side of the mattress. Not sure if the house is empty yet, I tip toe slowly into my attached bathroom and brace my hands against the vanity. Staring at my reflection in the mirror, I grimace at the state of my skin and hair. My auburn locks are dull where they were once shiny and vibrant. My skin has gone pale to the point of near transparency, especially around my eyes. If not for the dark circles gathered there, I wouldn't have any coloring to my face at all.

Turning away from the mirror, refusing to look any further at the toll the last year has taken on my body, I reach into the bathtub and turn on the water to warm for my shower. I knew it would be hard after my mother passed away, but I had no idea how hard it was really going to be just to survive. If it weren't for Ralph allowing me to eat at work, I wouldn't eat anything. Shivering in the cool air of the bathroom, I toss my discarded clothes into the hamper in the corner and step into the warm spray of the shower.

I can't help but wonder what the handsome stranger thought when he looked at me yesterday. The way he glanced at my mouth when I smiled at him, like he knows that my smile was fake but forced himself not to point it out. I felt the heat rushing to my cheeks as he continued to stare, and I wanted to run away. Hide in a corner where he couldn't see through my façade. I've never felt the need to hide from anyone before, knowing that they won't see beneath surface level anyway. But this man stared through me as if he could read all my secrets just by gazing into my eyes and it made me nervous.

I don't understand why I'm still thinking about him. I'll probably never see him again anyway. He was just passing through town and wanted to stop for a bite to eat before making his way back to the city. There's no way he'll come back here for me or anything else. Even still, I was so lost in my thoughts that I hadn't realized he'd left until it was too late. He left me a generous tip though. Along with a note that I still don't understand.

Thank you, Emi. Dinner was delicious. Perhaps next time we can eat together. Keep the change.

I wonder what he meant by that. It's not as if he would ever come into the diner again.

Stepping out of the shower, I grab a towel from the rack over the toilet and dry myself off quickly. I wrap the towel around my body while grabbing my comb and quickly raking it through my tangled tresses, pulling it into a ponytail without bothering to wait for it to dry. I'm anxious to get to the diner and get my day started. My stomach rumbles loudly as if agreeing with my decision to hurry.

After brushing my teeth and applying a bit of foundation to cover the dark circles under my eyes, I step into my bedroom and sip some more water to hopefully hold me over until I can get something to eat at work. Once I'm dressed, I unlock my bedroom door and hold my hand to the doorknob for a few seconds, my breath held in my lungs as I strain to listen for any sound on the other side of the door. After several seconds of complete silence, I open the door and step into the hallway. There's no one here and I can breathe easier knowing that I won't have any issues getting out of the house today.

The walk to work is relatively uneventful. I still haven't had a chance to mow the grass and it tickles my ankles as I amble through the tall blades. I don't bother following the sidewalk through town, instead cutting through yards and parking lots in hopes of arriving sooner than my normal thirty minutes. I'm already winded at the minimal exertion of the walk by the time I reach the back door of Freedom Diner and have to stand in place for several seconds to catch my breath before stepping inside. It's amazing how weak I've become over the last few days of barely eating. As if the effects of malnutrition hadn't already taken its toll on me.

"Your boyfriend's back," Ralph says as I step into the kitchen, his voice laced with amusement.

"What?" I stop in my tracks, grabbing my apron from the hook next to the door and wrapping it around my waist.

"You know. The guy that was here yesterday staring at your ass." Ralph openly laughs this time, but I watch as he nods his head in the direction of where the suited man from yesterday is sitting. "He's been here ten minutes already and won't let Amber take his order. He said he'd wait for you."

"Oh," I gasp not knowing what else to say. I didn't think I'd see him again, much less have him requesting me to be his waitress. Why is he back?

"Be careful with him, Emi." Ralph speaks over his shoulder as he walks back to the sink to clean some more dishes. "Guys like him are only after one thing."

Ralph is a good guy. He owns this diner; it's been in his family for fifty years. He's like an uncle to me and the other waitresses here. I know he means well, but if he really cared then he would be more concerned about me outside of just work. Not that I really ever expected him to be. No one in this town has ever cared enough about me to notice anything.

Checking to make sure my notepad and pen are in my apron pocket, I grab a glass of ice water and walk over to the table where the suit guy is sitting. He watches me, a smirk tipping up the corners of his full lips as I approach. A shiver runs down my spine at the gleam in his eyes as they lock with mine.

"Emi," he says in greeting as I place the water on the table. "I wasn't sure if you were going to be here today."

"I'm here every day." I reach into my pocket and pull out my notepad and pen. "What can I get for you today?" I chew the inside of my cheek while I wait for his response. It's taking all the willpower I have not to swoon at his feet with the way his hungry gaze is devouring me whole.

"Lunch, with you." He says matter-of-factly as he reaches for his water glass.

"Excuse me?" My head tilts to the side, my bottom lip catching between my teeth. I must have misunderstood him. He can't mean...

"It's quiet here. There's no one here besides me. Certainly, you can sit with me for a few minutes and have lunch."

"I just got here."

"Have you already eaten?" His brows rise as he asks the question.

"Well, no." He doesn't need to know that I don't eat anything at home. The only time I actually have enough peace to be able to eat is when I'm here at the diner. "I usually grab a turkey sandwich and some chips when I get here but I eat in the kitchen."

"Perfect. I'll have that and you can join me." He isn't going to take no for an answer. Normally, I would hate someone being so forthcoming with me, but with him I kind of like it.

"Okay." I take a minute to jot the order down on a ticket. "Would you like anything else to drink besides water?"

"No. Water is fine." Nodding my head, I place my notepad in my apron pocket and turn on my heel to walk to the kitchen. I can feel his eyes on me as I walk away.

Stepping around the counter, I walk directly into the kitchen to start on the sandwiches. Ralph watches me but doesn't say anything. He's used to me making myself a sandwich when I get here anyway. As I plate the two sandwiches and chips, I grab another glass of ice water and balance the plates on my forearm. Ralph watches me, one brow raised in question as I back out of the kitchen.

Suit guy is still watching me as I walk back to his table. He immediately grabs one of the plates when I'm close enough and I take the seat across from him in the booth. He watches intently and waits for me to take a bite of my sandwich first before he finally reaches for his own.

We eat in silence, me trying hard not to moan over the tangy mustard covered turkey. This is the first thing I've had to eat since lunch yesterday. I finish my sandwich and a few chips before washing it all down with a big gulp of water. When I turn my gaze across the table, I see he's already finished everything on his plate and is just watching me quietly. Heat fills my cheeks as I start to blush under his gaze.

"I'm sorry," I apologize.

"For what?" He furrows his brows and cocks his head to one side.

"I didn't realize how hungry I was until I started eating." It's a small lie but he doesn't need to know that. The truth is my stomach was on a mission to turn itself inside out and winning.

"That's nothing to apologize for. I was happy to wait until you finished. I didn't want to interrupt the love affair between you and that turkey. It looked like you were having a good time with it."

My cheeks really do fill with heat and blood now. I move my hands to my lap and turn my gaze down to the table. He reaches across the table, one finger going beneath my chin to turn my gaze back to him and I flinch away from his touch. I don't mean to, but in my experience, men don't reach out to touch you unless they mean you harm. My eyes pinch shut at my reaction – I don't want to see the hurt look of pity on his face.

"Hey," he starts. "I'm sorry. I shouldn't have touched you. I just wanted you to look at me."

I lift my head and look in his eyes. I don't see pity there like I was expecting. I'm not sure how to read his expression exactly since I don't really know him. "I'm sorry. I shouldn't have reacted that way."

"Don't apologize. You did nothing wrong." He seems sincere but I don't know him well enough to judge his character. "Thank you for having lunch with me." I watch as a smile spreads across his handsome face, and it's glorious. I think he really did appreciate me having lunch with him. Again, I don't know him well enough to know that for sure, but it was nice to have someone to eat with besides Ralph.

I look over as the bell rings above the door, indicating that someone else is coming into the diner. "I'm sorry. I have to get back to work." I grab the empty dishes and stand to take them to the kitchen. "I'll be with you in just a moment." I announce to the newcomers. "Just have a seat anywhere."

After getting waters for the new customers and making sure they have menus, I return to suit guy's table to see if he needs anything else.

"No, I don't need anything." He smiles at me again as I lay the ticket for his sandwich on the table. I'm almost disappointed that he's going to be leaving. I'm angry that more customers came in and I didn't even get a chance to talk to him or get to know him a little better. "I'll see you tomorrow, Emi." I watch as he takes another fifty-dollar bill out of his wallet and places it on the table. "My name's Landon by the way."

He doesn't wait for me to say anything before he stands and walks to the door. What did he mean about seeing me again tomorrow? Surely, he isn't driving here from the city just to eat in this little diner.

Chapter
SEVEN

LANDON

IT TAKES EVERY OUNCE of strength I can muster to walk away from Emi again. Pausing with my hand against the diner door, I look over my shoulder and see her standing by the table with the fifty-dollar bill clutched in her tiny fist. Her brows are furrowed as she watches me and as much as I want to march back over to her and wipe away the wrinkle between her brows with the pad of my thumb, I toss her a wink before pushing my way out the door.

Images play through my mind like images on a reel as I drive through town. The way she closed her eyes as she took the first bite of her sandwich. The sounds that escaped her throat as she moaned around each bite like it was the absolute best thing she'd ever eaten. I can't understand how that's even possible – it was just a turkey sandwich. It was nothing special, certainly not something that she could have had at one of the Michelin restaurants in the city. I wonder how she would react to something she eats there. I wonder what I'll have to do to find out.

Pulling into the driveway at my grandmother's house, I'm immediately greeted by the moving crew. They are just stepping out of the truck when I arrive so thankfully, they haven't been waiting for me long. Not that I'd care if they were, having lunch with Emi was more important than anything I have to do at this house today.

Thankfully, my grandmother was meticulous about cleaning her house. There isn't much to do after the furniture is all moved out besides run a vacuum over the floor to remove the impressions in the carpet. Still, it takes several hours to get everything moved out and loaded into the back of the truck.

I lock the house up after they leave and go back to my apartment in the city for the night. I don't have any meetings tomorrow that I need to attend so I'll be able to go straight to the diner for lunch with Emi again before meeting with the realtor.

I'm anxious to see her again. I don't like the way she flinched away from me when I tried to touch her chin. I wasn't going to hurt her – I just wanted her to look at me. There's no reason for her to act so shy around me. But still, that flinch just about broke my soul. She's obviously been hurt. Her demons started to show and now I want more than anything to get to know her better. I need to fight those demons. A woman as beautiful as her has no reason to flinch like that.

She should never be made to feel afraid of a gentle touch.

I've never had the reaction to any woman that I'm having for Emi. I feel overwhelmingly protective of her. I want to wrap her in my arms and make sure nothing and no one can ever hurt her again.

I rush through a shower after a quick dinner and my thoughts still go back to the way Emi flinched away from me. Fuck, I can't stop thinking about her. About the haunted look in her beautiful blue eyes. What is she doing right now? Is she at home having dinner with an abusive boyfriend? Is she stuck in a dead-end relationship that she doesn't know how to escape from?

My sleep is fitful, and I wake to the incessant ringing of my cell phone. Without opening my eyes, I reach to the nightstand and grab it, pressing the answer icon on the screen without even looking to see who it is. "Yeah?"

"Mr. Strong," my assistant Melodee says, her voice shaking with nerves. "I'm sorry to bother you so early and I know you said you weren't coming into the office today."

"What is it, Melodee?" I rub my free hand over my forehead while swinging my legs over the side of the bed.

"It's the foreman sir." I listen as she takes a deep breath, obviously trying to calm her nerves before she continues. "He's having an issue with the crew. Something about a disagreement on the blueprints."

I groan and squeeze my eyes shut. We went over those blueprints meticulously before scheduling the build. There shouldn't be any issues with any of it. "Tell him to figure it out."

"He says he needs you to come help…"

"He can figure it out," I interrupt her. "He's the foreman. He's paid to control his crew. He can either figure it out or I'll give the job to someone else."

"Yes sir. I'll let him know."

I disconnect the call before she can respond again. It isn't her fault, she's basically the middleman. But I shouldn't have to babysit the foreman just to make sure that he can handle the responsibilities of his job. I have lived and breathed my company since I started it four years ago and the one day I decide not to come into the office, this is the shit I wake up to. I'm not dealing with it today. There are plenty of other candidates out there that can do a better job at managing a construction crew. If my foreman can't figure it out, I'll just let him go. But not until I get back to the office tomorrow.

After a quick breakfast, I kill time moving the boxes that came from grandma's house into my bedroom closet. I'll deal with them another day. There's someplace else drawing my attention today and it's a forty-five-minute drive to get there.

The drive there is uneventful. Thankfully, even the traffic is cooperating with me today. It helps that the sky is full of pregnant clouds, the threat of rain keeping most people indoors.

Looking through the diner window I can see Emi wiping a cloth over the counter, a faraway gaze in her eyes. I sit in my car for several minutes just watching her and wishing I could read her thoughts. Her hair is pulled back in the same high ponytail I've seen her in the last few days I've come by. Today, however, there are several strands loose and hanging around her face giving it more of a disheveled appearance. She's wearing the same sweater I saw her wearing yesterday, the sleeves long enough to hang over the backs of her hands as she works. Her long fingers curl tightly around the cloth as she drags it over the spotless countertop.

I watch as the other waitress walks up beside her, her lips moving silently in a conversation that I can't hear. She obviously doesn't get the response she hopes for as she stops moving and lifts a hand to Emi's shoulder. My heart skips erratically in my chest as I watch Emi jump in surprise away from her friendly co-worker. Obviously, I'm not the only one she flinches from.

Enough.

I'm getting to the bottom of this today.

EMILEE

"I'M SORRY EMI," Amber pulls her hand back into her chest as I flinch away from her. "I didn't mean to scare you."

Closing my eyes, I chastise myself internally while attempting to steady my breathing. "You didn't. I just wasn't paying attention. I didn't hear you walk up to me." She doesn't understand the reason that I flinch every time she sneaks up on me, I don't expect her to.

"I was talking to you the entire time." I open my eyes and watch her shake her head slowly side to side. "You didn't hear anything I was saying? Where are you today?"

"I didn't get much sleep last night. I'm just tired today." Pulling my hand away from the counter, I toss the cleaning cloth into the bucket of soapy water beneath the counter. Grimacing at the ache in my hand, I flex my fingers in an attempt to relieve the cramping in my joints from having clutched the cleaning cloth so tightly.

I need to get a hold of myself. I've spent far too much time daydreaming these last few days. It all comes back to a certain suit wearing man that I can't seem to get out of my head. Landon, he said his name was.

My daydreaming is causing me too many issues and I need to get my head together. Last night, I was so caught up in my thoughts that I burned Charlie's dinner. I tried to cover it up by adding more sauce to his steak, but it only resulted in the entire plate being thrown against the wall. He screamed at me, which was nothing new, but he grabbed me when I tried to clean up the mess he created on the wall and the floor. He threw me against the counter, the edge biting into my back with a sharp pain, before wrapping his hands around my biceps and squeezing hard.

The resulting bruises on my arms are nothing new, they blend in with the already discolored patches lining both of my arms. However, he escalated from slaps and bruising grabs when his eye caught the steak knife that I'd already tossed into the sink. My life literally flashed before my eyes as I watched him reach for the knife, knowing I'd never be able to get away from him before he inflicted the pain I knew was coming. The evil glimmer in his drunken gaze as he dragged the knife along the flesh of my inner forearm will haunt me for days if not years. My screams as the blood trickled to my fingertips only further fed the hatred in his laughter.

In all the time that I have been forced to be the victim of his abuse, I've never seen that aura of hatred surrounding him that he had last night. This was something new, he'd never escalated to the point of purposely drawing blood before. Oh, I've bled plenty of times because of his actions against me, but it was mostly from being cut by flying shards of glass. My only fear is that he will appreciate his appetite for blood, now that he's had a taste of it, and become more of a pit bull than ever before. I don't know how I'll be able to escape his wrath in the coming days now that he's escalated to this point.

"There you go again," Amber drawls next to me. "Really, Emi. It's like you're up on cloud nine today. Where is your head at?"

Shaking my head, I make a sound that I had hoped was a giggle but sounds more like a gag to my own ears. Looking at Amber, I'm relieved to see that she didn't notice the sound. She isn't even looking at me anymore but toward the door. Following her gaze, I see Landon walk in wearing a t-shirt and dark blue jeans – much different than the broken suits I've seen him in the last two times he's been here. A tingle races down my spine and I realize that I like this look on him much more than the suits. A casual Landon is a sexy Landon.

"Wow," Amber whispers as her eyes grow impossibly wider. "He's definitely not from here."

I take a deep breath, my eyes trailing Landon from his tennis shoes up to the messy locks of his dark hair. It looks like he's been running his fingers through it, maybe pulling at it in his own fists, and I wish I could do the same. "No," I whisper back as I my eyes lock on his. "He isn't."

Landon smiles a crooked smile as his eyes lock on mine. My heart practically skips in my chest as he begins to walk closer to the counter, directly toward where Amber and I are currently standing.

"Hey, handsome." A stab of jealousy punches me in the gut at Amber's words. I'm honestly envious of her ability to talk to people and the way she speaks her mind regardless of the consequences. But still, I've never felt such pain as I do at her words toward Landon. Yes, he's obviously handsome. But I don't like the fact that she's noticed.

The one thing that I wanted to be able to keep for myself was the attention that Landon has been paying me the last two times he's been here. I want to take the feelings that I have for this man and lock them in a box. Somewhere that they can't be taken from me like everything else in my life tends to be.

He's the only thing that I have to look forward to from one day to another. Honestly, I think the only reason that I was even able to drag myself to work today was the hope of seeing him again.

His eyes still locked with mine, I see the slightest flinch at Amber's words. He doesn't respond to her greeting and a calmness washes over me at the realization that he only has eyes for me.

"Okay," Amber breathes out before turning her attention back to me. "I see you have it handled here. I'll leave you to it."

I watch from the corner of my eye as she grabs the bin of washed silverware and carries it to the other end of the counter to begin wrapping. The pain in my stomach dissipates as I continue to stare back at Landon. "Hi," I whisper in an attempt at a greeting. "You came back."

"I did." He takes another step toward the counter, and I stand frozen in his path. Honestly, it's almost comical how I continue to stand in one place, barely even breathing, as he approaches me. I guess this is what a deer feels like when it's greeted by the headlights of an oncoming car. My feet feel as if they're filled with lead and I'm not able to move from this spot.

"Would you like something for lunch?"

"You." Just one word, and I can feel the blood rushing through my veins lighting up all my nerve endings like a lightning strike. Dangerous. That's what he is. But oh, so tempting. But then what is life if not a series of risks and what-ifs? This is a risk that I'm willing to take. It can't be any worse than what I have already waiting for me at the end of my shift.

Chapter
EIGHT

LANDON

"EXCUSE ME?" I WATCH as her brows lift to her hairline, my lips twitching slightly.

"I would like for you to have lunch with me again," I respond. Honestly, I'm not even hungry but I would give anything to be able to sit in her company again today. After today, there really isn't any reason for me to return to town. The house will be on the market, my realtor will handle everything from here leading up to the hopeful sale of the property. I have so much going on at work lately with the new build that I don't know when I'll have another chance to return to this diner, to Emi's presence.

If there was a way for me to wrap her up in a package and put her in my pocket, I would gladly carry her with me everywhere I go from here on out. But I don't see that happening. She obviously has a life here and I would be a monster to take her away from that.

But I need the opportunity to get to know her better. I just have to figure out a way to make that happen. I'm not ready to give up yet.

"Okay," she breathes, and I feel myself relaxing. The tension of awaiting her response a palpable thing.

Already, I'm amazed at the reaction I have in her presence. Like I'm elated to be around her. Yet there is still so much that I don't know about her. I want to know everything about her.

"I'll just have a seat over there," I gesture toward the booth against the window and watch as she nods her head in agreement. "You can join me after you decide what we'll have for lunch today." I wink at her before turning to walk toward the booth. I chuckle to myself when she immediately lowers her head to hide the blush creeping into her cheeks, but I don't miss the way her lips tip up at the corners.

Small victories and all that.

Moments later, her co-worker appears with two glasses of water. She sits one in front of me and the other in front of the seat opposite. I nod my head in thanks before she smiles and walks away without a word.

Emi walks over a few minutes later with two plates, a serving of meatloaf and mashed potatoes on each one. She smiles as she sits across from me, and my heart nearly leaps out of my chest at the sight. Her smile is genuine and the most beautiful thing I've seen in all of my twenty-seven years. I know without a doubt that I will do anything in my power to make her smile at me like that again. As many times as possible.

"Wow." The words are released on a sigh before I have a chance to hold them back.

"What?" Her brows furrow in confusion, and I'm immediately disgusted with myself for breaking the moment. Fear sits heavy in my gut as I worry that I won't be able to get another smile from her.

"Your smile," honesty is the best way to go here. I don't know how she'll react to my words, but I have to try. "It's beautiful." I watch as a light blush blooms across her cheeks and my stomach does a little dance when the genuine smile, yet again, spreads across her perfect mouth. "There it is." Finally picking up my fork, I cut off a bite of the delectable meatloaf and place it in my mouth. Neither of us talks as we eat our lunch.

She peeks up at me every now and then between bites of her own meal, the blush a constant reminder of her bashfulness. She's adorable, even if she's still a little guarded – a wall that I hope to be able to tear down soon. "So," I begin as I finish off my meal and reach for the glass of water. "Tell me about yourself, Emi."

"What's there to tell?" She sets her fork down and wipes the corners of her mouth with a napkin. "I've lived here my whole life. Grew up here. Went to school here. I've never been anywhere else. I work here at the diner every day." She lowers her gaze to the table where her hands are twisting together nervously.

I want to reach out and soothe her, let her know she has no reason to be nervous around me. But the last time I tried to touch her, she nearly jumped out of her skin. I refuse to be the cause of her anxiety again. Instead, I place my palms on the table directly in front of where her hands are held together, barely an inch of space separating us from touching. I'll get close and let her close the distance between us if and when she's ready. "Hey." I lower my head so I'm within her viewing range and wait for her to turn her eyes to mine.

She lifts her head, her bottom lip is pulled between her teeth. "Hey," she says in return.

"Don't ever be ashamed of where you come from. I grew up here too."

"Really?" Her brows furrow in confusion. "But you seem so normal."

"Normal?" I chuckle at her response. "As opposed to what?" I watch, fascinated at the blush darkening her cheeks and trailing down the smooth slope of her neck.

"You know," she starts before gulping down another drink of her water. "This town is so old school. Like everyone lives in the past."

"Yeah, I know exactly what you mean." My head nods slowly as I turn my gaze out the window to the street beyond. The ever-present decorations on the light poles lining each side of the street, aged horribly over the years but never replaced with updated versions.

"It's like there's this force field around the entire town. Kind of like the movie *Pleasantville*, only nothing here is actually pleasant. Everyone acts like they know everyone's secrets, but they don't." The gleam in her eyes vanishes, her demons pushing to the surface, and I watch as she lowers her gaze back to the table. "They don't know anything." My heart is breaking for this girl, I realize that she really is stuck in this town. She's like two sides to the same coin. I watch as the life visibly drains out of her, and it takes every ounce of restraint that I have not to scoop her into my arms and run away with her. Get her away from this town and the secrets that she wants so badly for someone to see. "They don't even care."

My phone buzzes in my back pocket and I'm pulled from my thoughts of running away with Emi. Pulling the phone out, I see a text message from my realtor letting me know she'll be at the house in five minutes. Shit, I lost track of time. But I can't leave Emi like this. Not when I've finally gotten her to start opening up to me.

"Emi." I wait for her to look back up at me. She finally does and I'm gutted by the sorrow pooling in her eyes. My heart is bleeding for her. As much as I want to wrap my arms around her and tell her everything will be okay, I know I can't do that yet. She has to trust me first and I have no idea what I'll need to do to earn that. I take a minute to put my phone back in my pocket and place my hands on my thighs, palms down. Looking around the diner, I see all the other tables in the dining area are empty. Emi's co-worker is still folding silverware on the counter. "Are you able to take the day off?" I ask Emi hopefully.

"Um," she looks around before answering. "I think so. But why?"

"There's somewhere I have to be but I'm not ready to leave you yet. I'd like for you to come with me. Spend the day with me. I want to get to know you more."

She doesn't even hesitate before responding. "I'd like that."

EMILEE

I HAVE OFFICIALLY LOST my mind. There is no other explanation for the fact that I'm sitting in Landon's car and driving away from the diner where I'm supposed to be working all afternoon. As elated as I am to be spending additional time with him, I can't clear my thoughts of what Charlie would do if he knew I was shirking my responsibility.

Neither one of us says anything during the drive. I watch out the passenger window as the neighborhood flies by until Landon pulls into a driveway in front of a gorgeous blue house. The house isn't very big but has a beautiful porch with a swing. My mother always wanted a porch swing. She saved up every penny she could until she was able to buy one but couldn't get anyone to hang it for her. Years later, the swing she purchased is still sitting on the porch floor, pushed into the far corner like a discarded memory.

There's another car in the driveway and I watch as a woman steps out. She has a camera in one hand and a tablet in the other. I didn't realize we were meeting with anyone else and a pang of jealousy shoots through my stomach. I internally chastise myself for the evil green monster washing over me. I don't even know this man, much less the woman stepping out of her car. I have no business feeling so possessive of him.

I wait as Landon steps out of the car and walks around to my door. He opens it and waits for me to step out. He doesn't reach for me and keeps a respectable distance when we walk closer to the other woman standing in front of her car.

"Nice to see you again, Landon." She reaches out to shake his hand. "And who is this?" I watch silently as she turns her gaze to me.

"This is my friend, Emi." He turns his gaze to me, "Emi, this is Rachel. She's with the realty company up the road. She's here to take pictures of the house for me."

I don't say anything to either of them, just nod my head in agreement, suddenly feeling a little out of place. I stand out of the way while they both walk up the porch. Landon doesn't follow her inside after he opens the door. Instead, he steps off the porch and sits on the stairs. I laugh as he comically taps the step next to where he's sitting in invitation for me to sit beside him. Which I do, leaving a couple inches of space between us.

"So," I begin tentatively. "You're selling your house?"

"My grandmother's house. It's the reason I've been here the last few days. I was cleaning it out and donating all of her things. She passed away recently and left it to me."

"Oh. I'm sorry."

"Thank you." He turns his head toward me with a crooked smile. "I'm sure she had hopes that I would return to this town after she passed." He pinches his lips together and looks out over the yard, shaking his head slowly side to side. "I left ten years ago and haven't been back since. I have no desire to move back here."

"I don't blame you. If I had a way of leaving, I wouldn't want to return to it either." He doesn't say anything in response, but I see him nodding his head in agreement. Maybe he gets it. Maybe he knows how this town has a way of sucking you in and never spitting you back out.

Moving my feet up another step, I pull my knees to my chest and wrap my arms around my legs. The motion pulls at my lower back, and I grimace slightly at the pain, hoping he doesn't catch it. Fidgeting with the sleeves of my sweater, I pull them down further, so the edges are nearly covering my fingertips. It's hot outside today and I can feel the sweat rolling down my back. The fact that I'm nervous doesn't help.

From the corner of my eye, I can see Landon watching me. The hairs on the back of my neck stand on end under his scrutiny. Clenching my teeth tight enough to crack, I wait for him to ask me questions that I'm not ready to answer. I don't know if I'll ever be able to tell him my truths, not that he's going to be around long enough for me to do that. After his house sells, I'll probably never see him again. It's not like I can expect him to ride in on his mighty steed and save me.

Fuck. I'm a damsel in distress. Only, instead of being trapped in a tower waiting to be rescued, I'm stuck in a small town and Charlie is the evil dragon. If only fairy tales were real. Maybe then he really could be my knight in shining armor. But, instead of riding in on his white horse, he'd rescue me in his silver Mercedes.

"All done," Rachel announces as she steps out of the house, pulling me from my thoughts. "I'll get the listing drawn up and send it to your email for approval before it goes live."

"Thanks, Rachel." Landon stands and walks with her to her car. I stay seated on the porch until she pulls away and watch as Landon returns to lock up the house. He steps off the porch and stands in front of me, fidgeting nervously with the house keys before placing them in his pocket. "Will you have dinner with me?" he asks, both hands going into his front pockets while he waits for my response.

"Um..." I start before looking around skeptically. "You can't possibly want to eat at the diner again."

He chuckles and moves one hand to the back of his head, gripping the base of his neck.

I suppress a smile as I watch his movements. Honestly, the fact that he's nervous right now is a little endearing.

Turning his gaze toward his feet as if suddenly bashful, "No. I don't want to eat at the diner. I was thinking of taking you to the city."

I tilt my head, lowering my brows as I study him as if waiting for him to suddenly say it was a joke. This isn't real right? I mean, he's gorgeous. Nervous Landon is adorable even. He could have any woman he wants to have dinner with him. And I'm me – just plain, simple, easily forgotten Emi. But the offer is tempting – I've never been to the city before. But then if I go to the city with Landon, I won't make it home in time to make dinner for Charlie. My thoughts are at war inside my head – do I go? Do I decline? Ohmygod, I don't know what to do here.

"I'm serious, Emi." He interrupts my thoughts as if he can sense the war waging inside my head. "I want to take you to dinner. You deserve to have a nice meal. Not something you could get from the diner."

"Okay," I answer before I have a chance to come to my senses. I have no idea how I'm going to manage to eat another meal today. I don't know what makes me more nervous – going to the city with someone I only just met a few days ago or forcing myself to eat another meal that I know my body will immediately reject.

"Great." He smiles, the most perfect smile I've ever seen. His eyes shine even brighter as they fill with pure joy. He doesn't move or reach out to help me stand, which I appreciate more than anything right now. I don't know if I can handle being touched and I've already flinched away from him once before. I don't want to ruin his good mood by flinching from him again. He waits until I've reached the side of the car before opening the door for me, closing it behind me once I'm seated and fastening my seatbelt. I watch as he walks around the front of the car, butterflies taking flight in my belly at the prospect of spending more time with him.

LANDON

MAYBE I'M A BASTARD.

I'm definitely selfish.

I'm not blind – I saw how nervous Emi was when I asked her to have dinner with me. She told me over lunch that she's never even left Independence before. She deserves something other than diner food. And I can't wait to see how her eyes light up when she sees the city as the sun sinks over the horizon. The way its rays shine off the buildings downtown. It's one of my favorite things, seeing the sunset painting the city buildings in a variety of colors. The way the light is reflected off the windows and steel framed buildings, illuminating the entire city scape in the brightest oranges and reds.

Reaching over, I turn up the air conditioning. I know there has to be a reason why she's still wearing that sweater this time of year. Summer hasn't started yet, but the humidity alone is enough to make an extra layer of clothes feel like a heated blanket. I'm determined to find out what that reason is, but I won't rush her. She'll tell me when she's ready. Maybe she's self-conscious and uses the long sleeves as a shield. That's a thing, right? No matter, the baggy top leaves enough to the imagination. She'll be a delicacy to unwrap, one that I'll be sure to savor.

It takes nearly all the self-restraint that I have not to reach over and touch her. Place a hand on her thigh. Hold her hand, our fingers twisted together. But I won't, not until I know she's ready for it. I refuse to be the cause of her discomfort. I'm still uneasy about the way she flinched from me yesterday, and her coworker today. There's only one reason I can think of for someone to flinch the way she did, and I hate to think that I'm right. The innocent creature sitting next to me doesn't deserve to be treated poorly by anyone. Nobody deserves to be treated in such a way that would cause her to be so jumpy around another person.

I grew up surrounded by love by both of my grandparents. Not only toward me, but toward each other. I've never laid my hand on another human being for any reason. But I can put two and two together. The way she watches her surroundings nervously, the long sleeves covering her arms, the way she was flinching away from a gentle touch, the limp to her gait. My gut clenches at the thought of someone laying a hand on her. She may not know it yet, but she's safe with me. I'll keep her safe any time she's with me, protect her as long as she'll let me.

The drive to the city is quiet, if not tense. I know she's still nervous but there isn't anything I can do about that right now. I can only hope that she loosens up a bit with a nice meal and conversation. I'm desperate to get to know her better.

We arrive at the restaurant and are seated immediately. I discreetly handed the hostess an additional fifty dollars to make sure we got a quiet booth in the back.

Within only a few seconds of seating, a waitress comes to our table with two glasses of water and two menus. "Can I get you anything else to drink while you look at the menu?"

I look across the table and watch as Emi takes a tentative sip of her ice water. She's probably near dehydration by now after sweating all day in that hot sweater. "Water is fine for now. Thank you," I tell the waitress. She smiles and nods her head once before turning to walk away. I already know what I want, this restaurant has the best steaks in the city. Still, I look over the top of my menu, my gaze focused on Emi as she reads her dinner options.

"There are no prices on the menu," she whispers as if afraid someone else will be listening in on our conversation.

"And?" I cock my head to the side unsure of what that has to do with anything and place my menu down on the table.

"How am I supposed to know what to order if there are no prices on the menu?"

I never thought that was a problem. Even now, I don't understand why that matters. "What do prices have to do with what you order. Order whatever you want to eat, Emi." I'm not rich by any means but I do have money to live comfortably on. I have no issue with being able to treat a beautiful woman to dinner and I don't care what the cost is.

"Okay," she relents and places her menu down on top of my own. I watch curiously as she picks up her glass of water and takes another sip. She looks around the restaurant with wide eyes, her nerves just below the surface but visible in the slight tremor of her hands as she places her glass back on the table. With the way she keeps looking around the restaurant, if I didn't know better, I'd think she was looking for someone to jump out of one of the dark corners or out from under a table.

The waitress, ever attentive of our table, comes over as soon as she notices our menus being set down. She is definitely earning her tip tonight. "What can I get started for you?"

"I'll have the ribeye," I start. "Medium rare, baked sweet potato with the butter on the side, and green beans."

"Excellent choice. And you ma'am?" She turns her attention to Emi, and I hold my breath waiting for her to order something other than a salad.

"I'll have the chicken marsala and a side salad, no dressing."

The waitress leaves without writing our orders down. I know from having been here before that they rarely write anything down, however they always get everything right.

"So," Emi begins before taking another sip of her water. "What is it that you do in the city?"

"I'm an architect and I own a construction company. Same as my father before me and his father before him. New construction mostly but we have done a few remodels during the slow seasons."

"Wow. That's amazing."

"Thank you." I smile proudly before reaching for my own water glass. "I learned everything I know from my grandfather. I knew early on that I wanted to be an architect. It's a rewarding job, being able to drive around the city and see the buildings that I designed in completion."

"I bet. I'd love to see them sometime."

My chest blooms with pride and desire. Just the idea of spending more time with her, showing her around the city that I've grown to love so much over the years does something to me. "I'd love to give you a tour. During the day of course, when you can appreciate the glow of the sun reflecting off the windows."

"Of course." She fidgets with her napkin, and I suddenly wish that I was a mind reader so I knew what she was thinking.

"What about you?" I ask, hoping to continue our small talk. Now that I've got her talking to me, I'm in no hurry to make it end. "Did you always want to work in the food industry?"

"Oh no." She giggles and a chill runs down my spine at the sound. "I wanted to take pictures. But I didn't finish school. I dropped out when my mother got sick. I wasn't able to go back after she died, so I kind of fell into waitressing." She fidgets a little more and turns her gaze down to the table. There's more to this story that she isn't telling me yet, but I don't want to rush her.

"What kind of pictures?" The waitress returns with our food before she gets a chance to respond. "This looks amazing, thank you."

"All kinds. I took some photography classes in high school. I liked scenic photos better than people. I always wanted to travel and take photos of historic places."

"That sounds lovely. I bet you were good at it. Do you still have any of the photos that you took in high school."

"No." Her voice is quiet enough that I barely hear her answer. "I don't..." I watch as she swallows a few times as if looking for the words. "I don't have them anymore."

I want to ask her why, but she picks up her silverware and begins to cut into her chicken. I'll leave it alone for now. Let her enjoy her meal.

Neither of us say anything else as we enjoy our food. The only sound being the occasional moan coming from Emi's side of the table. I knew she would love her dinner and I was right. Something grows and builds deep in my chest, a feeling that I'm not familiar with. But this, right here at a nice restaurant, with Emi enjoying a meal with me just feels right.

"Would you like dessert?" I ask as Emi places her fork down and wipes the corners of her mouth with the napkin. She didn't finish her food, barely ate half of it actually.

"No thank you. I couldn't eat another bite." Her smile is one of pure joy and it warms me from the inside knowing that I was able to help put that smile on her face.

"Perhaps next time then." I wave my arm in the air for the check and hand the waitress my credit card when she approaches. As soon as she returns with it, I sign the slip, being sure to indicate a twenty five percent tip. "I should probably take you back home," I whisper to Emi and her eyes go wide, the fear evident in her gaze as she quickly turns and looks out the window at the dark street beyond.

Chapter
NINE

EMILEE

"OH NO. NO, NO, NO." I stand up from the table, spinning around wildly as I look through all the windows and see the darkness beyond, as if the view will change depending on the direction I'm facing. How did I let this happen? What is he going to do when I get home and he realizes that I've been gone all day and not at work? I wasn't home in time to make his dinner for him.

"Hey," Landon takes a step closer to me. He begins to lift his hand out in my direction before thinking better of it and dropping his arm back down to his side. Even though I know I would flinch away from his touch, I want nothing more than for him to wrap me up in his arms and tell me it will be okay. I wish I could let him hold me and chase away the terror burning through my veins like acid. "What's going on?"

I lift my eyes and meet his gaze. The expression I see there is not only confusion and concern, but there's a tenderness there as well. That's something I've haven't seen anyone express toward me in a long time. I'm the unlovable one, the forgettable one. At a loss for words, I can do no more than shake my head side to side, fear roiling deep in my gut. Not only fear of going home and facing the wrath of Charlie. But fear of disappointing the gorgeous man standing in front of me. The one that thought I was special enough to treat to a fabulous meal at a restaurant that doesn't even list prices on their menu.

My stomach churns wildly and it takes all I have not to double over from the pain. Not only from having eaten a second meal in one day – something that I haven't been able to do in quite some time so my body doesn't know how to digest it – but because I know what torment I will have greet me as soon as I walk through the door at home. After the way Charlie escalated the other night, I'm afraid that I won't survive what awaits me after being gone all day. I wrap my arms tightly around my waist hoping to hold back the nausea that threatens to move into my throat.

"Come on," he says and reaches an arm out toward me. Not to touch, but to direct me to walk ahead of him as we exit the restaurant. "Let's get out of here. We can talk in the car."

I walk to the door, he only steps around me to hold it open for me before handing the valet ticket to the guy standing outside. We stand side by side, not talking as we wait for his silver Mercedes to arrive at the curb. He holds the passenger door open for me, same as before, and waits for me to buckle my seatbelt before closing the door and walking around to the other side.

He begins talking again as soon as we're on the street and pulling away from the restaurant. "What's going on, Emi? You're worrying me."

"I'm sorry. I'm so sorry. I didn't realize it was so late."

"Do you have somewhere better to be?" he asks before turning his gaze to me at a red light. He has one brow lifted and one corner of his mouth is tilted up, so I think he's joking. Maybe he's trying to lighten the mood. If only he knew.

"No, but I should have been home hours ago. I have responsibilities. Things that are expected of me."

"Emi," he grips the steering wheel tighter, and I watch as his knuckles begin to turn white. "I don't know, maybe I should have asked this before. Do you have a boyfriend?"

"What? No." I fidget with the sleeves of my sweater, pulling them far enough down my arms that I can wrap my fingers in them and hold the fraying threads in my fists. He blows out a slow breath at my response, as if he was waiting to breathe until he got the answer he wanted.

"I didn't think so. At least I had hoped not." He flips on the blinker and sits at another red light waiting for the arrow to light up.

I have no idea which way we're going, I've never been to the city before and I have no way of knowing if we're even on our way out of town or headed back to my home. Part of me hopes that he isn't, I don't know if I will survive another night with Charlie, especially after being gone all day. There's no telling what he'll do to me when I walk in the door and find him drunk in his recliner chair wondering why he didn't have dinner waiting for him when he got home.

Neither one of us says anything else as he continues to navigate through town. He continues to drive while I mutilate the inside of my cheek with worry. He's made so many turns I would have expected us to be back in front of the restaurant again, but we aren't. When he finally stops, we're parked in front of a beautiful three-story office building with a fountain in the front. The fountain is lit up with multi-colored lights as it sprays water in all directions. In the center of the fountain is an angel, her wings stretched far behind her, and her arms spread wide as if inviting everyone into her calming embrace.

"Where are we?" I whisper as I gaze at the beautiful angel in the center of the fountain.

"One of my buildings. Well, I don't own it, but I designed it. Including the fountain." He unbuckles his seatbelt but doesn't turn off the car or make to open the door. "This is the only building of mine that's still as beautiful at night as it is during the day."

"She's beautiful."

"She is." He inhales deeply before continuing. "She's my grandmother. Well, she was modeled after my grandmother. She was my angel in so many ways when my parents died. She took me in without a second thought and put up with all my shit. She always had a smile on her face and a tight hug anytime I needed one."

I feel a tear slip down my cheek but don't make any move to swipe it away or hide it. That's what I've been missing, someone to be my angel. Someone to look over me and take me in when I needed it. I've been on my own dealing with life for so long. "I wish I could have met her."

"Me too." He fists his hands together in his lap, still not looking in my direction but keeping his gaze on the angel in front of us.

"What's going on, Emi. I know it's something and I want to be able to help you. I've seen how you flinch away when someone touches you and I can see the fear in your eyes now. I don't like it, but I want to understand it. Will you tell me?"

"It's been so long since I've had anyone that wanted to help me. I don't know how to accept it."

"What about your friends at work?"

"I don't have any friends at work. At least not anyone that I would consider friends outside of work. Not anymore at least. No one really pays attention to me. I've been invisible for too long."

"Emi." My name slips out of his mouth on a single breath. "You're not invisible. I see you."

LANDON

AS SOON AS THE WORDS are uttered, the floodgates are opened. I watch as Emi breaks down next to me and there isn't a single thing I can do. I want nothing more than to scoop her up in my arms and take all the pain away. But I know that she isn't ready for that, she isn't ready for me to touch her yet. My heart is shattering into a million pieces as I watch her break down knowing that I can't comfort her.

"It's my stepfather," she gasps between sobs.

Reaching into the center console, I grab a pack of tissues and hand them to her. She takes them with a nod of her head and begins to wipe the tears from her cheeks. Her eyes are puffy and red but she's still the most beautiful woman I've ever seen in my life.

I sit silently and let her get it all out as soon as she's composed enough to do so. She tells me about how her mother shielded her for years from her stepfather's drunken rage. But how he turned on her once her mother had passed away. She tells me about how he takes her tips from her to spend on alcohol and makes her take care of the house and cook for him.

"Why haven't you told anyone else?" I ask and immediately regret the question when her fury filled gaze turns my way. Her red-rimmed eyes are suddenly full of anger and regret.

"You think I haven't? You think I never told anyone what was going on at home? I've told several people, and no one will listen to me. My stepfather is a legend in our small town. He was the captain of the football team in high school and if it wasn't for him, our school would have never broken so many records. He's a god in our town. No one would ever listen to me."

That's one of the things that I always hated about that small town. I know exactly what she's talking about, no one ever forgets a high school legend. Even when they grow up to be a drunk abuser like her stepfather. It's one of the many reasons why I fought so hard to get out of that town and never look back. Only I had help. I had resources. My grandparents made sure that I would be able to take care of myself when I graduated high school and encouraged me to grow my business. To be successful. If it wasn't for them, I'd be just like her stepfather and still be stuck in that small town.

I had someone there for me. Someone that meant so much to me that I designed an homage to her in the center of this fountain.

Emi has nobody. It dawns on me in an instant like a swift punch to the gut and I know exactly what I have to do.

"Will you come to my apartment with me?" I ask. "I have a guestroom. You can stay in there as long as you want to."

"I don't know." She looks around, taking another tissue and wiping beneath her eyes. "I don't want to impose."

"You wouldn't be an imposition, Emi. I can't bring myself to take you home knowing what's waiting for you there. I want to help you. Please let me help you." There's no way I can take her home now that I know what she has waiting for her. I'd be just as much of a monster as her stepfather if I took her back to him.

"Okay," she whispers, and I don't waste any time. I put my seatbelt on and flip the car around to get back on the road.

It's late enough that there isn't much traffic, so it only takes us a few minutes to reach my apartment building. "You live here?" she asks as she bends forward and tilts her head to the side to look up out the front window.

"Yeah." It really isn't much to look at, well at least it isn't for me since I've been here for four years. But it's a nice building. I should know since I designed it. I own it too but I'm not going to tell her that yet. It was a good investment and I make a decent income on the rent from the other units in the building.

The building stands twelve stories. The bottom floor is a grand entryway and communal area for the tenants and their guests. The next ten floors house apartments, four on each floor which are all filled. I have the entire top floor to myself, which is a little extreme, but I do like my privacy. That means that not only will Emi have her own room if she wants, but she'll have her own bathroom too.

I'm willing to let her choose which guest room she wants for now. But I have no intention on allowing her to get too comfortable in it. When she's ready, I'm hoping that she'll move into my room with me.

Maybe I'm moving things too fast, but it feels right. Just in the few days that I've known Emi, I've realized that I want her to be a part of my life. Not just for now, this isn't a fleeting feeling. But for the long run. I plan to keep her around forever if she'll let me. I should be afraid of the feelings running through my head, I've never had such a visceral reaction to anyone before. But fear is the last thing that I'm feeling.

I pull my car into the parking garage below the building and lead Emi to the private elevator that will take us all the way to the top floor. Emi leans against the back wall of the elevator, her arms wrapped around herself defensively, as we ride up to the twelfth floor. When it stops and the doors open, I step out and turn around to face her. "Welcome to my home."

Emi steps out of the elevator slowly, her eyes wide with wonder as she takes in her surroundings. "This is amazing." Directly in front of us is a wall of floor to ceiling windows looking out over the city. The view really is breathtaking at this time of night. The city lights are able to be seen for miles.

Emi goes straight to the windows and looks out at the view. "You should see it during the day." I step up behind her, keeping a few inches between us so she doesn't feel crowded but close enough that I can smell the sweetness of her shampoo. "Let me show you around."

"Okay." She turns around and looks up at me. She's still close enough to me that I could touch her with just the movement of a single finger, but I dare not move an inch. I want to let her make the first move, so I don't scare her away.

I take my time leading her through the apartment. I show her the kitchen, the dining room, and the living room. We wander down the hallway and I show her my home office, my workout room, and the guest bathroom. I'm watching her as she looks around the space with wide eyes. I can see my apartment as if through her eyes and I realize that it's a sterile space. I've been here for four years and haven't done much in the way of decorating or personalizing my apartment. The walls are still white, a few rugs here and there offer a small amount of comfort and protection from sounds echoing through the wide-open space. But there are no pictures on my walls, no lamps on my side tables. I've never really bothered to spend much time at home, spending most of my time at my office tinkering with designs and blueprints. In a way, I guess it's like an empty canvas. Just waiting for someone to come along and give it some character.

We walk further down the hallway, and I show her where my bedroom is before leading her to the guest bedroom where the bed is already made up and ready for her. The door is directly across the hall from my own.

She spins around in the middle of the room, looking at her surroundings, before wandering over to the window. The view from the guest bedroom is almost as lovely as that from the entryway to the apartment.

"There's a lock on the door." I take a few steps back toward the door as I talk. "So, you can feel safe if you need it."

"Thank you, Landon. You have no idea how much this means to me."

"We'll talk more in the morning, Emi. Get some sleep." She doesn't say anything else. She nods her head once and turns her gaze back out the window.

Lowering my gaze to the floor, I walk out of the room before I do something stupid like take her in my arms and kiss away her pain and fears.

Chapter TEN

EMILEE

I WAKE SLOWLY AS the morning light filters in through the bedroom window. It takes me several minutes to remember where I am and shame washes over me when I think of my stepfather, Charlie. I didn't go home last night. I have no phone, so I didn't even bother to call him, not that he deserves that much. But what happens when Landon realizes that I'm too much and sends me home?

No. I refuse to think about that.

Throwing my legs over the edge of the bed, I stand slowly and walk into the attached bathroom to wash my face. I find a new toothbrush in the drawer next to the sink along with toothpaste and mouthwash. After brushing my teeth, I splash cold water on my face and glare at my reflection in the mirror. Running my fingers through my tangled tresses, I pull my hair up into a loose bun on the top of my head and secure it with the hair tie wrapped around my wrist.

There are still dark circles under my eyes, but they are lighter than they were yesterday. Unfortunately, I don't have any of my makeup with me so I can't even attempt to cover them up.

Walking back into the bedroom, the smell of bacon and coffee assaults my senses and my stomach growls loudly in protest. I dress in the clothes I took off yesterday, including the sweater I wear to cover the bruises and cuts on my arms. I have no other clothes here. A shudder runs down my spine, ice filling my veins at the thought of returning to my home to retrieve my belongings. I don't know if I'm ready to face the consequences of returning yet.

"Time to face the music," I whisper to myself as I open the door and step into the hallway. I didn't bother locking the door last night. I already felt safer in Landon's apartment than I have in my own home for years, so I didn't feel the need to. Maybe I'm crazy considering I've only known Landon for a few days, but I trust him.

I take my time tip toeing down the hallway, through the living room, and into the kitchen. Landon doesn't turn away from the stove until he hears me pull a stool away from the counter.

"Good morning," he greets me with a smile on his face. He looks so domestic, wearing low slung sweats and a worn black t-shirt. The sleeves of the shirt are tight around his biceps, and I watch in awe as the muscles ripple and flex against the threads as he turns the bacon in the pan with a pair of tongs. "How'd you sleep?"

"Very well, thank you." I stand and walk around the counter to grab a coffee cup that he has sitting on the counter next to the fresh pot of coffee. "The bed was way more comfortable than my own back home." I fill my cup with the dark brew and scoop in a spoonful of sugar before returning back to my seat at the counter.

"I'm glad to hear it." I watch as Landon reaches into the cabinet above the counter and pulls out two plates. He places the bacon down on each plate before walking to the refrigerator to retrieve the eggs. "I hope scrambled is okay. I don't do well with any other eggs unfortunately."

"Scrambled is fine." Dragging my finger around the rim of my coffee cup, I look around the kitchen. It's nice and modern with stainless appliances and an apron sink. It's definitely nicer than mine that's equipped in butter yellow appliances that survived the disco era. I'd bet anything that all the burners work on Landon's stove too.

I watch as he finishes the eggs and scoops them onto both plates. After grabbing forks from another drawer in the kitchen, he brings both plates to the counter and sits on the empty stool next to mine.

"Thank you." I pick up a strip of bacon and take a bite. "This is amazing." I don't even remember the last time I had breakfast. Usually, I don't eat anything at home and only grab a sandwich at work when it's slow enough for me to eat. I haven't eaten an egg since I was in school. The rich buttery flavor bursts on my tongue and I moan in pleasure as I chew it slowly, my eyes closed as I savor the yummy goodness.

When I swallow and open my eyes, I find Landon watching me with his fork held in front of his mouth as if he were about to take a bite. "Sorry," I say. I can feel the heat filling my cheeks as embarrassment washes over me. "I haven't eaten eggs in years. These are really good."

"Years?" He finally takes the bite that's been sitting patiently in front of his face.

"I generally spend as little time at home as possible. I don't eat there at all. I usually grab something to eat at the diner if and when there's time for me to actually eat."

"Wait." He places his fork down on his plate and turns slightly to face me. "So those two lunches I had you eat with me." He lowers his gaze to his lap, and I see it when the realization hits him that those meals were the only ones I had either of those two days. "I can't believe no one at the diner knew."

"No. Like I said. I'm invisible."

"That's bullshit!" he exclaims, his palm slapping down on the countertop. I jolt at the action and the look on his face softens when he notices. "How can nobody notice you, Emi? You're beautiful."

"I appreciate the sentiment, Landon. Really, I do. But not everyone sees me that way."

Huffing his frustration, Landon stands and takes our now empty plates to put in the dishwasher. He grabs the coffee pot and fills both of our cups to the brim before returning to stand beside me. "Seriously, Emi. If no one else noticed how beautiful you are then it's their loss. Maybe you were just waiting for me to notice. For me to find you and save you from your life in that miserable town."

I can't move. I can barely think. This man says all the right things and I want nothing more than for him to be able to wrap me up in his arms and keep me safe. Just when I think I've finally found my voice, his next words stop me dead in my tracks.

"Can I kiss you, Emi?"

LANDON

86

SHE SHUDDERS AT THE shock of my words, and I wonder if said something wrong. Maybe I overstepped. I haven't lied to her. She really is beautiful and if no one else sees that then that's on them. Their loss is my gain. I have the privilege of her company and I intend to cherish it for as long as she'll allow me to. But I really do want to kiss her. It's taking every ounce of restraint not to reach out and take her in my arms.

I wait patiently as she ponders my question, waiting for her to either accept my offer or reject me. It'll be painful but I'll reign it in if that's what she prefers. I'll help her in any capacity that she'll permit me to. But if she isn't feeling anything remotely similar to what I'm feeling for her, I'll take a step back. I'll give her whatever space she needs.

"I'm not sure how I'm supposed to answer that," she whispers.

"It's an easy question, Emi. I want nothing more than to kiss you right now but I'm willing to wait if you aren't ready for that. But I want you to know that's the direction this is going. I'll wait as long as I need to for you to feel comfortable enough for me to touch you." I watch as her expression changes from fear to embarrassment to lust and I can't stop the words from spilling out of my mouth. "I have this desire to protect you, Emi. I want to hold you and hug you and make you realize that there is peace and love in the world. That not everyone is as horrible as the people in that town. As horrible as your stepfather. But I'd give anything to be able to kiss you right now."

"I want that too." She visibly relaxes where she's still sitting on that stool. I watch as her shoulders drop from around her ears, and she breathes a sigh of relief as my words wash over her.

"Yeah?" My body tenses in order to keep from throwing myself at her. I need to take this slowly, let her know that I'm not trying to hurt her. I'll never hurt her.

"Yeah." She nods her head slowly and locks her gaze with mine as I step closer. She doesn't move or flinch away from me as I approach slowly, cautiously.

I lift both hands slowly, giving her enough time to change her mind. My palms caress her face, my thumbs tracing her cheekbones, the tips of my fingers wrapping around and teasing the fine hairs at the back of her neck. I pause only an inch from her mouth and move my gaze back from her lips to her eyes, giving her a moment of time to change her mind. I take the time to memorize her features, the beauty of her angelic face. She washed her face of all the makeup and concealer she had painted on yesterday. Just as I imagined, she has an adorable smattering of freckles over her nose giving her an allure of innocence. It's the haunted gaze in her eyes though, the darkened circles beneath them, that I'm desperate to erase.

To my utter surprise, she fists her fingers in the fabric at my chest and pulls me the final distance to her. My mouth presses furiously into hers, the pillowy softness of her lips welcoming mine with a burn of fire fueled by lust and intense chemistry. Cradling her face in my hands, I angle her head back and deepen the kiss. She gasps at the movement and my tongue slides home, twisting and mingling with her own. Her taste is now burned into my brain, the distinct flavor of cherry lip gloss and coffee.

I knew this was a bad idea. Part of me always knew that if I was able to touch her, I wouldn't be able to let go. If I was able to kiss her, I wouldn't be able to stop. Breaking the kiss slowly, I drag my mouth along her jaw and to her neck. She throws her head back to give me more room, her breathy moans fueling my desire to continue. Dragging my hands across her shoulders, I lower them down her arms and around her back. Pressing my hands into the small of her back, I pull her closer to me, pressing my hips against hers. I know she can feel my desire for her, and I can't bring myself to regret it in the least.

It's only when her moans transform into a yelp of pain that I break away completely. Like a bucket of ice-cold water being dumped over my head, I immediately regret pushing her too far too fast. "I'm sorry." I keep my hands up in front of me as I step back but she doesn't release her hold on my shirt, and I'm limited to how much distance I can put between us. I don't want to pull her off the stool in my effort of getting away from her.

"No," she whispers, closing her eyes and slowly releasing my shirt. "You didn't do anything wrong."

"I hurt you." I glare down at my own hands, willing to rip them from my wrists if it would keep me from ever being the cause of her pain again. "I didn't mean to hurt you."

"You didn't hurt me." I look up at Emi as she stands from the stool and steps closer to me as I take another step away from her. I try to take another step back, but she stops me with a word, "Wait." I pause and continue watching her, my eyes locked with hers.

"What are you doing?" I ask as I drop my arms down to my sides.

"Showing you." She slowly unbuttons her sweater and slips it off her shoulders. I follow the fabric with my eyes as it falls to the floor at her feet. "I wear the sweater to hide my arms."

Trailing my eyes back up her body, I see the purple and green bruises covering her arms from her wrists to her elbows. Many of them dark and demanding and I know they're from within the last couple of days. As my eyes trace up to her biceps, I see cuts and scabs in various stages of healing and rage boils in my veins. "Emi." Her name slips from my lips like a prayer. How can someone do this to such a beautiful creature? Her arms are so thin and frail looking. The way her tank top hugs her body shows the extent of her thin stature, her desperation for someone to step in and give a shit about her.

"That's not all." She whispers before reaching for the hem of her tank top.

"There's more?" I hold my breath as she pulls the thin top up, revealing her abdomen. The bones of her ribcage are visible beneath the pale complexion, the blue lines of her veins apparent through her near translucent skin. "Fuck!" I exclaim as I see the bruises lining her body just over her prominent hip bones. She turns and I see more discoloration marking her back. "I'll kill him," I hiss through clenched teeth.

"He's not worth you going to jail for, Landon."

"Maybe you're right." I rub my hand over my face, the rough texture of my beard scraping over my palm. "But either way you're not going back there. He'll never touch you again if I have anything to say about it."

"I have to go back at some point."

"No, you don't." I refuse to argue with her about this. Bottom line, she has no business being there with that monster. She's mine to take care of now. It's my responsibility to protect and provide for her from here on out.

"I have no clothes here, Landon. Everything I own is back there."

"We'll go shopping. I'll replace anything that you left there. You never have to go back there." She lowers her brows in frustration, a true show of her stubbornness. She isn't going to win this fight though. She's been looking out for herself for far too long. It's my turn to stand in as her protector, her enforcer. I want to provide for her more than I want to take my next breath or see my business succeed. Cocking my head to the side, I focus on her until I see her relent. Her expression relaxes, the fight draining out of her, and I see that I'm going to get my way after all.

"Okay."

Chapter
ELEVEN

EMILEE

"WHERE ARE WE?" I ask as Landon expertly navigates through the parking lot decorated strategically with flowering bushes and crape myrtle trees in every color imaginable. The colorful buds are vibrant on the branches, the sweet fragrance of each bloom carried on the breeze into the car through the cracked windows tickling my senses.

"The Village." His answer is short but doesn't help me to understand what I'm looking at. There are people everywhere, walking with shopping bags slung over their arms and pleasure filled smiles crossing their sun kissed faces.

"That doesn't tell me anything." I can't take my eyes off the buildings all around us as we finally pull into a spot on the edge of the lot. There are sidewalks in every direction, Dutch architecture buildings lining the makeshift streets and going on for miles in a multitude of colors. Pinks, blues, greens, all blending together from one shop to the next. Storefront windows decorated with the latest spring fashions and accessories. Without waiting for Landon, I open my door and step out of the car and pull my sleeves down to my fingertips before closing my fist around them to hold them in place. "I've never seen anything like it."

"You're going to love it. Everything you could ever imagine is available here. Come on." He walks around the front of the car and reaches a hand in my direction. He doesn't grab me, but waits for me to meet him halfway, allowing me to make the decision on whether to be touched. I don't hesitate to reach out and clasp his hand in mine and my heart does a little flip in my chest as the corners of his mouth tip up in a victorious smile.

"That still doesn't tell me what we're doing here," I say as I watch him out the corner of my eye.

He doesn't stop walking, pulling me across the street separating the parking lot from the entrance to The Village. "Shopping."

I stop walking as soon as we reach the sidewalk. He takes another couple of steps before my hand pulls him to a stop and he turns to look at me. Cocking his head to the side, he narrows his eyes before asking, "What are you doing?"

"I can't go shopping, Landon."

"Why not?" I don't answer him, and he steps closer to me. Releasing my hand, he reaches up and pinches my chin between his thumb and forefinger, tilting my face up to look into his eyes. "What's wrong, Emi?"

"I can't go shopping."

"You said that already." There's a cool breeze blowing today, and a few hairs have escaped from my ponytail, fluttering across my face, and tickling my nose. Letting go of my chin, he uses his fingertips to smooth the stray hairs away from my forehead, tucking them behind my ear and cupping my cheek in his palm. "What's going through that adorable head of yours?"

I don't break my gaze away from his. His eyes soften as he waits patiently for me to find the right words. But how do I explain to him what I'm thinking? How do I tell him I don't want him spending his money on me even though I don't have anything to spend on myself? A shiver runs down my spine and I pull my bottom lip between my teeth to avoid breaking the silence. I don't want him to pity me, I don't need his pity.

Landon takes another step closer, our toes touching when he stops moving. His thumb traces my cheekbone softly and I close my eyes, leaning into his touch. It's been so long since I've been able to actually enjoy the touch of another person, usually it would take time before I would even feel comfortable being this close to anyone, much less being touched by them. But with Landon, it just feels natural – right. I may not know him very well yet, but I know that he won't hurt me. We're like two lost souls that have been searching for our way back to each other. We recognize each other on a subconscious level.

"Come on," he starts before leaning in and pressing his lips against my forehead. The burn that starts at the point of contact runs down my entire body, igniting my toes on fire as they curl in my sneakers. I've read in several books about the sweet, intimate moments when the man kisses the woman on the forehead. A sign of respect and adoration. But having finally experienced such an act in real life is a totally different scenario.

It's almost overwhelming – the overload of all my senses in a single day. The feel of his hand as he continues to caress my cheek. The deliciously masculine scent of soap and musk. The warm press of his lips against my forehead. I could dissolve into a puddle at his feet right now and be the happiest glob of goo on the planet.

"You need clothes and things." He steps away from me finally, his hand falling away from my cheek. "And we have somewhere to be this afternoon, so we need to get a move on." He reaches out for my hand, twining our fingers together as we continue to walk again. "And just so you're aware, I'm paying for everything. I feel bad that I dragged you away from your home and your job. But I don't regret it after seeing what that monster has been doing to you. You deserve so much better than the life you've been living in Independence, and I feel a strong desire to take care of you. Will you let me do that for you, Emi?"

I don't answer right away. I'm still somewhat embarrassed at the thought of him paying for things for me. I mean, I don't even really know him. Not that I don't want to. I want to know everything about Landon.

He stops moving and turns to face me. "I mean it, Emi. I want to take care of you."

"Okay," I whisper, my gaze turning toward the sidewalk. Then, something else he mentioned strikes me as odd. "Wait. You said we had somewhere to be this afternoon. Where else could we possibly have to be besides The Village?"

"I called a friend of mine that works at a clinic. I made you an appointment to see a doctor there to have those cuts on your arms looked at. I want to make sure everything is healing up okay. Not to mention those bruises on your lower back."

"You didn't have to do that."

"I know. I just want to make sure you're okay, Emi. That's all."

"Okay," I concede, knowing there's no point in arguing. We start walking again silently, my hand still held tightly in his.

We visit several shops in The Village, loading up armfuls of clothing that I really don't even need if it weren't for the fact that all of my things are still at the house in Independence. I get about a dozen pairs of yoga pants and long-sleeved t-shirts, Landon thought they would be more comfortable than a heavy sweater while my arms are healing. We ended up in a boutique that specialized in hand made soaps and fragrances and he bought me several varieties of floral bath products that I fell in love with while in the shop.

"Are you hungry?" Landon asks as he puts the last of our purchases into the trunk of his car.

Shaking my head side to side, I look at him over the top of the car. "Not really." My body isn't used to eating more than once a day and we had a rather large breakfast before leaving the apartment this morning. I don't know how long it will be before I'm able to eat like a normal person again without feeling sick to my stomach. I guess I'll make sure to ask the doctor during my appointment this afternoon.

"Okay," he walks over and opens my door for me to get into the car. Once I'm in and my seatbelt is buckled, he tips his wrist to check the time on his watch before closing my door. "We have about forty-five minutes before your appointment but it's on the other side of town. It will probably take us about a half hour to get there and you'll need to do paperwork. If you're hungry afterwards, we can go out for dinner."

Wordlessly, I nod my head as he closes my door. My hands twist nervously in my lap as he drives across town. The traffic isn't as bad as I thought it would be in the middle of a weekday, so we arrive at the office after only twenty minutes.

"I'll come in with you and sit in the waiting room. I won't go back with you though when you see the doctor. I'll give you your privacy."

"Thank you," I tell him honestly. I'm nervous about seeing a doctor but I do want to go in there by myself. I do appreciate him not forcing me to have him go back with me though. Not that I'm worried about him hearing about anything that's gone on with me, but I don't know if I would be able to speak honestly with him there. I wouldn't be able to get the words out if he watches me with pity in his eyes.

After checking in with the receptionist, I take the clipboard and a pen and sit in an over padded leather chair next to Landon. The paperwork is pretty straightforward, but unfortunately, I don't know what to put for most of the information. I don't have insurance, or a phone number for contact. I don't even know who to put down for an emergency contact. Nervously, I tap the pen against the page. The constant *tap, tap, tap* of the pen hitting the clipboard is a constant focal point in my head, breaking through the erratic thoughts streaming through my head like a movie.

"Your birthday was yesterday?" Landon asks, his voice breaking me out of my anxious thoughts.

"Yeah," I whisper back. I fist my hand around the pen and force myself to stop tapping it against the page. "April fools, right?"

"I don't think I've ever known anyone that was born on April Fool's Day before."

I don't say anything back to him. My birthday is something that I haven't thought of since my mother passed away. She always made it a big deal, but instead of singing *Happy Birthday* to me every year, she would present me a mangled cake and scream "April Fools!" as she set it on the table. The cake was always atrocious looking but delicious. I think she prided herself on the one day every year that she could purposely destroy a perfectly good cake before presenting it to anyone to eat. It was like an annual challenge to see how bad it could look from one year to the next. I never thought I would miss those hideous looking cakes.

"Emilee Jackson?" I hear called from across the waiting room. Looking down at the clipboard, I see that I haven't even finished filling out the information.

"I'll wait here," Landon whispers in my ear, his hand pressing between my shoulder blades gently to help me stand.

Clutching the clipboard in one hand, the pen tightly in the other, I walk across the room toward the open door. I don't look back at Landon as I step closer to the nurse, her forced smile sending a shiver up my spine. I don't know why I'm nervous, I have no reason to be afraid of seeing a doctor. It's been a while since I've been to one so I'm not sure what to expect.

"I'll take that," she says as I step closer to her side. She holds the door wide with one hand, grabbing the clipboard with her other. She doesn't even look at the paper and I feel a little guilty for leaving so much of it blank. I watch out the corner of my eye as she places her tablet on top of the clipboard, effectively covering up my information. She steps inside the door, and I jolt in surprise at the loud click of it closing behind us.

Neither one of us speaks as she directs me to a small room where a table, chair, and scale sit against the far wall. She motions for me to step onto the scale, and I watch as she moves the small weights left and right until they balance out perfectly. She taps her findings into the tablet before directing me to sit so she can take my blood pressure with an electric cuff that feels like it's squeezing the life out of my arm. Maybe I should have said something about the bruises and cuts on my upper arm before letting her attach me to this machine. It hurts a lot worse than I thought it would and I grimace against the pain, biting the inside of my cheek hard enough to taste blood.

After removing the cuff from my arm, she directs me to another room where she has me sit on the table. Thankfully, she doesn't direct me to remove any of my clothing. "The doctor will be in soon." She closes the door without giving me time to respond and I'm left to my own thoughts while I wait.

After what feels like an hour, but may have only been a few minutes, a woman walks into the room. She doesn't look up immediately, her gaze focused on the tablet in her hand. "Good afternoon, Emilee," she greets me as she closes the door softly behind her. She looks to be in her mid-forties with her grey streaked red hair pulled back in a tight bun at the base of her neck. She's dressed in a loose-fit pant suit with a white lab coat covering her arms, a stethoscope peeking out of her jacket pocket. "I'm Doctor Casey. Do you mind if I sit with you for a few minutes?"

"Okay," I answer on a shaky breath. She sits and rolls the stool closer to the side of the table I'm sitting on, the tablet left sitting on the table on the opposite side of the room.

"So, what brings you here today?"

"Umm," I'm not sure how to answer that question. "To be honest, I didn't even know I was coming to see you."

"I see." She reaches over and picks the tablet up, tapping the screen once to wake it up. "That's fine. I have a few notes." She silently reads over whatever information is on the screen, humming a few times to herself as she nods her head. "So, you just turned twenty?"

"Yes."

"You're a little underweight, but your blood pressure looks good. Not too low. I'd like to get some labs drawn while you're here if that's okay."

"I guess so."

"Don't worry," she looks up at me with a soft smile. "My nurses are really good at blood draws. You won't even feel it." I nod as she turns her gaze back to the tablet. "Hmm." She stretches her arm out to set the tablet down again before rolling away from me and standing up. "Would you mind taking off the sweater?"

My lips are pressed tightly in a line as I lean forward slightly to pull the bottom of my sweater from beneath where I'm sitting on it. Slowly, I pull my arms out of the sleeves, careful not to upset my tender bruises. I hear the doctor gasp in surprise as my first arm becomes visible to her. She reaches out and takes the sweater from me once it's removed and sets it across a chair.

"These look like they're fading." She wraps her cold fingers around my wrist and twists my arm from side to side to get a better look. "This is healing nicely." I watch as she traces one of the cuts on my upper arm softly. "It might leave a scar. Do you have any more bruises besides the ones on your arms?"

"Yes." I lift the hem of my shirt and watch as she leans to look around to my back. My gaze never leaves her face as she assesses the bruises below my ribs and along my kidneys. Without saying anything, she nods her head a few times and steps away to sit back on the stool.

"Is there someone I can call for you? Do you need someplace to go?"

I'm not sure why she's asking me that. I'm here with Landon, and he's been keeping me safe since he took me away from Independence. My brows lower in confusion while she taps the screen of her tablet, obviously entering her own notes about her observations.

"Look, Emilee." She stands and steps closer before placing a hand softly on my shoulder. "I'm sorry that this has happened to you. But I want to make sure you're safe. If he's hurting you then I'd like to help you find somewhere safe to go so he can't hurt you anymore."

"I am safe."

"You don't have to defend him, sweetie."

It finally hits me what she's thinking, and I jerk away from her touch. "You think Landon did this?" She lowers her arm, and her brows raise in question. "It wasn't Landon. Landon got me away from it. Believe me, I'm safe."

"I'm sorry. I didn't mean to jump to conclusions. But you'd be surprised how many abusers bring their loved ones in here and pretend like nothing's going on. You can't fault me for making sure you were safe."

"Can I have my sweater back please?" I'm anxious to get this visit over with. Nodding her head, she reaches out for my sweater and helps me put it back on.

The rest of the visit goes by smoothly, if not a little quietly. She doesn't say much as she goes over some information with me. Another nurse comes in a draws two vials of blood, she has me pee in a cup because she says she's worried about the bruises over my kidneys. I'm given a few pamphlets on a suggested high protein diet in order to gain back some of the weight that I've lost since I've only been eating once per day. Of course, she also suggests that I start with small meals, so I don't make myself feel sick during the day. I have to reacclimate my stomach to eating regular sized meals again. She also tells me that when I start to gain some of my weight back and replace some of the nutrients that I've been neglected of, that my periods will start again. It's been more than a year since I've had one. I asked her about birth control, but she decided it wouldn't be a good idea until my cycles start again.

The nurse walks me back out to the waiting room where Landon is still sitting patiently waiting for me. He stands as soon as he sees me, and I walk straight toward him. He doesn't reach for me when I get near, which I appreciate, but holds his hand toward the door to direct me to walk ahead of him as we leave. He doesn't ask about the doctor, and I don't offer any information. I'm just ready to get back to his apartment and put an end to this crazy hectic day.

Chapter
TWELVE

LANDON

I WATCH AS EMI WALKS toward the nurse, she still has a slight limp to her gait, so I know she's still healing and sore. I only hope that she doesn't have anything seriously wrong, more damage than can be seen on the outside with the bruises and cuts littering her frail body. I know she's nervous about being seen by a doctor, but I only want the best for her. I probably should have talked to her before making this appointment for her, but I don't know if she would have agreed to be seen. If that makes me an ass, so be it.

I definitely feel like an ass knowing that her birthday was yesterday, and I didn't even know. Not that we know each other well enough to celebrate birthdays together, but I can't help but wonder how long it's been since she's been able to celebrate hers. I may not be able to do anything about the day itself, but I can at least get her something as a late celebration. I wonder how angry she'll be with what I have in mind for her.

One thing that I've learned about Emi in the short time that I've known her is that she wanted to be a photographer. I don't know what happened to her equipment, I know she had some at some point because she mentioned her mother working hard to get it for her. I can only imagine that her stepfather had something to do with it disappearing, the bastard. That's at least one dream of hers that I can help to bring to fruition.

Pulling my phone from my back pocket, I fill the time with research. It doesn't take me long to find what I'm looking for. Unfortunately, it isn't available anywhere local and needs to be ordered. I decide to order everything that I want and have it shipped to my office. It will take a few days to come in, but I can't wait to surprise Emi with it when it does.

Happy with my purchase, I'm just putting the phone back in my pocket when Emi comes through the door. I stand and she walks toward me, looking bashful and innocent. It takes all I have not to reach for her, offer her the comfort she so desperately needs. But I know she isn't ready for that yet. I don't worry about talking to the receptionist before we leave, I already made sure she had my credit card information for the bill. I suspect that Emi doesn't have any insurance working at the diner, something that I hope to be able to remedy soon.

"Are you hungry?" I ask her as I slide into the driver's seat of my car.

"No." She twists her hands in her lap but doesn't look over at me. "I'm actually a little tired. I think I'd like to lay down for a little while if that's okay."

"Of course, that's okay. You've had a long day, Emi. I tell you what," I start as I back out of the parking spot in front of the clinic. "We'll go home, take all these bags up to the apartment, then you can take a nap and I'll help you put everything away after you wake up."

"Thank you, Landon. For everything."

"You don't have to thank me, Emi." She turns her gaze out the passenger window and watches the city fly by as I drive down the street toward the apartment building. The rest of the drive is relatively quiet, no sound besides our breathing and the steady hum of the engine.

We work in tandem to remove the bags from the trunk of the car and carry them up to my apartment. As soon as I open the door, Emi walks in ahead of me and carries her bags to the guest room. I follow her in and set the bags on the floor inside the door. She doesn't say anything, just walks slowly to the bed and collapses on top of the blanket, immediately curling her body around one of the fluffy pillows. I watch her for a few seconds before backing out of the room and pulling the door closed quietly.

I want to know about the visit with the doctor, but it isn't my place to push. She'll tell me about it if and when she's ready.

Stepping into my home office, I boot up my laptop to check my email. Typing up a quick message to my assistant, I let her know that I'm expecting a package to be delivered to the office this coming week. Hopefully, it's delivered early in the week – I can't wait to see the look on Emi's face when she opens it up.

After answering a few more emails, and confirming meetings scheduled for the next couple of weeks, I decide to relax for a few minutes. I picked up a new book several days ago that I'm anxious to get started on. It's by a new author from California that writes realistic fiction based on true crime. It's different than some of the other true crime dramas that I've read in the past, but I've heard good things about it. Apparently, the author, Julie Adams, writes her stories based on actual events and unsolved crimes. Melodee, my assistant, mentioned it to me one day at work. After telling me that the proceeds from the book sales were donated to an outreach program in LA that rehabilitates abuse victims and helps them pay medical and legal fees, I just had to run out and buy the book myself.

I briefly wonder if I should start making something for dinner, I know Emi will be hungry when she finally wakes from her nap. Unfortunately, I don't want to make her sick either – I've never been much of a cook. Breakfast is easy, but anything else resembling a healthy meal, not so much. Much to my grandmother's chagrin, I wasn't a good pupil in the art of cooking. She tried, oh how she tried. She wanted me to be able to not only take care of myself but be able to woo a woman with my soulful cooking skills. As it turns out, I just don't have the patience for it.

I can design and build a house, a parking garage, or an office building. I can renovate buildings left dilapidated and forgotten, worn with the tendrils of time rotting away their existence, and turn them into modern marvels of engineering and structural durability. But I can't cook a simple meal that would satisfy the hunger of even a common cockroach without fear of food poisoning. Even a crock pot is a mystery to me for whatever reason. I can, however, order takeout. I have a plethora of takeout menus awaiting selection in a drawer in the kitchen. That would be the safer option.

Decision made, I can safely wait until Emi wakes up. That will give her the option of choosing where to order, anything that she craves can be ordered easily with a simple phone call. At least then I won't have to worry about causing her to get sick. I couldn't live with that.

I'm so caught up in the pages of my book that I don't even hear Emi coming down the hall. I don't realize she's even in the room until she sits on the couch next to me and curls into my side, my arm going around her shoulders automatically. My heart swells several sizes as I realize how comfortable she's becoming around me. She doesn't push my arm away or flinch away from my touch. I'm grateful for that little improvement in such a short amount of time. I'll take it as a point in the win column.

Gently folding over the corner of the page in my book, I set it on the table beside me before kissing Emi softly on the top of her head. The sound she makes is so quiet, I almost don't hear it. It's a cross between a moan and purr and a vision of a tiny, innocent kitten comes to mind. Smiling, I decide to kiss the top of her head one more time with a little more force and feeling.

"What are you reading?" she asks, lifting her head from my shoulder.

Reaching for the book, I hand it to her and watch as she flips it over to read the back cover. "It's by a new author I've never read before. My assistant recommended it to me."

"Looks interesting." She hands it back after flipping through a few of the pages, her brow furrowed in thought.

"So far, it's pretty good. This author writes fiction based on true crimes." She settles back in against my side and yawns sweetly. Her stomach rumbles and I'm reminded that it's been several hours since she's eaten anything. "I need to feed you."

She sits up as I move away from her to stand. "Yeah," she whispers. She takes my extended hand as I offer to help her off the couch.

"What are you in the mood for? I can order from anywhere."

"Order? Why don't we just cook something here?"

I pause and look down at her, my hand frozen on the menu drawer. "I don't think that would be a good idea. I'm not a very good cook."

"You did pretty well with breakfast this morning."

"That's different. And the only thing I can really cook successfully."

She walks closer and leans on the counter across from where I'm standing. "I'm a pretty good cook. At least I think I am. It's been a while since I've eaten anything that I've cooked myself." She turns her gaze down to the counter and I wonder what memory is afflicting her.

Walking around the counter, I nudge her chin, so she looks up at me. "I don't expect you to do the cooking, Emi."

"The doctor says I need to eat healthy. Lots of protein and smaller frequent meals. I have some time to make up for."

Damn, she's right. Takeout might be convenient, but it's anything but healthy. It's full of fat and fillers that her body really doesn't need right now. "Fine. I'm sure I can think of something that even I won't mess up."

"We can cook together." Her eyes glimmer with amusement as my brow lowers in frustration. I don't think she understands just how bad of a cook I really am. "It'll be fun."

"Sure," I relent, mentally cataloging what medication I already have on hand for in case of stomach issues later. "But we'll have to go out again for groceries. I don't have much here beyond breakfast foods. And from the sounds of it, you're going to need some snacks too. Do you feel like going shopping again?"

She smiles before pulling away from me and darting toward the front door. I watch as she bends and pulls her shoes on. "Do you have a piece of paper?"

"Are you wanting to make a list?" I open the junk drawer on the other side of the center island and reach for a sheet of scrap paper and pen.

"No. I just need the paper."

Confused, I toss the pen back into the drawer and walk over to Emi. She's still smiling when she takes the sheet from me and holds it in one hand. She waits for me to grab my keys and wallet before opening the door and we take the elevator down to the parking garage.

Chapter
THIRTEEN

EMILEE

LANDON KEEPS EYEING ME curiously as he drives through town. I'm sitting in the passenger seat with a sheet of paper in my lap and I know he wants to know what I'm going to do with it. An idea struck me as I flipped through the pages of his book and saw his dog-eared page. I've always hated it when I got a book from the library and saw the creases in the corners of the pages. Many may not see anything wrong with it, but after being folded several times, the paper becomes weak and will tear. No one wants to read a book that's been abused to the point of missing parts of their pages. I know Landon likes to read, I saw the bookshelves full of books lining his living room wall. You can tell a lot about a person by the types of books they read. But you can tell more about them by the way they treat those books too.

I fold the paper several times, making precise and purposeful creases along the sheet. I can feel his gaze wandering over to me several times before we get to the store, but I don't pay him any mind. I'm still folding and tucking the paper when he walks around the front of the car before opening my door and helping me out. Not even paying attention anymore, I've done this so many times it's all muscle memory at this point, I follow him into the store and watch as he grabs a cart.

I don't know what all we need since I didn't take time to go through the cabinets or refrigerator before leaving his apartment. I figure I can just throw out suggestions here and there and see where we end up. We start in the produce department, and I grab a bag of fresh Brussels sprouts and toss them into the cart. A giggle bursts out of me as he eyes the vegetables with a look of disgust.

"Seriously?" he growls low.

"What's wrong with Brussels sprouts?"

"My grandmother used to make me eat those. I've always hated them."

"Then she wasn't cooking them right." I toss him a quick smile before turning back to look for more fresh vegetables.

Challenge accepted.

"Okay," he starts as he pushes the cart along beside me. "But I make no promises."

"I can work with that." I grab a selection of peppers and toss them into the cart. Even if I don't use them for cooking, I can slice them for snacks. Ralph hated it when I would wander into his kitchen at the diner and eat peppers from the prep station. It's funny really. Something that I hated so much when I was growing up and now, I can't get enough of them. I'm still folding the paper into a smaller shape as we continue through the produce.

I grab several different condiments and toss them into the cart. Dijon mustard, mayonnaise, different jams and jellies. I don't know if he has any seasonings since he doesn't cook, but I assume he at least has salt and pepper, so I skip those. He grabs a few things that I don't pay attention to and tosses them into the cart as well. We finish at the meat department where I grab ground beef, a few different roasts, steak, and pork chops.

Finally finished with my paper folding, I slip it into my back pocket for safe keeping. I see him watching me, but he doesn't ask. I just smile innocently and continue walking beside him as we head for the checkout.

Mentally, I inventory everything we just picked up from the grocery store on the way back to Landon's apartment. I know for a fact that I'm going to make him Brussels sprouts, but what should I make to go with them?

Landon carries most of the bags from the trunk, leaving me with the lightest three of the bunch. Which is fine with me since I'm still sore, my arms hurt more than anything else right now. Finding a home for all the groceries once we reach the apartment isn't hard since there wasn't much food stored away to begin with. My eyes land on the pork chops and I toss the package on the counter rather than put them away. I know what I'm going to make.

"Are you ever going to tell me what you were doing with that paper?" Landon interrupts my thoughts and I laugh before turning to face him.

Pulling the paper from my back pocket, I tell him, "Go grab that book you were reading earlier." He cocks his head to the side in question before turning to go get the book from the side table in the living room. He carries it back into the kitchen where I stand still facing him with my hand outstretched toward him. He places the book in my hand and stands a few steps in front of me as I open the book to the page he dog-eared earlier.

"It may not mean much to you," I start as I smooth out the crease on the corner of the page. The paper I folded earlier is shaped into a square, one side divided in half diagonally with the ends tucked under to create an opening. "But I've always thought books were amazing escapes from reality. Some of us have realities worth escaping more than others. I used to go to the library and borrow books to read while I was hiding out in my bedroom at home. I hated it when I'd get to a page that someone had dog-eared the corner. Several times, I would get a book that had been dog-eared so many times that the pages were ripping, or missing parts and it killed me." I slip the folded paper over the corner of several pages in the book, showing Landon how it would mark his place. "Now, you have a bookmark to use. You don't have to destroy your books anymore." Closing the book, I hand it back to him.

"Thank you," he says, holding the book to his chest. I can't read his expression as his gaze meets mine but at least he likes the bookmark.

"You're welcome. So how about we start on dinner?"

He sets the book on the counter and walks around to join me in the kitchen. "What do you need me to do?"

"Well," I start, clapping my hands together excitedly. "I know where all the food is because I helped put it all away. But I need a few things that I have no idea where to get them from." He nods his head, ready to accept orders, and I smile at his sudden enthusiasm. "I need a baking sheet, a skillet, a knife, a cutting board, and a pair of tongues."

While he moves around his kitchen gathering the supplies I've requested, I step to the sink to wash my hands before gathering all my ingredients and setting them on the counter. Once I have the oven set to heating and the skillet warming up on the stovetop, I begin rinsing the Brussels sprouts and placing them on the cutting board a few at a time.

"Okay," he cries as he watches me work with the leafy vegetable. "I promised I would try."

"Yes, you did," I remind him playfully, elbowing him in the ribs softly. One by one, I slice each of the Brussels sprouts in half and place them on the baking sheet. After sprinkling them with some olive oil and a little salt and pepper, I set them aside to wait for the oven to finish heating.

"You aren't boiling them?"

"No!" I exclaim. "It's too easy to overcook them that way and then you get the nasty sulfur taste and miss out on the natural nutty sweetness of the vegetable.

"Hmm. Okay"

Taking the pork chops out of the packaging, I set them on the plastic cutting board and sprinkle pepper on each side. After drizzling a little olive oil in the skillet, I place both chops in the pan and let them sizzle then place the baking sheet into the oven.

"What's next?" Landon asks.

"I need a bowl and a whisk." I grab the Dijon mustard, chicken broth, and peach preserves that we bought at the store today and set it all on the counter.

"What on earth are you going to do with all that?"

"You'll see." I take a few minutes to flip each of the pork chops before returning to the counter where Landon has placed the bowl next to my ingredients. Scooping out a huge spoonful of the preserves, I dump it into the bowl, squeeze in some of the mustard and a splash of the broth. "Here, whisk this all together." I stand back and watch as he enthusiastically mixes the sauce for the chops, a smile on my face at the realization of how domestic this seems. I don't think I've ever had so much fun cooking a meal.

"How's that?" he asks as he sets the bowl back on the counter.

"Perfect." Checking the pork chops one more time, I grab the bowl and the spoon I used to scoop out the preserves and split the sauce between the two chops in the skillet. "Now we let those finish cooking then we're ready to eat."

"That's it?"

"That's it."

"You made that look so easy."

"Save the praise for when you get to taste it. I told you, I know how to cook. But I haven't eaten anything that I've cooked in a really long time. I don't know how good it's going to be."

"Well, it smells amazing." I watch as he walks back to the other side of the kitchen and grabs a couple of plates from the cabinet. He places knives and spoons on the breakfast bar and grabs two bottles of water from the refrigerator and places beside them.

Opening the oven, I see that our leafy greens are perfectly browned and crispy, so I pull them out and set them on the stove next to the skillet. Turning off both the oven and the stovetop, I start plating up the food for us. Holding my plate, Landon grabs his from the counter and I follow him over to the barstools on the other side of the bar. I wait patiently as Landon takes the first bite, of course choosing to try the pork chop first.

Smiling around the food, his eyes go wide as he looks up and turns his head toward me. "This is really good," he says as soon as he's swallowed. "Juicy and sweet. Probably the best pork chop I've ever had in my life."

"Thank you," I whisper, cutting off a bite of my own. He's right, it is really good. Tasting the Brussels sprouts, I'm pleased with how they turned out as well. Perfectly nutty and sweet without the sulfur aftertaste. I look over at Landon and wait for his opinion on the vegetable, I'm anxious to see if I've convinced him they were better than he thought.

"Okay, you win!" he exclaims. "These are really good too."

"I'm glad you approve." Giggling, I take a few more bites before I push my plate away. Landon finishes everything on his plate before reaching for his water to wash everything down. "So, what were you thinking about doing tomorrow?"

"Well," he starts before taking his plate to the sink to rinse before placing it in the dishwasher. Reaching into another cabinet, he grabs a plastic container and holds it out to me so I can save my leftovers for when I'm able to eat again. A warm feeling builds in my chest at the encouragement – it might seem weird, but he isn't pushing me to finish eating knowing that I have to start small. Especially now that he knows how long it's been since I've had a real meal more than once per day and this is technically the third time we've eaten anything today. "Did you ever learn how to drive?"

"What?" I freeze, my pork chop hanging at the end of my fork between the plate and the container.

"Driving. I was thinking about teaching you how. That is, if you don't already know."

"I've never driven. You know how it is living in Independence. The town is small enough that you can walk anywhere that you want to go. There was never any reason for me to learn, and Charlie certainly wasn't going to teach me."

"Then, that's what we're doing tomorrow. You should learn how to drive."

Oh boy. This is going to be a disaster.

Chapter
FOURTEEN

LANDON

"OH, MY GOD. I CAN'T do this!" Emi exclaims from the driver's seat of my Mercedes. Her hands are fisted so tightly around the steering wheel that her knuckles are turning white, and her legs are bouncing up and down nervously. She's as jumpy as a kitten on a catnip bender.

"Of course, you can." I pinch my lips between my teeth to stop myself from chuckling at her antics. I know she's nervous, but she has nothing to be nervous about. "Come on. We're outside of the city. It's a Sunday and there's nobody around. What could possibly go wrong?"

I fail miserably at not laughing when she turns her gaze toward me. Her eyes are huge, her lips are pursed into a tight frown, and a worried expression is on her face that shouldn't be funny, but I can't help it. She is fucking adorable. "Breathe, Emi." I watch as she takes a deep breath, but she's still too tense. "You need to relax. You're safe."

"I can't believe you're trusting me to drive your car." I never realized how much I've taken driving for granted. I remember learning with my grandfather. I'm sure I was nervous, I mean who wouldn't be? But I need to get her to relax.

"Emi, look at me." She does and her brows shoot up to her hairline. She's still chewing on her bottom lip but she's not frowning anymore so I'll take that as another win. "This car is full of safety features. It has lane assist so you don't have to worry about running off the road. It has stop assist so if you're about to hit something, it'll stop in time. We're taking it slow and there's no other traffic out here. We're just learning the basics today. Just relax."

"I'm trying, Landon." She takes several deep breaths and at least she's no longer in danger of hyperventilating. Her shoulders are finally easing away from her ears, so that's a good sign. Now if I can convince her to get the car to move.

"Are you ready?" I ask, watching her knuckles finally get some color back to them as she releases her death grip on the steering wheel.

"Yes," she whispers while shaking her head slowly from side to side. I chuckle at the cuteness, knowing that she'll be fine once she actually gets going.

I take several minutes to go over the basics with her. The car is an automatic, so she doesn't have to worry about shifting gears once she starts moving at least. I show her both the gas and brake pedals, how to move the gear shifter, turn signal, and how to adjust her seat and mirrors. Once she's comfortably situated, I have her put the car into gear and we finally begin to move slowly.

Her grip doesn't loosen on the wheel, her lip stays pinched between her teeth, and her eyes stay wide and rounded as we slowly begin to inch forward. "Give it a little more gas," I try coaxing her.

"Shit!" she yelps as the car lurches momentarily. I don't say anything as she pulls her foot away from the gas pedal before slowly lowering the toe of her shoe back down, pressing lighter than before. "Sorry."

"You're doing great, Emi." I spare a glance away from the road ahead of us to look over at her. The smile that spreads across her face is angelic, making her look even more beautiful than I've seen her before in the short time that we've known each other. She's loosening up, finally, as she begins to gain her confidence. Confidence that I can physically see as her features begin to relax, the capillaries in her fingers filling with blood, blooming pink into her once snow-white knuckles.

"I'm doing it!" Her excitement is intoxicating.

"You are." As much as I want to reach out, place my hand on her thigh and share in her happiness, I keep my hands folded together in my lap. We haven't gotten there yet, and I don't want to distract her. "There's a road up here I want you to turn on." Lifting my hand, I point out the front windshield to indicate the road ahead. "Lift your foot from the gas pedal and slowly press against the brake, just to slow us down." We jerk slightly forward as she taps the brake a little harder than she means at first. "Gently," I coax as she tries again, softer this time.

"Like that?"

"Just like that. Turn on your right turn signal. Good job." Like a pro, she turns onto the road I had indicated, albeit a little faster than I would have liked but we haven't left the road so she's doing great.

We spend another few hours just driving around rural roads outside of the city before the sun begins to fade beyond the horizon. We pull into a deserted looking driveway to swap places so I can drive back to the city. She's done good for her first time ever driving and I couldn't be prouder of her.

"That was amazing, Landon. Thank you for this."

"You did great, Emi." I smile at her before turning my gaze back to the road ahead. "What would you like to do for dinner tonight?" A chuckle rises out of me when her stomach begins to rumble at the mention of food.

"Sorry." I watch out the corner of my eye as she lays a hand across her stomach. "I didn't realize how hungry I was until you said something about food."

"That seems about right." She giggles sweetly and my heart fills to bursting at the sound.

I throw out a few options for places to take her for dinner. We debate fancy restaurants and fast food. But in the end, she decides to go back to my apartment and cook together again. I can't argue with that option, I had so much fun working with her in the kitchen last night. I'm itching to get the opportunity to work that closely with her again, maybe even try my hand at the helm and see if I can make something that won't land both of us in the hospital.

Thankfully, Emi decides on a simple dinner of grilled chicken breast and salad. Even I can't mess that one up. Emi picks at her food, moving greens around her plate while nibbling on a crouton as I regale her with stories of learning to drive with my grandfather. She laughs along with me when I tell her about breaking the passenger seat when I popped the clutch in his old Toyota Camry too hard, tossing him back against it, laying him flat back as it landed against the back seat of the car.

"I hated that car," I tell her once I've stopped laughing enough to catch my breath. "He swore it was the easiest thing in the world to drive. For some reason, I just couldn't get the hang of the clutch and stalled it every time I had to start moving from a dead stop."

"I can't imagine you failing at anything." She continues to laugh, her hand landing on my thigh and staying there, an electric current flowing from the palm of her hand straight to my cock. I clench my jaw, my teeth grinding together as I swallow the groan building in my chest. "How did you finally end up learning to drive?"

Clearing my throat to find my voice, I tell her "We used my grandmother's car. Much to my grandfather's disappointment, I never did learn how to drive a manual transmission." She still doesn't move her hand from my leg, and I don't push her away. She doesn't move at all, her fork still pinched between two fingers with the tines resting against her plate. Her gaze locks with my own, a fire burning in those azure irises that probably matches my own. There's so much life in those eyes, so much more than when I first met her at the diner.

Has it really only been a month since I first saw her? How is it possible to have so many feelings toward her after only a month? I feel like there's still so much that we don't know about each other. But I want to. I want to know everything about this woman; her likes, her dislikes, her dreams, her nightmares. Her walls are falling down around her, everything that she'd built up over the last several years to protect herself. She's starting to open up and become a completely different person. I'm intrigued by the woman sitting beside me, even more so than I was when I first saw her in the diner.

"Are you done?" I ask as I push away from the counter. If I don't move now, I'll end up doing something that I'll regret. It's not that I don't want to get closer to her, but I'm afraid of scaring her. Her hand falls from my leg as I stand, bringing my plate with me.

"Yeah." She starts to stand but I stop her and take her plate.

"I got it." I walk around the counter, careful to keep turned just enough that she doesn't see the bulge in the front of my pants. Taking my time rinsing the plates after scraping them into the trash, I place everything in the dishwasher and wipe down the counter and stovetop.

Turning to the side, just enough to be able to see her where she continues to sit at the table but keep the evidence of my arousal hidden, she seems lost in thought. It's nice to see that she isn't torturing herself beneath the thick layer of her normal cardigan, I made sure to buy her several varieties and colors of long-sleeved t-shirts when we were out the other day at The Village. She still fidgets with the sleeves, pulling them over her fingertips and fisting her hands to hold them in place. I know it'll be a while longer, while the bruises and cuts on her arms heal before she feels comfortable enough to ditch the sleeves all together. But I still hate seeing her so self-conscious when it's just the two of us together. A final barrier that I want to tear down, let her be her true self around me.

It's late, but it isn't late enough to sleep. My brain is still running a mile a minute and there's no way I'll be able to shut it down enough to get any rest. After hanging the hand towel on the front of the oven door, I walk back toward where Emi sits, her fingers still working nervously beneath the cover of the shirt sleeve. "You wanna watch a movie?"

She lifts her gaze to me, her eyes wide with wonder like I'd just offered her the world when in reality it's only whatever we can find on Netflix that I haven't already seen a million times. "Yes," she whispers, finally releasing her hold on the threads of her shirt and relaxing her fingers.

I let her pick. I've probably already seen everything a hundred times. I have a tendency to leave the TV on while I'm working out, just letting it play senselessly in the background. I'm not even sure if I can remember anything that I've seen, to be honest. It's just background noise majority of the time, something to drown out the millions of thoughts and to-do lists running through my head at any given hour of the day. Even now, I'm more intrigued by watching her as she concentrates on every word and scene playing out on the screen. If I didn't know better, I'd say it's been a long time since she's watched anything on a television. Probably never even been to a movie theater, which isn't something that I do often myself.

She giggles several times throughout the movie, each time sending a bolt of lightning down my spine and straight to my cock. When she gets more relaxed, she moves closer to me on the sofa, curling into my side with both of her hands fisted together in her lap. My arm lays loosely across her shoulders, putting the lightest amount of pressure against her skin or pulling her into me. It's comfortable, intimate, this connection building between us. I love that she feels safe enough to sit so close to me, even though we hardly know each other.

When her breathing evens out, long and slow breaths hissing out between her parted lips and teeth, I know that she's fallen asleep. The movie is still playing on the TV when I reach toward the coffee table to grab the remote and turn it off. I don't want to move her, but I can't let her sleep in this position. She's so small curled into my side, her cheek pressed against the side of my chest, her ponytail fanned out over my arm. The purring noises that come out of her as she sleeps peacefully are so kitten-like that I have to bite back the chuckle threatening to escape my chest.

She doesn't stir when I stand, scooping her up in my arms. She remains relaxed as I cuddle her to my chest and carry her down the hallway toward the guest room. Walking forward until my shins brush the side of her bed, I lean down and pull back the blanket with one hand before laying her down. She immediately curls to her wide, pulling her knees up to her chest and wrapping her arms around them. I remove her shoes and set them on the floor next to the bed, so she'll find them in the morning, pull the blanket up to her shoulders, and bend down to kiss her on the top of her head. "Goodnight, Kitten," I whisper against her temple before standing and walking out of the room, pulling the door shut behind me.

Chapter
FIFTEEN

LANDON

PULLING INTO THE PARKING garage at my office, I get a notification on my phone letting me know my packages are arriving today. Perfect timing considering I stopped off at the store this morning to pick up a phone. Emi has been staying at my apartment for a week already and it pains me to leave her every day without a way to reach out if something happens. No one has landlines anymore, me included, and there's no reason for her to be stuck without some way to get hold of me if she needs anything. Even something as simple as needing me to pick something up from the store on my way home. And God forbid she get sick or hurt and not be able to call for help.

The past week has been amazing. I never thought I would be comfortable having someone else living in my apartment – I've been living on my own for almost ten years. But I didn't realize how lonely I had been until there was someone else there to talk to. Even doing simple things like grocery shopping is more fun with someone else. I've never had so much fun bickering over fresh produce before. And yes, before you ask, Emi has convinced me that those evil little green monster Brussel sprouts are actually quite amazing. My poor grandmother would be rolling over in her grave if she knew there was another way to cook and eat those pathetic cabbages.

Despite Emi's attempts to teach me to cook, I'm still a lost cause. Actually, that's not true. I've kind of been sabotaging her teaching efforts. What can I say? It's been more fun to watch her immerse herself in cooking – she's magical as she navigates my kitchen like a master chef. And she is a master chef. That woman can definitely cook, and I realize that her gifts were wasted in waiting tables. Ralph could have made bank in his little diner in Independence if he would have given her a spatula and access to the stove.

I know her heart isn't in cooking though. As much as she loves to do it, and as good as she is at it, I know that she wants to get back behind the lens of a camera. She's told me about her photography from high school and how supportive her mother was of her hobby. She's told me more than once about wanting to make a career of it but never having gotten that chance. I hate to think of what might have happened to her equipment but knowing about Charlie and what he's put her through since her mother passed away, I think I can figure it out. That's what makes today so perfect.

"Good morning, Mister Strong," Melodee greets me as I step off the elevator.

"Good morning, Melodee." I don't bother looking up as I walk past her desk to my office. I'm pulling up the tracking app to see the estimated time that my packages will be here. "I have packages being delivered here today. Please make sure they bring them to my office for me."

"Yes, sir."

Stepping into my office, I close the door behind me and walk over to my desk. I want to program the phone for Emi before the rest of her belated birthday gifts get here, but I need to plug it in to charge first. Yes, these things usually come out of the box with a charge, but I want it to be fully charged and ready for her when she takes it back out of the box. Smiling to myself, I envision taking her to the electronics store later to pick out a case and wonder what flashy color she'll choose for her phone. I didn't bother ordering one for her because I'm interested in what she'd choose for herself. Hopefully something that shows off her adorable personality.

Once the phone is plugged in, I power it on and skip through most of the initial setup steps. I enter in a few numbers that I want her to have quick access to – my personal cell, my office number, Melodee's desk for in case she can't reach me directly. Then I power it back off and set it aside to finish charging. There's a knock on my office door as soon as I reach over to power on my laptop. "Come in."

"Mister Strong," Melodee enters with her tablet in hand. "You have a few meetings today to go over the new build across town. Rob will be here in a half hour to discuss the crew and dates for breaking ground. The permits came in first thing this morning, you should see them there on your desk."

"I do. Thank you." I push the permits closer to the edge where the blueprints are rolled up, so they'll be ready for Rob when he gets here. Melodee continues talking about the rest of the meetings scheduled for today. Looking over the calendar on my laptop, nothing seems like it's overly important and I wonder if I can push some of them to another day. Especially if her packages get here sooner rather than later – I'm anxious to get home to give them to her if they do.

"Are you okay?" Melodee asks as she sits in one of the leather armchairs across from me. Shocked, I turn my attention to her, and I feel my brows lift in confusion.

"Of course," I answer easily. I've never been better honestly.

"You just seem a little distracted lately," she observes.

Taken aback by her observation, I push back against my chair and grab the armrest on either side. "I'm not sure what you mean, but I can assure you that I'm not distracted. There's just a lot going on lately and you know this is the start of our busy building season." Melodee has been with me since I started the Strong Designs four years ago. She probably knows me better than anyone else that works for me, so I can't help but wonder if she's right. I do get a little nervous though when I look closely at her and see a gleam in her eye that I've never seen before.

I watch her as she lowers her gaze to her lap, setting her laptop across her thighs and crossing her hands over the top of it. She almost seems...nervous? Melodee is three years younger than I am and she's a really great administrative assistant. She's always had a little bit of a crush on me honestly, but I've never bothered to pursue her in any way outside of work. I know she tends to party on the weekends and loves the club scenes. If I was about five years younger, I might be into that scene more myself. It just isn't what I've been looking for though. Sure, Melodee would be great to have some fun with. But she isn't the girlfriend type, and I just don't have any interest in a fling. Especially not with my assistant. Just thinking about that reminds me of the lawyer and the obvious affair he was having with his assistant and a shiver runs down my spine.

"I just think you work too hard sometimes," she says quietly. "You spend so much of your time here at the office and in meetings. I just wonder if you have a way to unwind after a long day at work."

Oh, shit. Part of me knew this was where she was going with this. I need to put an end to it before it starts. "Melodee," I try to interrupt her.

"I was wondering if you wanted to go out to dinner sometime. With me?" She finally looks up from her lap. The shyness that I see in her eyes is so different from the confident assistant that I've come to know over the last four years, it almost hurts me to have to let her down. But I've always made it a point of keeping my personal life out of the office, so she doesn't know. She couldn't possibly know, but I'm putting an end to this now.

"Melodee, stop." I raise one hand in front of me and watch as she pulls her bottom lip between her teeth. "I'm flattered. Honestly. But you need to know that I'm currently seeing someone." Okay, that's kind of a lie. I mean, I do have a woman living with me but we're not technically together. Not that I'm opposed to it – I would love more than anything to build more of a relationship with Emi. I'd like to think that we've become close friends over the last several weeks since I first saw her at that diner. I know she's scared, and she's been through a lot. She's probably hesitant to get too close because I know she's been hurt. I don't know if she's ever been in a relationship before, we haven't had that conversation. But, knowing what her stepfather has put her through, I can't imagine that she's had time to date previously. I've moved slow, not wanting to pressure her into anything that she isn't ready for. But I knew – I knew it the moment she let me kiss her – she's it for me if she'll have me. When she's ready of course.

"Oh," she responds. She sits straighter, her brows lifting in shock. "I had no idea."

"It's fairly new."

"Well, who is she?" Her gaze immediately falls to the floor in front of her. "I mean, not that it's any of my business. But I haven't heard you say anything about seeing anyone."

"Her name's Emilee," I admit, my mouth curving into a smile at just the feel of saying her name. I figure if I mention her name, maybe Melodee will realize that I'm serious. "Well, Emi. She's not from here though. I met her when I went back to Independence to clear out my grandmother's house. She's a waitress at the diner there." Well, she was a waitress. Now that I think about it, I should feel guilty about taking her away from her job. I should, but I really don't.

"Oh." She stands and clutches the tablet back to her chest. "That's great. I'm happy for you." I can hear the tone of disappointment in her voice. I watch her as her gaze sweeps around my office as if she's suddenly uncomfortable, her eyes pausing when she notices the phone charging on the corner of my desk. "Alright, well. You know where to find me if you need me."

"Thank you, Melodee. Don't forget about my packages." She doesn't say anything else before walking out and closing my door behind her. Wow, what a way to start the day. That's one uncomfortable conversation down. Hopefully the last one of the day.

I'm up to my elbows in emails when there's another knock on my door. Looking at the clock in the bottom right corner of my laptop, I see twenty minutes has already passed. "Come in," I announce while pushing my laptop off to the side and watch Rob, my foreman, walk into the office. He's dressed casually today in a light blue polo shirt and khaki slacks. It's always a shock to see him in regular street clothes rather than dusty work clothes. At least the shoes don't look so out of place – the steel toes of his work boots have a light coating of dried mud. Standing, I reach out to shake his hand before he sits in one of the available chairs in front of my desk.

Nodding once in a silent greeting, Rob sits before leaning back comfortably in the chair and resting his left ankle over his right knee. This is normal for him, he's not a man of many words. Well, not to me at least. It would seem that he vents most of his frustrations to Melodee, making her the middle man so to speak. I know that he's had a few issues with members of his crew but hopefully he's managing them more appropriately on his own. He's basically their boss, being the foreman of the crew. I don't interfere with how he manages them unless it becomes a problem.

Our meeting is fairly straight forward, thankfully. We go over the plans on breaking ground, discuss some last minute changes on the blueprints since the original design, and lay out the number of crewmen it'll take to complete the entire job. I want to make sure it's budgeted properly so everyone is paid fairly.

We both stand and shake hands again before I hand Rob the rolled up blueprint and the manilla folder with copies of all the permits he'll need for the build. I walk with him toward the elevator, giving myself several minutes to stretch my legs before my next meeting is scheduled to start. Part of me wants to ask him about the crew members and make sure that he's already hashed out any issues that occurred a few weeks ago with the last team. But

I forget about it quickly when I see the parcel delivery stepping off the elevator.

"Landon Strong?" the delivery driver asks as he walks toward me, three boxes stacked in his hands in front of him.

"That's me." I motion for him to walk ahead of me to my office where he can set the boxes on my desk. He hands me a handheld device to sloppily sign my name using a broken stylus before taking it back from me and walking back out the door. I'm thankful for no small talk as I step around my desk to sit and focus on opening the packages to check the contents. I'm sure everything is fine, and I'm thankful that it's not all crammed into one oversized box, but it's a habit of mine that I've never been able to break. I want to make sure it's all in one piece before I give any of it to Emi.

Everything got here earlier than I thought it would, which I'm grateful for. That just means that I can get home earlier than anticipated. I'm excited to see Emi when she opens everything up and sees what I got for her. I only hope that she likes it.

Packing everything back up and putting the phone back in its box, I stack the boxes from largest to smallest and step out of my office. "Can you reschedule everything else I had on my calendar for today please?" I ask Melodee as I step closer to her desk.

She looks up at me, confused. "Umm…"

"Something came up, and I'll be taking the rest of the day off. I'll be back tomorrow."

"Okay, Mister Strong," she concedes.

Nodding once, I walk back to the elevator, ready to head back home to my Kitten and watch her open her gifts.

Chapter

Sixteen

Emilee

LANDON HAS TAKEN ME out driving every afternoon for the last three days. He leaves for work in the morning after we have a quick breakfast and coffee together, spends a few hours in the office or in meetings, then comes home in the early afternoon ready to take me out for another driving lesson. After a couple hours of driving aimlessly, we return to the apartment where I get to take over the role of instructor and continue teaching Landon how to cook.

That first afternoon that I got to drive his Mercedes was the most nerve-wracking, frustrating, and terrifying thing I've ever done in my life. Despite everything that I've been through in the past several years, since Charlie came into mine and my mother's life, I was still terrified of getting behind the wheel of that car. I've never known anyone to be as patient and attentive as Landon though, the way he was while I was shaking nervously behind the wheel of his car. He took his time to help me calm down and encouraged me the entire time I was driving.

I'm happy to say that I've gotten much better over the last couple of days. At least, I don't worry so much about giving him whiplash while he rides in the passenger seat. And we've even moved our lessons into the city so I can get more practice driving with traffic and through the residential neighborhoods. He took me to the DMV yesterday afternoon to get my learner's permit too. Another few weeks of practice and he says I should be able to take the driving test for my actual license. Not that I need it, really, since I don't have anywhere that I need to go. I don't even have a car.

Despite the nerves, I've actually had a really great time learning how to drive. I don't know if it's the driving that I enjoy, or the fact that I get to spend so much time with him in the enclosed space. I never thought I would be so comfortable being that close to another person, much less a man. It's been a long time since I've been able to open up to anyone, to get close to anyone. I've had a wall built up around me because I'm used to people ignoring me or taking advantage. I've been hurt so many times over the years – not just physically but emotionally too. I had started to think that I was destined to continue living the life of hell that I was orphaned to. That's what I was – orphaned – since the only person that ever cared about me died. The only one that actually saw me and made me believe that I wasn't invisible.

Until now.

Until Landon.

Somehow, he *sees* me.

I've already been staying with Landon for a week. His apartment is amazing, and he wasn't kidding about the view from the windows during the day. It's absolutely breathtaking. I feel like I sit here, in front of the floor to ceiling windows, for hours every day just looking out over the city. I've even gone so far as to move one of the armchairs from the living room area closer to the window so I could enjoy the view while reading one of the thousands of books Landon has.

He has an endless collection of books, anything from sci-fi and fantasy to true crime and suspense. I hadn't realized he was such a nerd before but it's honestly somewhat endearing. You can tell that every book he has on his bookshelves has been read not only once, but hundreds of times. They're well-worn and loved. Thankfully, he hasn't dog-eared any more pages since I made him the bookmark. Of course, I had to make another one for myself since I've started to dive into several books in the week that I've been here.

Landon has done exactly as he promised, he's been a perfect gentleman since I've been here. He's let me continue to sleep in the guest room and hasn't tried to persuade me otherwise. He hasn't even kissed me again since that first morning we spent together over breakfast.

I've healed quite a bit over the last week and my bruises are finally fading. The cuts on my arms are healing nicely and I'm sure I won't have many scars. The bruises have finally faded to a soft yellow, enough that I'm wearing a short-sleeved shirt today for the first time in more than a year. While you can still see the discoloration against my pale skin, it isn't as stark a contrast as to warrant any questions from strangers. While my pain fades, my heart continues to swell within my chest as my feelings for Landon grow daily. I've even put on a little weight since being here, now that I'm finally able to eat three full meals without feeling like I'm going to be sick.

But today, I have a plan. I went snooping after Landon left for work this morning and found an electric pressure cooker in the back of his pantry. He might be disappointed that he doesn't get to help with dinner when we get back from my driving lesson tonight, but I'm sure he'll quickly forget about it when he finds out what I have planned for him. I set the timer on the cooker, and by the time we get back to the apartment, we should have a perfectly cooked pot roast ready to eat.

We'll enjoy a meal together and talk about his day at work – like a normal couple. Because that's what I want us to be – a normal couple. I started falling for Landon the first time he came into the diner and my feelings for him have only grown stronger. He makes me feel safe and cared for – something that I haven't felt since before my mother passed.

I'm tired of being alone. I'm tired of trying to be who everyone else expects me to be and pretending that everything is okay when it's not. Like I'm waiting for the walls to close in on me, the other shoe to drop. I don't want to do that anymore and I know that with Landon, I don't have to be anything other than myself. That he appreciates me, possibly even loves me, for who I am. With him, I feel like anything is possible.

I'm pulled from my daydream, the book slipping from my fingers and falling into my lap, when I hear the click of the lock disengaging on the front door. Startled, I look around the room and wonder how long I've been sitting here, staring out into the cityscape, and suddenly feeling guilty for wasting so much time rather than getting ready to go out with Landon to drive again. I haven't even taken a brush to my hair yet today. Rushing over to the bookcase, I set the unread book back on the shelf where I had taken it from earlier and turn to the door right as Landon pushes his way through with a stack of boxes tilting precariously to the side in his arms.

"Landon," I gasp as I hurry over to the door to help him.

"I got these, Kitten," he smiles as he steps over the threshold and walks to the coffee table in the living room. I freeze, my palm resting against the door as it clicks shut, as my cheeks grow warm, and butterflies take flight in my stomach. Did he just call me Kitten? I don't think I've ever had a pet name before, but I think I like it.

Stepping away from the door, I look toward the clock hanging over the mantel and finally see that it's earlier than he usually gets home from work. "You're home early today."

"Yeah." He stands straighter and turns to face me. "I only had a few meetings this morning and then wanted to get back home. I've been waiting for some things to get delivered for a few days and they finally showed up today." He points his thumb over his shoulder, toward where he left the boxes sitting on the table. There are four boxes total in different sizes.

"Oh," I respond, not sure what I should be doing. I shouldn't feel so awkward just because Landon came home early today. I mean, we have our routine sort of figured out. He comes home after work, we go out for a while to practice driving, then we come home and eat before watching a movie and going to bed. A few extra hours together on a workday shouldn't be such a big deal, should it?

"Did you eat lunch today?" he asks, stepping closer to me as I stand frozen in place completely dumbfounded.

"I did." I watch as he takes another step closer to me, his eyes trailing down my body slowly.

He stops moving, mere inches separating us and my heart pounds nervously in my chest as I look up at him. He tilts his head to the side, his brows furrowing slightly, and I see his hand reaching toward me slowly as I lock my knees, forcing myself not to move away from him. I want him to touch me, any way that he can. I'm not afraid of him. His fingers graze my wrist softly before pulling my arm away from my body. "You're not in long sleeves today." He reaches out with his other hand and does the same to my other wrist.

My arms seem so small cradled in his hands. His thumbs trace my pulse points, and a shiver runs through my body at his touch, goosebumps rising instantly beneath his fingertips. "No."

"I like it." He cradles my hands against his chest, capturing both wrists in one hand and reaching up with the other to move a strand of hair away from my forehead. He pauses, his fingers lingering behind my ear, and I close my eyes and lean further into his touch. We stand like that for several seconds before I feel his lips press firmly against my forehead. "Come on," he drops his hand from my head and wraps the other around my fingers. Opening my eyes, I watch as he turns, pulling me along with him and walks toward the sofa. "Sit with me for a few minutes. I got you something."

Following him, I sit next to him with only a few inches separating us. He doesn't release my hand, his thumb is slowly tracing my knuckles and I watch him as he stares at the boxes lying on the table in front of us. If I didn't know better, I'd think he was nervous.

"Landon," I place my hand on his thigh softly and watch him as his eyes flutter closed. "What is all this?"

He draws in a long breath before opening his eyes, his gaze turning and locking with mine. "So," he begins as he releases his hold on my hand and reaching toward the stack of boxes. Grabbing the smallest box on the top, he wraps his fingers around it as he brings it to his lap. "I've been thinking a lot." He pauses and blows out his cheeks and I fold my hands together in my lap as I patiently wait for him to find his words.

"I really like you, Emi," he continues. "I'm sure you know that." He pauses and I nod my head once encouraging him to continue. "I hate that I took you away from your life."

"No," I interrupt him, shaking my head quickly from side to side.

"That's not what I meant." Closing his eyes, he hangs his head and rakes the fingers of one hand through his hair in frustration. "What I mean is that I'm glad I got you out of that town and away from your stepfather. But I'm sorry that I have to leave you here all day while I'm at work. I hate what you've had to live through and I'm sorry that I didn't find you sooner. I hate that you didn't get to celebrate your birthday. I don't even know when the last time was that you got to celebrate it."

"It's been a few years."

"So, I got you a few things."

"Landon," I gasp. "You didn't have to get me anything."

"I know." He scratches his beard nervously. "But I wanted to."

"Okay," I whisper.

"I got you a phone first of all."

"A phone?" My head tilts to the side, my eyes narrowing in confusion.

"Yeah." He reaches out and hands me the box. Looking down I see that it's a new iPhone, much more sophisticated than anything

140

that I had before. I mean, I've seen the newest iPhone because Amber has one that she can't stay off of when she's supposed to be working. But the last phone I had was a cheap pre-paid smartphone that I don't even know the model of. "I figured I could take you out later to get a case for it or something. And I programmed a few numbers in it already so you'll be able to reach me during the day when I'm not here or if you're out somewhere by yourself. You should be able to reach out if you need something."

"Thank you." I have no idea how I'm going to afford to pay for this phone since I'm pretty sure I don't have a job anymore, not that I want to go back to the diner anyway.

"I added it to my plan, so you don't have to worry about having it activated," he states plainly as if reading my mind. "It doesn't cost much to have it on my bill, so I'm not even worried about you paying for it or anything."

The other boxes on the table are much larger than this box was and the butterflies are back in full flight in my lower stomach as I anticipate what else he could have gotten for me. It's been a long time since I've had presents to open and I can't help but be a little giddy with excitement.

"I have an idea." I watch as Landon reaches out and grabs the next box on the stack and carefully brings it over to his lap. He smiles at me before turning his gaze over his shoulder and looking toward the windows. "You really like the view from that chair. I've found you sitting there every day when I get home from work, usually with a book in your hand that you're not even reading."

He pauses and looks back at me as a giggle escapes my lips. He isn't wrong. As much as I want to read some of the books that I've found hidden in his collection, I can't pull my attention away from the amazing view from that window.

"You should see it from the roof. The sky is so clear today I just know it'll be breathtaking. Let's take this one up to the roof and you can open it there."

I watch him, my brows furrowed in confusion, as he tucks the box between his elbow and ribs and reaches out his free hand to grab my hand. Our fingers entwined together, he pulls me gently behind him toward the door and I follow him willingly. We're already on the top floor and I know the elevator doesn't go any higher, so I have no idea how to get to the roof from here. My question is answered quickly when we walk down the hall toward the stairway, and I see a flight of stairs leading up.

So, I follow him. My heart is racing a staccato rhythm against my ribs with excitement. But I know beyond the shadow of a doubt that I would follow this man anywhere.

Chapter
SEVENTEEN

LANDON

I DON'T COME UP TO the roof very often. To be honest, I don't generally spend much time back at my apartment, which is something that has definitely changed over the last few weeks. I've been mostly caught up in everyday life, building my business and making it profitable. I've rarely taken the chance to enjoy my surroundings or time spent alone with my own thoughts. I've finally had the opportunity to view the world through a different set of eyes, through Emi's eyes, and I'm anxious to see her view of the world from the roof.

Stepping over the threshold onto the roof, the humid air immediately hits me in the face. I'm actually thankful that Emi has been able to go without the sweater today. She still has the slight discoloration on her arms, though they've finally faded to soft butter yellow. It still hurts my heart like a fist straight to my chest when I see it, but she's healing. She's coming out of her shell. I've had the pleasure of witnessing her personality as she heals and strengthens every day that she's with me. And let me tell you, it's a hell of a thing to witness. The man that shoved her into that dark, cold box that she's been forced to live in should be given a one-way ticket to that special room in Hell that's been reserved for him and his counterparts. Those being anyone else evil and twisted enough to snuff out the light in such an incredible human being as Emi.

Looking over my shoulder, I watch as Emi follows me through the doorway. She steps closer to me as the door closes behind her and I watch as her eyes widen at her surroundings. When I designed this building, I decided to give it a flat roof with the intention of making it into a private oasis. Over the years, it's been grown and utilized by all the tenants and has become a beautiful, secluded getaway. There is a steel and glass railing surrounding the entire border of the building that stands just under four feet in height. The steel bars framing the glass give the illusion of safety without obstructing the view.

The entire space has been landscaped with raised flowerbeds and planters in various sizes. There are paths covered in pea-sized gravel leading around the entire rooftop, culminating in the middle with plush oversized outdoor furniture. It's the perfect place to relax and escape the confines of everyday life and demands.

I don't know why I haven't brought Emi up here before now. If anyone has something they need to escape from, the need to find a little paradise in the middle of a mundane existence, it's her. Watching her now as she takes in her surroundings – enveloped by the vast oasis of greenery and newly blossoming flowers, the fragrance of Spring filling her lungs and awakening her senses to the possibility of a new life – is truly a magical experience.

"Wow," she gasps as she releases my hand and steps ahead of me. Holding her arms out to her sides, she spins around in a circle slowly as the smile on her face grows wider. My chest expands with pride at the sight of pure joy glowing in her angelic features. "I had no idea this was here."

"Yeah." I walk several steps behind her as she slowly follows the path around the garden, knowing that it'll lead us to the center where we can sit while I give her the gift pinned tightly against my hip. "I wanted something secret and special just for the tenants in the building. It was a lot of fun to design and watch it all come together."

"You designed this?" She stops walking and turns to face me and I remember that I haven't told her yet about the building. "Wait, did you design the building?"

Busted. "I did."

"No wonder you have the top floor." She giggles as she turns around and starts to move again along the path. "I guess that's a perk of designing the building. You get first pick of the best apartment."

"Yeah, about that." I watch as she turns back to face me. "I own the building." My teeth clamp down on my bottom lip as I wait for her to say something else. She just stands there watching me for what feels like forever, chewing the inside of her cheek like she's thinking of what to say, and my lungs freeze as I wait anxiously.

"Huh," she finally says on an exhale. "I had no idea."

I finally release the breath that was held captive in my chest as she turns back to the path ahead and starts to move again. I don't know why I was expecting that conversation to go differently. Neither of us say anything else as we walk, her several steps still ahead of me. When we reach the center of the roof, I move ahead and motion for her to sit on the stuffed love seat before sitting next to her and moving the package to my lap. She folds her hands together and waits for me to speak and I chuckle as her eyes jump from the package to my own eyes and back again.

The corner of my mouth tilts up in a crooked smile and I reach one hand out to move a wayward wind-blown hair away from her forehead, tucking it behind her ear. My heart grows three sizes when she doesn't flinch away from me, and I'm amazed at how far we've come in such a short amount of time. I want to open myself up to her – just slice open a vein and bleed out the truth about my growing feelings for her.

"So," I begin, reaching out to wrap my fingers around her small hands which are still folded together on her lap. "I've been thinking about what you've told me about yourself. About your dreams and desires growing up." Her brows knit together making an adorable wrinkle in the middle of her forehead as she raises her gaze to mine. "I've really enjoyed having you here, Emi."

"I've enjoyed being here. I feel comfortable here." That makes me smile.

"I'm glad. But I don't want you to have to sit around all day while I'm out working or stuck in meetings. I took you away from your job at the diner." She starts shaking her head back and forth and I push on before she can interrupt me. "I don't regret getting you out of that town, Emi. Don't think for one second that I regret anything I've done. I'll never regret getting you away from that monster."

She turns one of her hands over and wraps her fingers around mine. My stomach flips wildly when her thumb runs back and forth over the back of my hand – such a simple gesture but it means so much considering where we started. But it's enough to help me to continue my train of thought.

"I wanted to get you something to help you. Something to remind you to chase your dreams, no matter how big or how many obstacles you think have gotten in your way. I probably went a little overboard, honestly. But I want you to know that I will support you, in whatever capacity you need." Releasing her hand, I raise my hand to cup her cheek and wipe a tear away with my thumb. She presses her cheek against my hand, so I keep it there for several seconds longer than probably necessary.

Releasing a sigh, I grab the box in my lap with both hands and hand it to her. Her eyes stay locked on mine as she grabs the box with both hands, not looking down until she has it lying in her lap. Slowly she pulls the open flaps on the box to the sides and gazes at the contents for so long I'm sure she's gone into shock and my nerves have detonated once again.

She hates it.

She's angry that I got it for her.

She's going to think it's too much.

"OhmyGod," she rushes out on a breath, so quietly that I nearly missed it. It's probably too much, but I know that she's missed being able to take her pictures. She told me how it was something that her mother supported her on and encouraged her to pursue a career in photography. I want to do that for her. I want more than anything to stand behind her and watch her achieve all her dreams. She deserves it more than anyone I've ever known in my life.

I got her the best, it's supposed to be the top of the line in digital cameras. I even got all the attachments and additional lenses that were recommended for this particular model. Of course, the boxes still downstairs in the apartment contain a photo printer and a laptop, which she'll probably actually get angry about but that's beside the point. What's the point in having a digital camera if you don't have any way to enjoy the final product?

Her hands are shaking as she sets the box down between her feet. She reaches into the box and pulls the camera out, leaving everything else inside the box to look at later. I watch her curiously as she powers it on and goes over all the features and modes using the tiny display. Without saying anything, she stands and begins walking toward the railing at the edge of the rooftop. I stay seated, giving her space to explore through the lens of her new camera, knowing that she needs a few minutes to herself to enjoy it. She holds the camera clutched to her chest as she spins from side to side, looking out over the cityscape. Slowly, she lifts the camera to her face, and I watch as she presses her eye close to the viewfinder and presses the shutter button several times.

Obviously satisfied with the pictures she's taken, she turns and my stomach flutters when I see the happiness in her smile. She skips closer to me, a movement that I've not had the pleasure of seeing her do since we've met. It's surreal that she's so much happier now than when I first saw her at the diner that she's able to act almost giddy. She carefully sets the camera into the open box before standing to face me. Suddenly, she throws her arms around my neck and embraces me in a hug and I'm thrown against the back of the sofa with the force of her movement. My arms immediately wrap around her waist, pulling her into my chest and turning my face into the space where her shoulder and neck meet. Inhaling deeply, I breathe in the intoxicating scent of her coconut shampoo and revel in the closeness that I've craved with her more and more over the last few weeks.

"Thank you, Landon," she says softly, her voice muffled against my shoulder. Placing her hands on my chest, she raises just enough to look into my eyes and I'm gutted by the unshed tears I can see glistening in her eyes. "I don't know what to say. This is the most thoughtful gift I've ever been given. You have no idea how much it means to me." Her voice is breaking with emotion, and I want nothing more than to bring back the happiness. I'll give anything to see her smile like she was not even five minutes ago, every day for the rest of my life.

Looking at me through hooded eyes, her gaze lowers to my mouth and I moisten my lips without thinking. I don't move for fear of breaking our moment. My breathing shutters to a stop in anticipation of what I can only hope is coming next. Her hands trail up my chest and shoulders, cupping around the base of my neck and I gulp audibly in response to her touch. I wait patiently as she leans closer wanting her to make the decision on her own, I don't want to coax her or force her movements and I damn sure don't want to scare her away. I want her to make the first move.

My fingers dig into her hips, holding her tight enough to bruise but not able to loosen my grip. It's a battle of restraint and taking everything I have in me not to toss her over my shoulder and march back downstairs to my apartment. I see the moment clarity overtakes her expression, the ferocity of her desire drying up her tears as her eyes move back up to my own and I see my reflection in the darkening blue of her eyes. She moves to straddle my lap before crashing her lips against mine, nipping and biting at my bottom lip until I'm forced to take over the kiss.

She melts against me immediately, her trust in me not to hurt her is a heady feeling and something that I will fight to keep. The tip of my tongue traces along her bottom lip, coaxing her to open for me, and our tongues tangle together. She purrs against my mouth, a rumble building in my chest in response to the sweetness of her taste. My kitten is a livewire as she presses down against my lap, electricity like a direct lightning strike blazing up my spine as my cock hardens against her.

Fuck. This isn't happening here on the roof where anyone can walk out and see us. She deserves to be laid out on my Egyptian cotton sheets and worshipped, for me to take my time making her comfortable and sated. I break the kiss slowly and watch as she sits back and looks up at me.

"Can we go back downstairs?" she whispers.

"Anything for you, Kitten." Closing her eyes, she whimpers softly at the pet name and my cock throbs against my zipper. I help her stand, making sure she's steady on her feet, before grabbing the package and leading her back to the door.

Chapter
EIGHTEEN

EMILEE

HOLY SHIT. I CAN'T believe the way things are moving along today. All day, I've been thinking of how I can let Landon know that I'm interested in him. I want to be more than the inconvenient roommate that I've become over the last few weeks. I want to be more than his friend. I never thought I'd get to the point of actually wanting a relationship, but here we are.

His fingers twine around my own as he leads me back down the staircase and through the hallway to his apartment door. He stops inside the apartment long enough to place the box back on the coffee table with the others before turning to face me. His eyes are darker than usual, I can see the desire burning in his blown pupils as the tip of his tongue comes out to moisten his lower lip. He looks positively hungry, and I don't think it's for the pot roast that's waiting to start cooking in the pressure cooker.

My entire body is lighting up like a Christmas tree. Nerve endings that I never thought about before are tingling all over my body and it's all I can do to stand still under his scrutiny and not turn away. I'm nervous though. I've only done this once before and it wasn't a memorable experience for me. Landon is a big man, and I should be intimidated by the way he's looking at me. Instead, I find myself clenching my thighs together tightly to release some of the building pressure in my core. He hasn't even touched me yet and I'm melting beneath his gaze. If I'm already having this kind of reaction to the way he's looking at me now, I can only imagine what it'll be like when he finally touches me.

I back up two steps against the door when he finally moves toward me and grabs my waist. He grips my hips with near bruising force, pinning my body against the door. He closes the distance between us, pressing his erection into my belly and slanting his mouth over mine. Gasping, I open immediately for him and our tongues tangle together again in a dance similar to what I can only hope we'll be doing within the next few minutes. If we don't, I promise I will explode into a million unrecognizable pieces and may never be able to be put back together again.

"Tell me you want this as much as I do, Kitten," he growls against my mouth and shivers run down my spine at the raspy sound of his voice. Damn, an aroused Landon is a sexy as fuck Landon.

"Yes," I exhale breathlessly as I lift my chin and offer him my throat. He doesn't disappoint, lowering his mouth to my pulse point and nipping softly. My nipples tighten almost painfully and I'm suddenly aware of every fiber of my scratchy clothing as it rubs against my over sensitized body with every panting breath.

My fingers twist into his shirt as I drag it up his torso, pulling it out of the waistband of his slacks. He pulls away from me, giving me enough room to lift the shirt high enough to expose his abs. Damn, those abs. All this time that I've been staying here, Landon has remained a true gentleman. He's worn tight enough t-shirts around the apartment that I know he's ripped, he obviously works hard to keep a healthy and fit lifestyle. But to see his body now, this is almost as exciting as opening the gifts that he brought home for me today. I finally get to see and touch him in ways that I've only fantasized about recently. The tips of my fingers trail lightly over his sculpted abs, and I giggle as they ripple beneath my touch.

Landon releases my hips before unbuttoning the top three buttons on his shirt, ripping it over his head and tossing it over his shoulder. My breaths quicken at the sight before me, my eyes widening at his chest. He doesn't move, giving me time to gaze over his body, the chest he's bared for me for the first time only to find it inked in the most beautiful pair of angel wings I've ever seen. There are three sets of Roman numerals etched below the wings and I make a mental note to ask him about them later.

His eyes lock with mine, a silent question in his gaze, as he pinches the fabric of my shirt in his fingers and begins to draw it up. Lifting my arms above my head, I give him the permission he seeks and allow him to remove my top. My body tenses, my bottom lip pulled between my teeth, as he traces the backs of his fingers down my ribcage softly. I've worked hard to gain some weight since I first got here. I've slowly built up my tolerance to eat more without getting sick and I hope that he can appreciate it.

"Fuck, you're beautiful." I shudder at his words. Bending forward, Landon grabs the backs of my thighs and lifts me off the floor. "Wrap your legs around me, Kitten. And don't let go of my neck."

My legs wrap around his waist, my ankles crossing behind his back. My hands fist together behind his neck as he moves one hand to squeeze my ass, the other pressing against my back between my shoulder blades and pressing my breasts tightly against him. He steps back away from the wall, kisses me softly on the forehead, and turns to walk through the living room toward the other side of his apartment. My heart is pounding so hard against my ribs that I'm sure he can feel it against his own.

His eyes stay locked on mine as he walks through the apartment. I don't look away, completely transfixed by his expression as he moves his gaze over my face like he's looking for a hidden clue, something that tells him to stop what he's doing. He won't find anything. I have no intention of stopping him. He stops abruptly when his shins bump into the bed and his brows furrow slightly, his gaze dropping to my mouth. Unclenching my hands, I move a palm to cup his square jaw, the two-days growth scraping roughly against my skin and causing goosebumps to bloom up my arm. He presses against my hand as his eyes flutter shut, his lips pinching together as a rumble builds in his chest, the vibration teasing my nipples softly.

Neither of us speak as he places a knee on the bed behind me and bends down to place me softly on the mattress. He lifts me softly to slide me toward the center of the bed before slanting his mouth over mine and kissing me deeply. His hips thrust against me roughly and I immediately regret the layers of clothing that still separate us as I tighten my legs still wrapped around his waist, pressing my thighs against him and moaning softly against his mouth. My hands fist in his hair when he breaks the kiss, almost wanting to hold him against me so I can drink him down like an elixir of life. We share a breath before he moves away, dragging the stubble of his jaw across my cheek and down my neck, stopping only to nip at my ear and send a shiver down my spine.

His hands planted on the bed on either side of my hips, he continues to drag his chin down my body, placing the occasional open-mouthed kiss against my skin. I can feel the tip of his tongue peeking out occasionally as if to steal a taste.

I move my hands and arch my back hoping to reach behind me to unfasten my bra, but he grabs my wrists to stop me. "Not yet," he growls against my stomach before dipping his tongue into my belly button. "I don't think I'll make it if it comes off yet."

He hooks his fingers into the waistband of my yoga pants and drags his chin back and forth above the elastic, the scrape of his beard against my skin like a million tiny fingers, as his eyes lock on mine. I can see the silent question in his eyes, making sure I'm still okay before he proceeds, and I appreciate it more than he could ever know. I can't form any words, but I manage a quick nod of my head. My body is practically buzzing with excitement, wound up so tightly that if he were to stop now my head would literally explode. My eyes close of their own accord as my hips lift for him to slide my pants down my legs along with my panties. Lifting my legs one at a time, he removes my shoes and pants, letting them all fall to the floor at the foot of the bed.

My eyes open to look down at him, immediately missing the feel of his hands on me, and I notice that he's chewing on his lip as his eyes wander over my body. He must see the discomfort on my face, the blush a stark contrast against my still pale skin, because his eyes turn sympathetic before his hands reach out and land on my thighs. He swipes his thumbs back and forth softly against my inner thighs in a comforting gesture.

"Fuck, Kitten." He drags his hands over my thighs softly before pushing them apart and narrowing his gaze on my core. I watch him curiously as he lowers himself down to the mattress, laying between my legs and inhaling deeply. "I want to taste you." He practically growls the words as he traces his fingertips up my thighs, closer to where I need him the most. I nod my head once even though I know he wasn't asking for my permission this time.

"Oh, God!" I exclaim, louder than I mean to. My head falls back against the mattress, my hands fisting in the duvet tightly. I've read about this, even heard stories from Amber since she enjoyed bragging so much. But I've never experienced anything like this. There are so many things going on at once, I can't concentrate on anything but the massive amount of pleasure shooting through my entire body. I can feel Landon as he nibbles on my labia, running his tongue from bottom to top and focusing on my clit. When he circles his tongue around that bundle of nerves, my hips thrust against his face, the scratchy hairs on his cheeks scraping against my inner thighs as I try to close my legs around him on instinct. He chuckles against me before pushing my legs apart and pinning them against the bed, his breath sending another wave of pleasure up my spine.

I always thought I would be embarrassed to do anything like this, but embarrassment is the last thing going through my mind. There's a spring inside me that runs from my lower abdomen up to my shoulders and it's winding tighter and tighter, my toes starting to curl so tightly that I can feel a cramp starting in the balls of my feet. My back arches off the bed, my eyes are squeezed shut so tight it almost hurts and I don't know if I'll ever be able to see again. He growls as his lips wrap around my clit and he pulls it into his mouth, I can feel his tongue flipping against it quickly.

The spring finally bursts, and I see stars. My heart pounds so hard against my chest that I fear it may burst through my ribs. Fireworks literally explode behind my eyelids and my ears are filled with the sound of a high-pitched cry. It takes several seconds before I realize that sound is coming from me. I lay still for several minutes while my breathing and heartrate return to normal before I realize that Landon is no longer touching me. Opening my eyes, I see him standing next to the bed. He's stripped down so he's completely naked and my eyes trail down his body, from his sculpted chest and abs to his impressive, sheathed cock. He chuckles as my eyes widen at the sight of his cock standing proudly and pointing directly at me.

Kneeling on the bed, he moves over me, and I lift my gaze to his face. The smile he awards me with is magnificent. Cupping his jaw, I run my thumb over his bottom lip and smile when I wipe my own wetness away, smearing it slightly into the corner of his mouth.

"You're amazing," he says, his voice raspy with arousal. I lift my head and lick his chin and bottom lip and he growls as his eyes flutter closed. Leaning away from me, he balances his weight on his knees between my legs and reaches beneath me to release the clasp on my bra. His fingers drag lightly down my arms as he lowers the straps, his eyes staying glued to mine until he tosses my bra to the floor next to the bed. "Are you ready?" Of course, I am. I know I am, but I still appreciate him making sure I'm comfortable with everything that's happening.

"Yes," I whisper.

"I'll go slow, Kitten." Reaching down, he fists his cock and swipes the tip through my slit several times before lining it up with my opening. "Let me know if it's too much and I promise you I'll stop." The emotion in his gravelly voice almost undoes me entirely. I watch his face while he focuses his gaze on where we're about to be connected. His jaw twitches as he grinds his teeth together and I know he's on the verge of losing control.

He inches in slowly, a tremor visibly running through his body. My breathing stutters as he stretches me, a burning pain slowly changing over to pleasure. He draws back before pushing forward again and I know he's still not all the way in. My fingers curl around his shoulders, my nails digging into his skin sharply and probably leaving crescent shaped marks against the surface. Pulling back one more time, he thrusts forward a little harder and lets out a harsh breath before stilling his movements completely.

Bracing his elbows near my shoulders, Landon lowers his mouth to my neck. He nibbles lightly below my ear and growls "You feel so fucking good, Kitten." Dragging his tongue down my neck, he lowers his mouth to my breast and sucks a nipple into his mouth. Balancing his weight on one elbow, he moves his other hand down my body and grabs me behind my thigh, lifting it to press against his hip and I can feel him slipping deeper into me. He starts rocking his hips against me in rhythm with his sucks against my breast. I'm lost in sensation as my hips begin to rock against him matching his movements. He switches to my other breast and pays it equal attention and I can feel the spring winding tight again in my lower belly.

Releasing my thigh, he lifts his hips enough to make room for his hand, placing a finger against my clit. "Landon," I moan as my fingers trail down his back feeling his muscles ripple beneath my touch.

"I can feel you trembling around me, Kitten. Let go for me. Let me feel you come on my cock." His words are my undoing and the spring inside me bursts again. The fireworks behind my eyelids are even brighter and more spectacular this time than they were before. "That's it, baby." His movements slow as he draws out my release and I know that I'll never be the same again. His mouth crashes into mine as his movements become more erratic. He groans into my mouth, deepening the kiss as he stills against me, and I can feel his body shudder beneath my palms.

My eyes are still closed when I feel him pull away from me. I hear him walk across the room before coming back a few minutes later. The mattress dips as he climbs onto the bed beside me and pulls me closer so I can curl into his chest. The feeling of his arms wrapped around me is comforting and soothing, being caged in the safety of his body is my new favorite place. He places a kiss against my forehead, the warmth of his lips heating me from the top of my head down to the tips of my toes, and a sound vibrates in my chest like a purr.

"Are you okay, Kitten?"

"Mmm."

He chuckles at my nonverbal response and pulls me tighter against him. "Sleep, baby."

"Mm-kay."

Chapter
NINETEEN

LANDON

IT'S THE MIDDLE OF the afternoon and I'm daydreaming in my office. I know I'm daydreaming, and I should be replying to the mountain of emails that are sitting in my inbox waiting for updates and designs. But I can't get my mind off of Emi and the way she fell apart in my arms yesterday afternoon. I've had plenty of sexual experiences over the years since I've been on my own, but never anything as fucking hot as Emi was yesterday. She was putty in my hands, her moans filling my soul with longing and devotion knowing there isn't anything that I won't do to make her happy and hear those sounds from her every day for the rest of my life. My heart now beats for her moans and purrs. The sweet juices that flowed over my tongue are now the elixir of my life and I'll require a sip every day in order to sustain my existence and quench my thirst.

I knew beyond the shadow of a doubt that I would never be able to get enough of her. And I was right. Once will never be enough. Even now, I'm sitting here harder than I've ever been in my life and there's nothing I can do about it. I have another meeting in a few minutes that I should be preparing for, but I can't get my mind off of my sweet Kitten long enough to do anything. At this point, I don't even know if I'll be able to move from my desk. My God damned dick is so hard, I'm surprised I'm still conscious. All the blood in my body is pooled into my cock leaving nothing left for my basic functions and decision making. Yet, I expect myself to be able to run my company wisely knowing that there's nowhere I'd rather be right now than buried between Emi's legs.

Fuck, what am I supposed to do now?

As much as I want to cancel the rest of my afternoon and go back home to her, I can't. I have a meeting with my foreman, Rob, in about twenty minutes that he says can't wait. He's having issues again with someone on his crew and he wants to talk to me about it before he makes any final decisions. As much as I want him to manage his own crew, I can't fault the guy for wanting council with me. It's hard to make tough decisions where someone's livelihood is concerned. No one should have to make those decisions themselves and I've always prided myself on being open and honest with my employees. I like to support their growth and potential but some of them need a little more push than others. Rob is good at his job, but he definitely needs that extra push when it comes to making decisions.

Picking up my phone, I send a quick text to Emi. I feel my lips curling into a smile at knowing that she's only a quick text away now. I should have gotten her a phone when she first started staying with me. Better late than never I suppose.

Me: Hello, Kitten. How is your day?

Thankfully, I don't have to wait long for a reply. I find myself smiling again when I see the three dots appear almost immediately.

Emi: Great. I'm learning the new photo software on the laptop you got for me. I can't even tell you how much I appreciate the gifts you got for me.
Me: I'm glad you like them. I knew you'd make good use of everything.
Emi: I still think it was too much.
Me: Nothing is too much for you, Kitten.

We napped for only a few hours yesterday before I woke up to the amazing fragrances coming out of my kitchen. Apparently, Emi had found an electric pressure cooker that I didn't even know I had in my pantry. She had set it to cook a pot roast while we were out practicing her driving so it would be ready when we got back to the apartment. Unfortunately, we didn't get a chance to go driving but I'm not complaining. She had wandered out while I was still sleeping to open the other gifts I brought home for her and was in tears when I wandered out to the living room.

"What's wrong, Kitten?" I kneel down next to her on the floor, pulling her into my lap and wrapping my arms around her. It's an amazing feeling, my chest swelling with protectiveness and pride that I'm able to be this open with her. That I can finally touch her without her pulling away from me. She reaches out and swipes her hand over the laptop sitting on the coffee table and I think I know what's wrong with her.

She's so overwhelmed with emotion, I don't think she knows how to process everything.

"I can't believe you did all this." She sobs against my chest and my brows lower in confusion.

"I told you already, Emi. I want to support you in any way I can so you can follow your dreams. You don't have to worry about anything else stopping you. You want to pursue photography? I want to help you do it."

"It's too much, Landon. You shouldn't have done all this."

"It's not too much, Kitten. Nothing is too much for you." She doesn't say anything else, just closes her eyes and fists her hands in her lap. Pinching her chin between my thumb and forefinger, I turn her to face me before lowering my lips to hers. I kiss her softly and sweetly before kissing the tears away from her cheeks. "Nothing will ever be too much for you."

"I don't know what to say."

"Just say thank you."

"Thank you, Landon." Her forehead rests against my chest and I rub soothing circles across her back.

"You're welcome, Emi."

I shift my seat on the floor, so my back is against the couch, settling Emi between my legs. I reach my arms around her to adjust the coffee table close enough to reach from our position and open the laptop. I had plugged it in at work earlier to make sure the battery was fully charged for her to use right away.

She reaches for the box containing the camera and its attachments and pulls it closer. She grabs the camera and the USB cable to connect it to the laptop and I sit back, keeping my hands on her hips, as she works with the device to upload the pictures she took earlier. She clicks the files one at a time to view the photos and I'm in awe of the images displayed on the screen in front of us. They're practically perfect, no editing needed as far as I'm concerned. I'm immediately impressed and anxious to see what other kinds of pictures she intends to take in the days to come.

The next photo she clicks to is of me and I'm surprised. I had no idea she had even taken it. She got me in perfect profile, my elbows resting on my knees as I sit on the rooftop waiting for her to finish taking her photos. I watch as she clicks a few buttons on the computer and changes it to a black and white portrait. She stands and steps away from me and I miss her warmth immediately, but I watch her curiously to see what she's going to do. She grabs the printer from behind the laptop and carries it over to the entertainment center. I watch her as she plugs it in and loads the photo paper into the pullout tray beneath it. Walking back to the table, I wait for her to sit with me again, but she doesn't. Instead, she presses another few buttons on the laptop and I hear the printer whine to life before it shoots out a printed picture.

Grabbing the paper, she skips the few steps back to me and settles on the floor between my legs. "I think I want to frame this one." She holds the portrait up in front of her and tilts her head as if admiring it on a gallery wall.

Wrapping my arms around her shoulders, I kiss her temple softly and watch her eyes flutter closed. "That looks amazing." I make a mental note to pick up a frame for her after work tomorrow. I'm amazed at the difference in the picture just making it black and white. It gives it more depth and meaning than it had originally. Rather than just looking like someone waiting patiently on the sidelines, I look like a man deep in thought. Possibly contemplating all the mysteries of this woman sitting in front of me.

"You need some photos in here. Your walls are a little boring. This can be the first one you hang on your wall." She turns her head side to side as she looks around my living room. I've never taken the time to

bother hanging anything on the walls in the four years that I've lived here. I don't know why, it was always something that my grandmother believed. She said, 'a house is not a home until you've hung something on your wall'. I should have hung something years ago.

"There are boxes in my bedroom closet full of pictures that came from my grandmother's house. You're welcome to go through them anytime and see if you find anything else worth hanging up."

"Really?" She turns and looks at me excitedly. "You don't mind me peeking through your things?"

"I have nothing to hide from you, Kitten." I move a stray hair from her face with my fingertips and tuck it softly behind her ear. "And I would love for you to take more photos that you want to hang up. I've been here for four years, and this apartment has only recently started to feel like a home." I chuckle when her brows furrow with confusion. "I think it's because you're here."

"I love being here, Landon. It's been a long time since I've felt safe anywhere and I feel safe here. With you."

"I'm glad," I tell her honestly. There are more words that I want to say to her. More reasons why I want her to stay here with me forever. But we're not there yet, it's still too soon. Thankfully, I don't have to worry about those words slipping out because her stomach rumbles loudly. Another thing to be thankful for, her appetite has definitely returned. "Come on." Standing, I pull her to her feet and watch as she sets the photo on the coffee table. "Let's eat."

"Mister Strong," my assistant Melodee's voice brings me back to the present. Looking up I see her standing in my doorway.

"Yes, Melodee?"

"Rob is here. Should I send him in?"

"Yes, please." Standing, I wait for Rob to step into my office. I extend my hand as he approaches my desk which he shakes before sitting. Nodding my head in greeting, I sit and fist my hands together over top of my blotter. "What can I do for you today, Rob?"

"Mister Strong," he begins but I hold a hand up to interrupt before he can continue.

"Rob." Pausing, I shake my head slowly side to side. "You've been with me for four years. I think it's okay for you to call me Landon."

"Of course, Landon." He swallows audibly before continuing, trying to calm his nerves. My own nerves begin firing erratically in his stead as I imagine what drama he's about to reveal on the job site this time. "I wanted to talk to you about one of my crewmen."

"Right." Sitting back in my chair, I move my hands to my lap and swipe my palms over my knees a few times to remove the sweat that has collected. "Is this the same one that you've been having issues with?"

"It is. But he's getting worse." Cocking my head, I lower my gaze to his knee that has started to bounce quickly. It's a nervous habit that I recognize as one that I've seen Emi do repeatedly since moving in with me. Something that she's developed over the years of living on the edge of fear. It makes me wonder just what this crewman has been putting Rob and his other workers through and I'm suddenly anxious to get to the bottom of it so Rob can make the decision that he's so hesitant to make.

"Worse how?"

"He's more agitated lately. I mean, he's always had an attitude. But lately, he's been getting mouthy with everyone on the job site. He appears unkempt like he hasn't been sleeping. He comes in hungover and late every day which is a risk in and of itself. He doesn't care anymore when I send him home, I can't let him work on the site when he's hungover. He's a danger to the entire crew."

"You're right." I move forward in my seat and rest my elbows on my desk. "So, what is it that you need my help with. Why haven't you let him go?"

He blows out a long breath as his gaze lowers to his lap. "I wasn't sure if you knew him. I wanted to make sure I wasn't stepping on any toes, sir."

"I don't understand. Why would I know him?" Yes, this is my company and I try to make it a point to interact with everyone in my office. But I leave the hiring decision of crewmen to Rob since he's the one that will be working with them directly.

"He's from your hometown. I know Independence is a small town and generally everyone from small towns know each other."

This is new information, and my curiosity is suddenly very intrigued. "What's his name?"

"Charlie Tillman."

My brows lower as I search my memory of anyone by that name but coming up blank. "I can't say that I do."

"Right." Rob seems to relax in his chair, his knee finally stops bouncing. "He is a bit older than you. He would have graduated probably ten or so years before you did."

There's only one Charlie that I've heard about recently. It would fit, honestly given the age. But it couldn't be. Could it? "You said he's escalated recently?"

"Yes, sir."

"Does he say anything when he comes to work agitated?"

"Quite a bit, sir."

"I'm assuming you've been documenting everything?"

"Of course. I wanted to make sure we were covered if he were to pursue an unemployment claim." Good thinking on his part. At least he's thought to cover his bases.

"Anything that I should be aware of?"

"Not really. I guess he had some girl at home doing things for him, cooking his dinner and taking care of the house. Says he didn't do enough to keep her in her place, and she took off. Plans to teach her a lesson if he ever finds her. Things like that."

My blood turns cold, instantly freezing in my veins, as the reality of the situation reveals itself. I guess this Charlie could very well be the one that Emi is running from. Time to teach him that lesson. "Let him go." I growl out between clenched teeth. "Send me a copy of your documentation, everything you have on him. And Human Resources. I don't want him to have a chance of filing for unemployment."

"Got it."

"Thanks for bringing this to my attention, Rob." He nods once before standing and walking out of my office and I'm ready to be done with this day.

Chapter
TWENTY

EMILEE

I'VE TURNED AN ENTIRE corner of the guest room into a photo studio. When Landon got home from work yesterday, I was sitting in the middle of the living room on the floor with my laptop set up on the coffee table. After spending most of the day tinkering with it, I think I've figured out most of the editing software – at least enough to get started taking some pictures. Landon walked into the apartment and immediately froze, his lips curved down into a slight frown, and I could see the deep wrinkle between his eyes from across the room. He didn't say anything, just came over and helped me up off the floor, kissed the top of my head, and told me to put some shoes on. When he tossed me the car keys as soon as we stepped off the elevator in the parking garage, I didn't ask any questions.

We walked around the furniture store for more than an hour before he found what he was looking for. He picked an adorable wooden desk just big enough to hold my laptop and photo printer, a fluffy but comfortable office chair, and a small Tiffany lamp to set in the corner. It was still early enough in the day that he was able to have it delivered to the apartment, so we spent another half hour driving around town before going home to start dinner together. We had the delivery guys set everything up for us in the guest room – since I'm not sleeping in there anymore, he thought it would be a good idea to turn it into my temporary office.

Now, I'm standing back on the roof of the apartment building. The views from twelve stories up are amazing – even better than from the floor to ceiling windows in the apartment. I've photographed everything, gotten the city from every angle possible and even a few of the landscaping that the tenants have helped to work on over the years. But now I'm thinking I need to get a few of the building itself. Landon designed the building himself and I think he would like some pictures for his office. Or a portfolio of sorts, something that he can brag about.

I step into the apartment to grab a few things first. Throwing the apartment keys and my cell phone into the camera bag, I sling it across my chest and walk to the elevator. Stepping into the lobby, my breathing stops. Turning my head side to side, I view a part of the building that I hadn't seen before. Every time we've come back to the apartment, we take the elevator from the parking garage underneath the building. I've never seen this amazing space before and am amazed at the complexity of the architecture. The space is wide open with floor-to-ceiling windows all the way around. The ceiling has to be at least twenty feet up, completely open to expose heavy wooden beams running the length of the building.

Hundreds of pipes hang from the ceiling in a crisscross design with lights on the ends of them and I can imagine it giving a starry night feeling when the sun goes down.

The elevator door starts to close, pulling me from my dazed staring, and I hold my hand out to stop the doors from trapping me inside. Stepping out into the lobby, I spin around to take in all the glorious sites around me. There's a desk in the middle of the room – not a normal desk. No, this desk is round and completely encloses the person standing in the middle of it so they can talk to anyone no matter which side they're standing on. There's a man in a suit sitting behind the desk, his head barely peaking over the top before he stands and watches me approach.

"Good afternoon, Miss Jackson." My brows lift to my hairline in surprise at his greeting.

"How do you know my name?" My suspicions are on alert, even though I know that's crazy. Landon probably told him I was here. He doesn't answer me, just smiles, and nods his head once before sitting back down. Shaking my head, I raise my camera and search my surroundings through the viewfinder. This lobby is hard to resist photographing. I spend several minutes walking around, taking in the lobby from every angle. The plants placed strategically around the open space, the sitting area with the soft suede material and colorful accent pillows. The entire space is a modern twist on industrial.

Pushing my way through the glass doors, I step out on the sidewalk and breathe deep. The smell of blooming honeysuckle assaults my senses immediately and I'm flooded with memories of my childhood – back when things were still good, and it was just me and my mom. We had a huge honeysuckle bush in the back yard that I used to sit in the middle of when I got home from school. Mom used to get so angry at me when she'd find me crouched down in the center of the bush, destroyed flowers littering the ground around me where I had discarded them after sucking the nectar off the stems.

Following my nose, I turn to the left and walk to the edge of the building. Peeking around the corner, I see the source of my nostalgia. There's a small, grassy courtyard on the side of the industrial masonry building with honeysuckle bushes and Crape Myrtle trees budding along the edges. This little slice of Spring paradise in full bloom is hidden away like a secret garden in the middle of the city's business district. It's beautiful and unlike anything I've ever seen before.

Good thing I brought my camera.

I take pictures of everything – the beautiful courtyard, the building itself, a bird nesting in one of the Crape Myrtle trees. I'm lucky enough to notice a hummingbird hovering over the honeysuckle and it gives me a chance to play with shutter speeds on the camera. I'm anxious to see how that picture turns out when I upload it to my laptop later. Walking back to the front sidewalk, I increase the shutter speed to take a few shots of the entrance as people walk past the building. My hope is to blur the walkers as they pass by. Since there's a lot of traffic on this street, I take a few extra minutes to walk across the street for a head-on picture of the building. I take a few with the slower shutter speed to blur the cars and people going past, then increase it for some normal photos to edit as well.

Holding the camera in front of me, I scroll through the selection of photographs that I've taken today. My stomach flips with excitement as I look over the shots I've been able to capture. I can't wait to show them to Landon when he gets home this afternoon. I can already visualize them hanging on the walls in Landon's apartment. That reminds me of the boxes he mentioned in his bedroom closet. I wonder if there are any pictures in there from his grandmother's house that he would like to have displayed. His walls are so boring as they are now, basic white painted drywall. He says he's been in this apartment for four years but there is no character – no personality – to his living space.

Mind made up, I open my camera bag to pack up the camera after powering it down to save the battery. The hair on the back of my neck stands, a chill running down my spine, as I zip the pouch closed. It's a feeling that I'm not unfamiliar with – like someone is watching me. Straightening my spine, I spin slowly to see if I can see anyone that might be watching me. There's no one there. "It's all in your head, Emi," I say aloud to myself. Waiting for a few passing cars before crossing the street, the feeling grows stronger. My hands fist at my sides, tight enough that I know there will be crescent moon shaped indents in my palms from my fingernails. It takes all the patience I can summon not to dash across the street as if I'm being chased by the boogeyman.

I don't breathe as I cross the street and stop in front of the apartment building. Pausing with my hand on the door, I turn my head over my shoulder and look back across the street where I had been standing only a few minutes ago. Still, there's no one there. I mean, there are people. This is a busy part of town after all. But no one that I recognize or that looks like they are watching me. Turning back to the door, I yank the heavy door open and step inside. I don't release the breath that I'm holding until I'm standing back in the lobby. Still watching over my shoulder, I walk toward the elevator. I'm anxious to get back to the apartment.

"Miss Jackson," I startle at deep voice before I remember the gentleman sitting behind the desk. "Are you okay?"

"Yes," I answer, my voice a little shakier than I would have liked. Smoothing down the front of my t-shirt, I take several deep breaths to control my nerves. I step closer to the round desk and lean against the top. Smiling nervously, I reach my hand out toward the man behind the desk. "My name is Emilee. But my friends call me Emi." I laugh at myself at that, I don't really have any friends that I can name.

"It's nice to meet you, Emi." He takes my hand as he stands with a warm and welcoming smile peeking out beneath his walrus mustache. I immediately like this man – he reminds me of Tom Selleck from one of my favorite TV shows, *Blue Bloods*. He's probably the same age as him too, his dark hair and mustache peppered with the perfect amount of grey. "I'm Steve."

He releases my hand but hesitates before sitting back down behind the desk. He looks over my shoulder, through the front windows, before nodding his head once and sitting down. I watch as his attention changes to something else and can't help my curiosity. Leaning forward, bracing my elbows on the countertop, I peer over the edge and notice several small computer monitors lining the space. He must notice me being nosey because he chuckles, the sound a deep rumble in his chest. "Do you want to see?" he asks me and I pull my gaze up to meet his, my eyes widening at his question.

"Can I?" I don't know why I feel so giddy all of a sudden. The feeling is similar to what I imagine spending time with a grandfather would be, but I didn't have one of those growing up. I'm suddenly very interested in seeing what he does all day behind this desk. I watch as he swivels his chair around before standing again and walking to one of the rounded edges of the desk, opposite where I'm standing. He flips a switch, and a section of the desk pulls back toward him, opening up a doorway, or gate, that will allow me to enter his area. Smiling like a kid on Christmas morning, skipping around the desk where he's holding the doorway open for me to enter.

"Have a seat." He motions to his vacant chair, and I step closer before taking a seat.

Looking at the monitors, I see different camera angles both in and around the apartment building and parking garage. "What is all this?"

"This," he points to the monitor in the middle, and I see a black and white view out the front door of the building. I turn my head to look over my shoulder and see a camera on the end of one of the pipes where a light bulb would have been otherwise. I hadn't even noticed it before. "This is a view of every angle of the building." Looking at the other monitors, I see everything. Each monitor, except for the one in the middle, is split into four screens showing different angles or floors of the building. There's even a view inside the elevator which I decide to store away for future reference just to make sure I don't do anything that I don't want any witnesses to with Landon. There are six monitors in total showing twenty-one different views at a time.

"How do you keep up with all this?" It's a little overwhelming. I don't know how anyone can view all the different angles at once and not miss something important. Not that this isn't a safe building, but one thing I've learned over the years is that you can never be too trusting of those around you.

"Oh, it isn't just me." He admits with a chuckle. "There is a security team in an office downstairs. There are five of us on shift at any time throughout the day and night."

"Wow. I had no idea." No wonder Landon said I'd be safe here. I wonder what reason he had to make sure there was so much security available in the building at all times.

"You can never be too careful these days." Steve laughs at my expression no doubt seeing my curiosity. "I saw you taking pictures earlier. Did you get some good ones in the courtyard?" I relax at his friendly conversation.

"I did." Pulling the camera out of my bag, I power it on and flip through the photos to find the one of the hummingbird and hold it out for him to view it.

"Wow!" he exclaims. "That's amazing."

"Thank you." Heat rises to my cheeks at his praise. It's been a long time since I've shown my pictures to anyone else. It's an amazing feeling to have someone who appreciates them with me and I get anxious all over again at the prospect of showing them to Landon. I want to rush up to the apartment and print this one out as it is so I can show it to him as soon as he gets home. I grab the camera as Steve hands it back to me and stand. "Thank you for letting me bother you for a little while."

He smiles again and I notice a dimple just on the outside of his mustache, again reminding me of Tom Selleck's handsome smile. "Any time, Emi." He walks back to open up the desk area for me to exit and I toss him a wave over my shoulder as I walk to the elevator. I definitely feel better about being here knowing there's so much security in the building. My nerves are finally settled since feeling like I was being watched across the street earlier.

My camera still clutched in my hand, I pull the keys from my pouch and unlock the door to the apartment. Walking in, I make sure the door is locked behind me and go straight to the guest bedroom to upload my photos to my laptop. "Wow," I say to myself. "Most of these are ready to print." I'm amazed at the photo quality of this camera and proud that I'll be able to save so much time on editing. I do take the time to make a few of the pictures black and white and save them as a copy so I can have both options. The one of the front of the building from across the street is one of my favorites – the one with the blurry cars and people. I select three photos to print – the hummingbird, blurry cars, and one of the cityscape from the roof. As the printer warms up, I walk into Landon's bedroom and open his bedroom closet.

Pulling out each box, I walk them to the living room one at a time and set them on the coffee table. I want to start going through them before Landon gets home and see if there's anything that would work for the walls. After grabbing my printed photos and setting them on the breakfast bar in the kitchen, I sit on the sofa and open the first box. There are three larger frames sitting on the top of everything in the box with bubble wrap separating them and protecting the glass. I pull out the first one and my heart stops, and I almost drop it as if it burned me. Grabbing the next two frames, I burst into tears. I'm clutching two of the frames in my tight fingers as I slip from the couch to the floor on my knees. I'm a sobbing mess when I see the front door open from the corner of my eyes.

Chapter
TWENTY-ONE

LANDON

MELODEE IS IN RARE form today. Even more so than usual. Not that she has an attitude every day at work, but I don't know her well enough to know what the issue is. She's been my assistant for the past four years, so I should really know her better than I do. For all I know, she has a rough home-life. Maybe something happened this morning before coming to work. Hell, maybe she just has PMS. No, I won't go there. My grandmother would smack me upside the head if I went accusing every woman with an attitude of having PMS. But what else am I supposed to think? She's not usually so short with me.

My phone has been ringing off the hook since I got here today. Usually, Melodee fields my calls. For whatever reason today, she's sending everything to my desk. Honestly, I'm ready to just send her home for the day. She isn't doing me much good being here with whatever has her distracted from doing her job.

"Landon, are you listening to me?" Rachel, my realtor asks through the phone.

"Yes. Sorry." Holding the phone to my ear with one hand, I rest my forehead against the other as my elbow lands on the desk. Today has been a nightmare that I'm anxious to wake up from.

"I was telling you about the offer on the house. It's full asking price and we're just waiting for financing to come through. This is good news, Landon."

"Yes, it is," I agree. I knew the house was going to sell fast with the price we were asking. As soon as the financing goes through, I can be done with it and officially wash my hands of anything and everything in Independence.

"Okay." Rachel sighs. "I won't keep you. I know you have enough going on at work. I'll send you the details once everything is written up. We should be able to close this sale by the end of the month."

"Thank you, Rachel." My forehead hits the desk harder than I meant once the phone is placed back on the base. I'm ready to unplug the thing so I don't have to talk to anyone else today. I have a million emails sitting in my inbox, because apparently Melodee isn't fielding those today either, and every time I start trying to work through those my fucking phone rings again. At this point, I should just send her home. She isn't doing anything for me today anyway.

The phone rings again and I throw my hands in the air in frustration. Ignoring the phone, I stand and walk to my closed door. Pulling it open, I immediately see Melodee leaning back in her chair with her cell phone held in front of her face. Her thumbs are moving across the screen at lightning speed, her brows furrowed in obvious frustration at whatever texts she's responding to. My blood heats furiously.

"Melodee," I call out to her, my voice low and full of frustration.

"What?" she snaps back without looking away from her phone.

"What are you doing?" I'm not a helicopter boss. I don't micromanage my employees like a lot of other bosses do. I like to think I'm lenient on a lot of things and let my employees get away with things they probably wouldn't anywhere else. But enough is enough.

"Texting."

"I can see that." This conversation is getting us nowhere.

Melodee huffs under her breath and tosses her phone onto her desk. "Did you need something?" Seriously?

"Yes." I lean against the doorframe and cross my arms over my chest. "I'm trying to get some work done but my phone is ringing off the hook. Are you planning on doing some work today?"

"Fine, whatever." I watch as she scoots her chair closer to her desk and turns on the computer. Obviously, after already being here two hours, she had no intention of getting any work done today if her computer wasn't even turned on.

Stepping away from the door, I walk across the space separating my office from the reception desk. Leaning forward, I place both palms on her desk and wait for her to make eye contact with me. "Look," I start when she finally looks up at me. "I don't know what you have going on today. If you need time off, just let me know. Otherwise, you're here to work and I expect you to do that."

"That it?" Moving her gaze back to her computer, she punches in her password to log it in. If she hits the keys any harder, they may end up flying off the keyboard.

"For now." Standing, I walk back to my office and slam the door shut. Hopefully now my phone will stop ringing long enough for me to get through these fucking emails.

It takes a few hours to get through them all. I work through lunch just to make sure I'm not missing anything important while scrolling through the massive number of messages in my inbox. Several are emails that I've been waiting for – permits and things that we need for our next build. After getting them printed out, I stack them on the corner of my desk to wait for Rob to come in to pick them up.

I've had enough of today already. Thankfully, my phone finally stopped ringing once I got Melodee to start actually doing her job. I'm anxious to get back home and see what all Emi was able to accomplish today. Looking up at the clock hanging over my office door, I see it's late enough to cut out for the day.

Standing, I grab my jacket off the back of my chair and toss it over my arm. "I'm leaving for the day," I announce as I step out of my office. Melodee doesn't look up, not that I expect her too. But two can play at this game. I don't say anything else to her before stepping to the elevator.

Once home, I take the elevator up to the top floor from the parking garage. My keys are already in my hand when I step off the elevator in front of my apartment door. I stop moving, cocking my head to the side as I listen to the noise coming from inside. I can hear Emi crying from here and I'm immediately put on alert. Did something happen today?

Throwing the door open, I storm into the apartment ready to fight whatever awaits me. She's been so happy lately, she's been healing and is healthier with each passing day. I don't like the thought of anything setting her back in her recovery. Whatever has happened to her to put her in such despair, we'll deal with it together. What I don't expect to see when I step into the living room is her on the floor, on her knees, with picture frames clutched to her chest.

A quick scan of her surroundings shows the boxes from my bedroom closet sitting on the coffee table in front of her. She's been going through the photos that I brought home from my grandmother's house. I have no idea what she may have found in the boxes to put her in such a state though.

Kicking the door shut behind me, I'm to her side in two strides before dropping to my knees beside her. "Emi," I breathe as I reach out and pull the frames from her fisted hands. Setting them on the coffee table face down, I pull her into my chest. She settles against me willingly and my heart bleeds for the pain that's been caused by whatever she found in the boxes. "What's wrong?"

"Oh, my God," she sobs against my chest. Her tears soak into my shirt, warming my skin beneath. I run my hand over her head, smoothing her hair away from her tear-soaked cheeks.

Pulling away, I cup her face in my hands and smooth the tears away from her cheeks with my thumbs. "What happened? Why are you crying, Kitten?" I wait several seconds for her to collect her thoughts while my heartrate slows. Now that I know there's no immediate threat to Emi, I can breathe easier while she calms down enough to talk to me.

"It's the pictures," she mutters between sobs. She pulls away from me and I release my hold on her and let her go. My brows lower in confusion while I wait for her to explain. "Where did you get these?" I watch as she reaches out and grabs the frame on the top of the stack of photos. Turning it over so I can see it, she shows me one of the pictures of Independence that I got from my grandmother's house.

"My grandmother bought them at the library. She had them hanging over the mantel at her house." I'm still confused about why she would be so heartbroken over seeing these photos and wondering if there's more to them than I know.

"I can't believe you have these." She reaches out and turns over the other two frames. Pushing the boxes to the other side of the coffee table, she sets the pictures side by side and runs her fingers over the glass of each one.

"Emi," I start as I place my hand on her shoulder. "I don't understand. Why were you crying?"

She closes her eyes, her hand lying flat over the photo in the middle. Lowering her head, she says, "I took a photography class in high school. It was probably my sophomore year, and I needed an extra class to fill the gap in my schedule. I figured it would be fun to take pictures, maybe join the yearbook committee. The teacher thought I was a natural. She told me I had a good eye and loved the pictures that I would turn in every week."

I don't interrupt her when she pauses. Her head shakes slowly side to side before she continues and I'm sure she's reliving those memories in her mind.

"We had a project at the end of the year as part of a fundraiser for the local library. It was actually that project that made me fall in love with photographing landscapes instead of people. Being able to capture nature in pictures, using the natural lighting instead of relying on artificial lamps and spotlights. I took so many pictures that year. I photographed everything, learning everything I could about setting up the perfect shot. My mother was so proud of what

I was doing, she hung just about everything I brought home to her on the walls all over our house."

I watch as she reaches out and picks up one of the pictures. She holds it in front of her and another tear trails down her cheek. Reaching out slowly, I swipe that tear away and she closes her eyes and presses her face into the palm of my hand.

"Everything is gone now. After my mother died, Charlie went on a warpath and destroyed everything. He took my camera away from me, trashed my laptop while I was at work one day at the diner. I came home one afternoon, and he was drunk and throwing things around the living room. All the pictures on the walls were gone, everything that my mother had framed and displayed proudly. Our family pictures, vacations, those of me growing up." She shakes her head and pinches her lips between her teeth. "There was nothing left. I ran through the house looking for where they went, even if the frames were broken maybe there would be something left that I could salvage. They were all gone. I have no idea what he ended up doing with everything, but they were nowhere in the house or the garbage cans outside."

Sitting back on my heels, I fist my hands into my lap and fight to control my breathing. I still don't understand, though, what these pictures have to do with anything.

"My photography teacher had picked three of my photos to donate to the library's fundraiser. I didn't think I'd ever see them again."

Drawing in a quick breath, my heart practically stops at the realization of what Emi is telling me. "Emi," I gasp as I reach out and grab one of the pictures from the coffee table.

"These were the photos that she donated. They're now the only remaining photos that I know of in existence from high school. These are pieces of my past. I can't believe that you have them."

And, if that's not fate, I don't know what is.

"In a world of billions of people," I begin, pulling her into my lap and cupping her face in the palms of my hands. "We've got the one thing that guides our souls back to each other. That's destiny, Kitten."

"Do you believe that?"

"Hell yeah, I do." Leaning forward, I kiss her forehead softly. "Come on." Placing my hands on her hips, I help her to stand before following her to my feet. "It's only right that these should be the first pictures we hang on the wall. Where do you think they should go?"

"Over the mantel." She reaches down and picks up each of the frames.

"That's perfect. We need to go to the hardware store. Then we'll hang them up when we get back."

"Okay. Can we get a few frames while we're there?" I watch as she sets the pictures down before walking toward the kitchen. "I printed these today."

Walking toward her, I look down at the counter at the three photos laying face up. "Holy shit." I pick up the one closest to me, a beautiful hummingbird caught mid-flight, drinking nectar from a honeysuckle flower. The bird is frozen brilliantly in time, the bright colors of its feathers illuminated in the natural outdoors. Not a single blur to be seen in its quickly flapping wings. "This is amazing." Holding the photo between two fingers, I look down at the other two. "You took these today?"

"I did."

185

One of the photos I know is taken from the rooftop. The other is the front of the apartment building. The way the cars driving past are blurred gives it life like I've never imagined before. I have no idea how she got the pictures to turn out the way she did, but her teacher wasn't lying. She really does have a natural talent for capturing life behind a lens. "These are amazing, Kitten."

"Thank you." I watch as she smiles shyly, the blush coloring her cheeks a beautiful shade of pink.

Pinching her chin between my thumb and forefinger, I tilt her face to mine and press my lips softly against hers. "You're amazing." Her shy smile morphs into one of pure beauty and sunshine. Her angelic features light up so brightly that it will forever be burned into my heart. "Let's go get some frames." Standing, I grab her hand in mine and pull her toward the door. "You wanna drive?"

"Yes!" Chuckling I open the door and usher her through before following her to the elevator. We'll get a few extra frames while we're out and she can frame and hang as many more pictures as she wants. She can decorate the entire apartment with her photos if she wants to and I won't stop her. Finally, after living here for four years, the place is finally starting to feel like home. And I have my Kitten to thank for that.

Chapter
TWENTY-TWO

EMILEE

THE LIVING ROOM OF Landon's apartment is starting to look like an art gallery. Don't' get me wrong, he needed something hanging on his walls, but I think I've gone a little crazy with the photographs that I've been taking all over the neighborhood while he's at work. Over the last week, I've gone out every day and taken more pictures.

After we got home from the hardware store the other day, we went through the boxes together that came from his grandmother's house. He didn't want to hang any of the other pictures that we found in those boxes. He did take a family portrait from when he was about five years old with his parents and put it on his dresser. The rest of the pictures stayed in the boxes and went to the back of his closet.

We've gotten back in the routine of going out every afternoon to practice driving. Now that I have my learner's permit, Landon has been making sure that I've had plenty of practice so I can take the driving test next week. I'm feeling more confident and comfortable behind the wheel lately but I'm not ready to go out on my own yet. Not that I have a car, but Landon does have a second car that he said I could drive after I get my license. I don't know yet how I feel about that to be honest. But we'll see what happens. It will be nice to be able to get around on my own while he's at work instead of having to walk everywhere or call an Uber.

Which is exactly what I'm doing today. Over the last few days, while we've been out driving around town, Landon has directed me to several of his buildings. The ones that he designed. Including the one with the angel fountain modelled after his grandmother in the front. Having made sure to take my camera with me anytime we leave the apartment, I've collected hundreds of shots of his properties from different angles over the last week. Today I'm printing and framing them and plan to surprise him later this morning while he's hopefully still at the office.

He hasn't taken me to his office yet. But a little internet sleuthing and I was able to find it online. My plan is to walk in with a box of photos and surprise him with them. He should have them hanging around his office where everyone can see them. Honestly, after having stalked his website, he needs to have more pictures of his buildings online. He doesn't even have an online portfolio that I've been able to find. Maybe that's something that I can talk to him about when I show up at his work.

"Oh shit," I groan to myself when I try to lift the box holding all the framed photos I want to take to Landon's office. "I think I majorly overestimated my ability to carry this box." Setting the box of pictures on the floor, I use my foot to slide it through the apartment to the front door. "What am I going to do now?"

Think, Emi. Think.

Leaving the box sitting by the door, I grab my keys and walk out to the elevator. Stepping off in the lobby, I see Steve working at the desk again. I'm glad, at least I've already met and talked to him so I shouldn't feel like a moron when I ask him for help.

"Emi," Steve stands as soon as he sees me step off the elevator. "Going back out for more photos?"

I can't stop myself from smiling as he greets me for the third time today. "Do you ever get a break, Steve?" Stepping up to the desk, I rest my elbows on the smooth surface and lean forward to view the monitors.

"Nope." He chuckles as he crosses his arms over his chest, his stance widening to make him appear intimidating with an aura of confidence. I know better, however. There is nothing ruthless about this man – he has a heart of gold and cares far too much about the tenants of this building. He's basically everyone's grandfather.

"I need your help with something," I mention before pulling my bottom lip between my teeth nervously.

"Anything. Just name it." He relaxes his posture as he awaits my request.

"I have a box of photographs that I've taken around the city. They're all of Landon's properties, the ones that he designed. I'm hoping to take them to his office and surprise him with them. But I hadn't realized how heavy the box was going to be and I couldn't get it downstairs. I have no idea how I'm going to get it to his office."

I watch patiently, still biting on my bottom lip, as Steve's brows rise toward his hairline. The corners of his walrus mustache twitch slightly and I know he's fighting a smile. "I think I have just the thing to help you." He holds up a single finger, indicating that I should wait here, while he turns and walks toward a door next to the elevator that I hadn't noticed before. From this angle, with the door standing open after he disappears through it, it appears to be a storage closet of some sort. He returns a few moments later pulling a cloth-lined wagon. "This folds down flat so it will fit easily into the trunk of a car. I assume you have an Uber coming?"

"I haven't ordered one yet, but that was my plan. Yes."

"Well, you're welcome to use this to transport the box. Will you be able to get it into the wagon?"

"I think so. It's sitting on the coffee table right now, so I'll probably be able to just scoot it off the edge right into the wagon." I reach for the handle as he steps closer to my side. "This is perfect, Steve. Thank you."

With a wide smile and a perfect glimpse of his dimple, he nods his head once before stepping back behind the desk. His attention immediately going back on the monitors.

Pulling the wagon behind me, I step into the apartment and over to the coffee table. Just as I expected, it's the perfect height to just slide the heavy box off the edge. Pulling my phone from my back pocket, I open the app to order my Uber. Hopefully, the driver won't mind helping me move the box and wagon to the trunk of the car.

Double checking that I have everything – box of photos, camera bag slung over my shoulder, apartment keys, phone – I step back into the elevator and press the lobby button. Stepping off a few minutes later, I toss a wave over my shoulder to Steve as I step out into the warm afternoon sun to wait for my ride. Thankfully, when they arrive and see me standing there with a wagon and full box of pictures, they don't hesitate to get out and help me load everything into the back of their car. It does take us a few minutes to figure out how to fold down the wagon though.

Settling into the backseat of the small SUV, I watch the city pass me by through the passenger window. The driver, thankfully, doesn't talk while we travel through town and I'm able to relax to the soft music playing through the stereo speakers. I know I have no reason to be, but I'm actually nervous about showing up at Landon's work with these pictures. Will he be upset that I came to his workplace unannounced? Will he be surprised to see me there in the middle of the day? I'd like to think he'd be happy to see me, but it isn't like he's given me the address. He's never offered to take me to the building he works in. He hasn't offered to show me his office. I'm probably massively overstepping here, and I can't help but feel a little insecure.

Chewing nervously on my bottom lip, I take several deep breaths to try to settle my nerves. The car begins to slow, and I look out the front window to see we're approaching our destination. Fisting my hands in my lap, I force myself to remain quiet, so I don't shout out to keep driving. The decision is already made, I'm not backing out now. I'll take whatever comes from his reaction to me just showing up here unannounced.

Thankfully, opening the wagon is easier than folding it down. We have the box loaded in only a couple of minutes and I'm walking toward the entrance. Looking up is a little daunting and makes me feel like I'm falling backwards, even though I'm standing upright. Taking a few minutes to just stare at the clouds moving above the building – it has to be at least twenty stories tall – I take a deep breath and lower my gaze to the doors ahead of me.

Removing the camera from the bag slung over my shoulder, I step closer to the building before dropping the handle to the wagon. Looking through the view finder, I raise the camera to point straight up. I move my view until the view shows the entire building at the front, the sky showing straight over head with the few clouds moving along the rooftop and snap a photo. Turning to my right, I angle the building to the left and take another photo. I want to immortalize the feeling of vertigo that I felt momentarily when I first looked up at the clouds. I don't know if Landon designed this building too, but if he did it will look good in the digital portfolio I'm putting together for him.

The lobby is wide open with marble flooring, four elevators lining one wall to the left, and three unlabeled doors on the wall to the right. The desk in the middle of the floor is lined with monitors with a single security guard sitting behind them. That's it – no receptionist.

Pulling the wagon behind me, I step closer to the desk and wait for the guard to acknowledge me – which he doesn't. "Excuse me," I say after a few minutes of silence.

He finally looks up, but he doesn't smile. He doesn't say hello – not that I expected him to. He just looks me over slowly, lifts his brows in question, and waits for me to say something else.

"I'm looking for Strong Designs."

"Top floor." He lifts his hand and points to the elevators to the left before turning his attention back to the monitors. I'm honestly shocked. If that's all it takes to gain access to the building, then why employee a security guard to work at the desk. There's nothing very *secure* about the way that anyone is permitted to enter the building.

He didn't even ask me about what I have in the box. It could be a bomb for all he knows.

Maybe I'm just being paranoid.

There's no reason for me to think that this building isn't safe. I've been safe ever since Landon took me out of Independence.

Stepping into the elevator, I look over the buttons on the inner wall to the right of the doors. The top floor is twenty-five, so I was close in my estimate of the number of floors in this building. Pressing my index finger to the twenty-five button, I watch as it lights up and the doors close with a soft *swoosh* sound. The ride up to the top floor is quiet, aside from the grinding of the gears overhead as the elevator is lifted along the tracks. I've never had an issue with small spaces, but being the only one in the quiet elevator is a little disconcerting. Landon's apartment building is only twelve stories, and even it has music playing in the elevator.

I watch the display above the doors as the numbers count slowly. It takes several minutes to reach the top floor before the elevator comes to an abrupt halt. The doors slide open with the same *swoosh* and I step out quickly, not wanting to be alone in the car any longer. Blowing out the breath that I held most of the way up, I step toward the reception desk. I see a nameplate that indicates the receptionist is named Melodee, and watch as the lady sitting behind the desk types on her phone, both thumbs moving quickly across the screen.

Huffing out a breath, she places the phone face down on her desk and looks up at me, her head tilting to the side. "Can I help you?"

"I'm here to see Landon."

Her brows raise at my request, obviously not used to anyone referring to him by his first name. "Do you have an appointment?"

she asks, her tone of voice showing her aggravation at my obvious interruption of her phone time.

"No, I…"

"You need an appointment," she interrupts me.

"I'm sure it's okay. If you'll just let him know that I'm…"

"Not without an appointment," she interrupts me again. She lowers her gaze and reaches back out for her cell phone, blatantly blowing me off.

Stepping back, I look around the open reception area to see if I can figure out for myself where Landon might be. There's a wall of windows behind where Melodee sits, separating us from what appears to be a conference room. Inside, a conference table is surrounded by empty chairs, all turned to face the large flat screen television mounted on the far wall. I assume that would be where he gives presentations or pitches for new building projects. There's a short hallway to the right of the conference room, leaning to my right I see a door at the far end that appears to be a restroom.

To the left of the reception desk is another door that's closed. It's the only other door on this floor that I can see and I'm almost certain that it's Landon's office. Deciding against being interrupted again, I choose to bypass Melodee all together and walk toward the office door. Of course, she doesn't appreciate that in the least.

"You can't go in there. I told you, you need an appointment," she raises her voice on the last word. Her annoyance shining through at how many times she's already used that word with me.

"I'm sure it's okay." I call over my shoulder, reaching toward the door handle. What I'm not expecting is the hard shove to my shoulder before I can push down on the handle and open the door. Losing my balance, I release the handle on the wagon and hit the floor, ass first, my legs sprawled out in front of me.

"I said, you can't do that!" Melodee stands over me, crosses her arms beneath her breasts, pushing them well above the low-cut neckline of her shirt, and furrows her brows in frustration. This isn't a good look on her. "I'm calling security."

"Sure," I yell in her direction. "Maybe he'll actually act like he works here for you. He certainly didn't when I was downstairs a few minutes ago."

"What is going on out here?" I hear Landon growl as his office door is ripped open from inside.

I watch, wide-eyed from my seated position on the floor, as he storms out of his office and looks down to see me on the floor. He narrows his eyes momentarily and I worry that I've upset him by showing up here after all.

Chapter
TWENTY-THREE

LANDON

THIS HAS BEEN THE day from hell. First, I come to work this morning and Melodee isn't here. She's always here before I am and makes sure that the office is opened up and all the lights are on. She didn't arrive at work until almost an hour after I got here.

I knew, starting with her attitude problem a few days ago, that something was going on with her. But now, I'm starting to wonder if she just doesn't want to be here anymore. She didn't say two words to me when she showed up and every time I step out of the office, she's on her cell phone again. I've already sent an email to HR to inform them about the corrective action that I'm going to be issuing to her tomorrow. I hate to have to replace her, she's been a great assistant for the four years that I've had her with me. I just wish she would talk to me – let me know what's happened in the last few days that caused her to start acting this way.

Then I got an email from the legal team letting me know that Charlie was pursuing an unemployment claim. Thankfully, Rob's documentation of the case against him is very detailed in the reasoning for his termination. I don't think we'll have any issues fighting the claim, but you never know. I've never had anyone file for unemployment against my company before, so I'm learning as I go here.

Looking at the clock on my computer screen, I see it's almost two in the afternoon. I worked through lunch again doing nothing more than answering emails and I'm suddenly ready to call it a day and get back home to my Kitten. Most of what I'd been doing the last several days – answering emails and phone calls because Melodee isn't doing a damn thing to field them – I could be doing from my home office.

I'm just finishing up another email when I hear a commotion out in the reception area. Cocking my head to the side, I try to make sense of what's going on out there. The voices are muffled so I don't hear the entire conversation, but I recognize Melodee's voice as it increases in volume, "*... need an appointment.*"

I'm not sure who would be here, with or without an appointment, at this time of day. I don't have any meetings scheduled until next week, and anyone else would have called first.

Closing the lid to my laptop, I push away from my desk and stand. I'm walking toward my door when I hear the doorknob rattle, before a *thud* sound as if something was thrown against the wall or dropped onto the floor.

"*I said, you can't do that!*" I hear Melodee yell. I don't know if I should be concerned that someone is trying to obviously bust into my office, or curious that Melodee is fighting with someone in the reception area.

I reach for the doorknob to open it and find out for myself what's going on when I hear Emi's voice, freezing me in my tracks. I have no idea what she's doing here. Is something wrong? Did something happen while she was at home today?

"*Sure,*" I hear her loudly from the other side of the door. "*Maybe he'll actually act like he works here for you. He certainly didn't when I was downstairs a few minutes ago.*" She sounds positively angry, and a chill goes down my spine. I've never heard her take that tone of voice in the short time that I've known her.

Ripping the door open, I step out into the reception area. "What is going on out here?" I demand, my eyes immediately going to the reception desk where I see Melodee reaching for her desk phone. I turn my gaze side to side looking for Emi before I find her sitting on the floor. Narrowing my eyes, I'm immediately concerned that she may have fallen, but that doesn't make sense. Not unless she was pushed.

Emi looks up at me, her eyes wide in fear, and I'm instantly set on edge. I never want to see that emotion come across her beautiful angelic features toward me. She'll never have a reason to be afraid of me. Kneeling beside her, I lay a hand softly on her shoulder and give it a gentle, reassuring squeeze. "Are you okay, Kitten?"

"Yes," she whispers. "Help me up?"

I don't hesitate. Standing, I reach for her hands, and she takes them into hers instantly. Pulling her to her feet, I place my hands on her hips to hold her steady, worried that she may be a little off balance from standing too fast. "What are you doing here?" I realize as she flinches slightly that my voice may be a bit gruffer than I intended, but I'm confused about what she was doing on the floor and concerned that she may be hurt.

"I wanted to surprise you, but your assistant refused to let you know I was here." She lowers her gaze to her shoes.

"It's okay." I lift her gaze with a finger beneath her chin. "You're welcome here anytime. I'm honestly surprised to see you. I was just thinking about coming home soon anyway. But what were you doing on the…"

No. No. Please tell me my *assistant* didn't put a hand on her.

Releasing Emi, I turn on Melodee and stomp the two steps to the side of her desk. "Did you touch her?" I demand.

"I told her she needed an appointment," Melodee answers nonchalantly with a shrug of her shoulders.

"Since when has anyone needed an appointment?"

"I know you've been super busy lately. I was doing you a favor." She sits behind her desk, her fingers going to her keyboard as if she's actually planning on doing some work. Or at least pretending.

"Only because you haven't been doing your job!" I exclaim. "Now, answer my question. Did. You. Touch. Her?" I ask again, forcefully.

"Landon, it's okay." Emi steps up beside me and places her hand between my shoulder blades.

Lowering my head, I take a deep breath to calm my boiling rage. "No, Emi. It's not okay." Turning to face her, I cup her face in my hands and rest my forehead against hers. "No one should put their hands on you. Never again." I pull her against my chest and thread my fingers into her ponytail. "I can't bear the thought of anyone hurting you again."

"It was just a misunderstanding," she says, her voice slightly muffled against my shirt. "I should have called first."

"That kind of ruins the surprise though, doesn't it?" The rage still settling in my veins nearly dissipates as she giggles softly. "Go home, Melodee," I say over my shoulder. "We'll talk about this more tomorrow."

"Fine by me."

I stay standing, my arms wrapping around Emi's tiny frame as I breathe in her sweet fragrance. She wraps her arms around my waist as we listen to the elevator open and close as Melodee leaves.

"We need to talk about that elevator," she says as she pulls back and looks up at me.

"What?" I chuckle at the serious expression on her face, her brows pulled together to form a sweet little line between them. I brush my thumb over the line to smooth it out. "What about the elevator?"

"Twenty-five floors are a long ride in a quiet elevator. It needs elevator music. Otherwise, it's just creepy."

"Huh." Stepping away, I reach for her hand. "Never thought of that before. I'm usually on my phone checking emails when I'm stuck in there." I turn toward my office and begin to pull her along. "Come on."

"Hold on," she stops me, and I turn to watch her grab hold of a wagon that I hadn't noticed there before. "Okay, I'm ready."

"What's this?"

"Your surprise." She smiles at me innocently and it lights up all her features. She truly is the most beautiful thing I've ever laid eyes on and I'm the lucky bastard that gets to call her mine.

Pinching her chin between my thumb and forefinger, I bend down and kiss her lips softly. "I love surprises." Placing my hand on her lower back, I lead her into my office and have her sit on the small loveseat in the corner. The wagon rests on the floor in front of us and I see a box full of picture frames inside. "What is all this?" Reaching out, I grab the first frame in the top of the box. My breath catches in my throat as I see the angel fountain that I took her to the first night I had her here in the city.

"Your properties," she tells me proudly. "Well, not yours, yours. But the ones that you told me you designed."

"Did you take all these?" Setting the angel in my lap, I reach out and grab a couple more frames from the box.

"Yep. I thought you could hang them around your office. Speaking of which, did you design this building too?"

"I did." I stack several pictures in my lap as I continue to look through the box. "These are amazing, Kitten." She has obviously been busy over the last few days. Some of the photos are printed in black and white while others are left full color. There are a few more similar to the one she took of the front of the apartment building with blurred people walking past the front.

"Do you own this building too? Like the apartment building?"

"No, I don't. The business does though. We rent the lower floors to other companies to use for office space and all the money goes back into Strong Designs. It was a solid business investment back when we first got started."

"That's smart."

"It was a wise decision. I rented an office space the first year Strong Designs was open and felt like I was throwing money away. So, after the first few big jobs we completed, I purchased an abandoned warehouse. It was beyond repair and needed to be bulldozed, but the location was perfect. I designed the tower, and our own construction team did the build. It didn't take long to fill the lower twenty-three floors and the building basically paid for itself within the first year after it was completed."

"Good to know. So maybe you can invest in some elevator music."

A laugh burst out of me before I can even stop it. Throwing my head back, the laughter bellows out of me until my stomach begins to cramp. How long has it been since I've laughed like that? "I'll do that," I concede, wiping the moisture from my eyes with the backs of my hands.

Standing, Emi takes the picture frames from my lap and places them all back in the box. I watch, my head tilted up to her face, as she stands in front of me. She reaches out slowly and cups my face in her hands before lowering herself onto my lap. Her knees press into the loveseat on either side of my hips, my hands immediately going to her hips to hold her in place.

She lowers her eyes to my mouth, and I watch as she pulls her bottom lip between her teeth. My hands instinctively move higher around her waist before pulling her tighter against me. I'm amazed at her courage as she takes the initiative to lower her head, her mouth pressing against my own softly, tentatively at first. Her tongue peeks out and trails over my bottom lip before I open for her to deepen the kiss. I let her lead, for now.

When she starts to melt against me, I pull her in tighter and take over the kiss. One hand remains on her lower back while the other cradles the back of her head, tilting her slightly for a deeper taste of her sweet mouth. Our tongues tangle together in a battle of lust and greed, desperate to soak her very essence into my own soul. She rocks her hips slightly against my growing erection and I don't stop her. The heat of her soaked pussy burning through the thin layer of her yoga pants. I wonder if she's wearing any panties underneath.

Groaning into her mouth, I suck harder on her bottom lip, and she purrs so sweetly against me. The taste of her cherry lip gloss is something that I'll never be able to live without. I'll crave it for the rest of my days, knowing that she's the elixir of life that I'll never be able to get over – an addiction that I'll never be able to break.

Breaking the kiss, I trail my lips along her jaw before nipping just below her ear. She throws her head back and grinds against my erection and it's all I can do to hold myself back. My hands move down to cradle her ass and a growl rumbles deep in my chest at how much healthier her body has become over the last few weeks. Just to be able to touch her now, to really feel her body without fear of breaking her fragile frame. "Fuck, baby. You feel so good riding me." I squeeze her rounded cheeks softly, directing her to rock her hips harder against me. "Are you wet for me, Kitten?"

She throws her head back, giving me more access to her neck. With soft bites and small teasing tastes as my tongue peeks out, I move slowly down to where her shoulder and neck meet and suck softly. I want to mark her but I don't want it to bruise. She's had enough of those to last her a lifetime and I don't care to ever see another lasting bruise on her silky skin.

"Take what you need from me, baby." Slipping one hand beneath her tank top, I cup her breast over her bra. My thumb grazes her nipple, rolling the hardened peak from left to right.

"Oh, God. Landon!" she cries out as she breaks apart in my lap. My hips thrust up against her once, twice more to ride out her orgasm before she collapses against my chest.

"Hold onto me, Kitten." She wraps her arms around my neck tightly as I stand, my hands moving beneath her thighs to hold her in place. Her legs wrap around my waist as I walk toward my desk before sitting her down on the smooth surface and reaching into my back pocket for my wallet. Removing a condom, I place the foil between my teeth and reach for my belt. "This is gonna be hard and fast, Kitten. Think you can handle that?"

"God yes," she reaches out and grabs the waist of my slacks. She's pushing them down my hips as I wrap my grab my hard cock roughly with one hand and bite the condom wrapper open with the other.

"Stand up and turn around, Kitten." She stands without hesitating and turns while pushing her yoga pants down her legs. As I suspected earlier, she isn't wearing any panties and that makes me smile. "Bend over and hold onto the desk, baby."

She bends down, flattening her upper body across the polished surface, her arms going out in front of her and her fingers wrapping around the end of the desk. The hem of her tank top rides up her back with the movement and I have the perfect view of her rounded ass as I line my cock up with her entrance.

I push into her in a single thrust, knowing she's wet enough to take me after her orgasm. She gasps at the intrusion, and I can feel her tightening against me. I give her only a few seconds to adjust before I begin moving, my fingers digging into her hips tight enough that I can only hope they don't leave marks. She meets my every thrust, pushing back against me every time. The only sound in the office the slapping of our skin and our ragged breaths.

I wanted this to be hard and fast, but there's no way I can do this without feeling her convulse around me. She has to get off one more time. Reaching around her hip, I rub circles over her clit with my middle finger. "That's it, Kitten. Let go for me." Closing my eyes, I concentrate on the pulsing of her pussy as she clenches down on my cock tight enough that I can barely move. She falls over that cliff and I jump over with her. We're falling together. It's a complete out of body experience as the heat builds in the base of my spine as my cock begins to pulse inside of her.

My eyes are squeezed tightly shut as her moans and cries begin to die down. I ride out the final shocks on my own orgasm, tightening my arms around her and pulling her to stand with her back pressed into my chest. My cheek rests against the top of her head while we catch our breath together.

"I like your office." She giggles sweetly as our bodies separate. This woman makes me laugh. It's a feeling I never want to forget.

As soon as our clothes are back in the right position, she turns to face me. She flattens her palms against my chest as I cup her face in my hands and lower my mouth to hers.

"I love you, Landon." My heart skips several beats at her proclamation. I've been falling in love with this woman since the day I met her, but I was afraid that it was moving too fast for her. I didn't want to scare her away. "I know it's fast and you probably think that I'm crazy. But I've never felt so safe as I do with you. You make me feel cherished and that's something that I didn't think I would ever feel with anyone."

I move the hair away from her forehead with the tips of my fingers, dragging it behind her ear before cupping her cheek. "I love you too, Kitten."

A single tear slips from her eye, and I catch it with my thumb.

"I think I fell in love with you the first time I saw you in the diner. I knew right away that I wanted to slay all your demons and keep you safe forever."

"You've done a really good job of chasing those demons away."

"And I'll never stop." I kiss her softly on her forehead before pulling away. "You wanna get out of here?" She doesn't answer, just reaches out for my hand, and nods her head. The smile on her face is brighter than I've ever seen it and I feel my own smile growing to match it.

Chapter
TWENTY-FOUR

EMILEE

THE MOONLIGHT SHINING THROUGH the bedroom window is the only thing lighting up the bedroom. It's still early, or late depending on who you ask, but I can't sleep anymore. My brain just won't shut down, the millions of ideas rushing through my head about setting up a digital portfolio for Strong Designs. I still haven't mentioned it to Landon yet, I wanted to have something put together to present to him first.

His bed is huge and comfortable, and there's more than enough room for me to sit cross-legged with my laptop without interrupting his sleep. Peeking over my shoulder, I see him sound asleep. He's lying on his back, one arm held over his head with the back of his hand pressing against the headboard, the other arm lying limply over his abdomen and the sheet pushed down to his waist. He doesn't snore even though his mouth is open slightly, but the sound he makes while sleeping is still adorable – it's more of a low growling sound similar to what I imagine a large cat or lion would make.

Just watching him sleep sets off a swarm of butterflies in my belly. I imagine this is what love feels like – the fluttering sensation I feel every time I look at him. When he touches me, I can't imagine being with anyone else. Landon is the first person that I've allowed to touch me in any way in so long. I didn't think I'd ever be able to allow someone to get close to me again. A month ago, I couldn't have imagined feeling not only safe but loved, cherished, protected.

One last look at Landon and my decision is made. He's given me so much in the last several weeks, the least I can do is showcase his business for him. A little internet sleuthing proves that he doesn't have an online presence at all. There is no digital profile for his business other than a Yelp listing. Do I want to manage his online presence? Not really. I don't know anything about TikTok or Instagram and doubt that I would be able to commit enough time to posting to keep up with whatever algorithm they use. I do have some experience with Facebook though. I had a profile of my own before my phone and laptop were taken away by Charlie. And I can set up a basic webpage with a gallery and contact information.

I don't want to throw anything online without Landon having a chance to look it over first, so I settle myself in with a throw blanket draped over my shoulders and my laptop balanced on my lap and begin creating a mockup. Deciding to go with a flip-book style gallery, I upload all the photos of Landon's properties and designs that I've been able to photograph over the last week into the mockup. I'm sure there are more that I haven't even found yet or that he hasn't told me about. Hopefully, when he sees the webpage design, he'll agree to take me around to any that I haven't already seen so I can get more pictures.

I realize I've lost track of time when the glare from the rising sun shining through the windows overtakes my entire screen, making it hard to see what I'm working on. I have to angle more to the left, turning my back to Landon as he continues to sleep beside me, just so I can see the screen and make sure the file is saved – I don't want to lose the progress that I've made on the page.

The bed dips behind me and I know that Landon is waking up for the day. Guilt washes over me when I look at the clock in the bottom corner of my laptop screen and I realize I should have made breakfast. We have a long day planned today. Landon is going with me to take my driving test and hopefully get my license before taking me to work with him so we can hang the pictures I left in his office yesterday.

"Mmm. Good morning, Kitten." I feel his warm breath on my neck below my ear just before his tongue traces a line down to my shoulder.

Tilting my head to the side, I give him better access. "Good morning." One hand resting on my laptop to keep it from falling from my lap, my other hand lifts to thread my fingers through his sleep-disheveled hair.

"What are you working on?" he asks, resting his chin on my shoulder and wrapping his arms around my waist.

"Just something I wanted to put together for you." Using the touchpad, I move the cursor around the page and navigate to the top first page of the mockup. I don't move, don't look for a reaction from Landon when he sees the home page for what could potentially be a new website for his business. I hadn't planned on showing it to him this early, but I'm not going to hide it from him either.

Releasing my waist with one hand, he scrolls through the mockup, clicking on a few of the links and flipping through the gallery. "You've been busy."

"Couldn't sleep."

"You nervous about today?"

"A little," I admit.

"Hey," he starts. Lifting one hand up to cup my cheek, he turns my face toward his. "You got this." His lips press softly against mine, his confidence bleeding into me through the simple touch.

"I know." He smiles at my response, the glimmer in his eyes as he pulls back and looks at me fills me with comfort. My head nods in understanding and realization that I really do *got this*. "I had a good teacher."

"Have you been studying the booklet?"

"I've been through it so many times I could probably recite it in my sleep."

"Good." He nips at my jaw. "What time is it?"

Looking down at the clock on my laptop I tell him, "It's almost seven."

"Mmm. Plenty of time." I watch as he pushes the lid down on the laptop before removing it from my lap and placing it on the nightstand.

"Plenty of time for what?"

"For me to make love to you." Grabbing the hem of my t-shirt, he lifts, and my arms instinctively lift for him. "Then we'll take a shower and I'll make you breakfast." He turns me around and gently pushes my shoulders, so I lie back on the bed before he crawls up my body and nips at my collarbone. "Your appointment isn't until ten. We'll go get your license then I'll take you to the hardware store for whatever supplies we need. Then you can spend the day with me at the office hanging pictures."

"You have the entire day planned out?" I giggle as he moves his mouth across my chest to nip at my other collarbone.

"Yep." He lowers his mouth again and draws my nipple into his mouth. Releasing it with a pop, he lifts his gaze to mine. "You okay with that?"

"Absolutely."

"Good. Now lay there and let me love you."

ALMOST THREE HOURS LATER, we're pulling into the DMV. We walk directly to the registration counter to check in and I'm immediately led to a glass booth to take the written exam. This part is going to be easy – I was always good at taking tests when I was in school. I wasn't lying when I told Landon that I'd studied the booklet enough that I could recite it in my sleep. There are thirty-five questions on the test, and I can't miss more than five.

It only takes me fifteen minutes to finish the test on the computer. When I step out of the booth, I'm greeted by a woman with bright pink hair. Her nametag says her name is Lydia.

"Have a seat while I pull your results and I'll call you up," she tells me as she extends her arm to indicate the row of chairs where Landon is already sitting.

"Okay." I practically skip over to Landon, and he smiles as he watches me approach.

"So," he starts as I take the seat beside him. "How do you think you did?"

"I feel pretty good about it." Smiling, I lay my head against his shoulder, and he wraps an arm around me, pulling me closer. "There was one or two questions that I don't know about, but I'm sure I passed."

I see the color pink out the corner of my eye and turn my head to see Lydia walking toward me with a clipboard. "Emilee?" she calls out to me. "Great job on the test. You only missed one. Are you ready for the easy part?"

I'm not sure that the driving test is going to be the easy part for me. If I'm being honest, I'm more nervous about that part than I was about the written test. "Yes," I say as I go to stand.

Landon stops me with his fingers wrapped around my wrist and pulls me toward him. "Good luck, Kitten. I'll wait here for you." Kissing my cheek, he releases me to stand to my full height.

Without a word, I smile at him before looking up at Lydia and following her out the front door.

She pauses on the sidewalk outside and turns to face me. Pointing toward Landon's silver Mercedes, I click the key fob to unlock the doors. "I'm over here." She doesn't say anything at all, which is making me more nervous. She just nods her head once and follows me to the car. She sits in the passenger seat and buckles her seatbelt while I pause with my hand still on the handle of the driver's side door. A chill runs down my spine and I get the sudden feeling that I'm being watched. "Don't be silly," I chastise myself. "You're just nervous." A few deep breaths and I open the door and slide into the car.

As soon as I have my seatbelt fastened, she finally speaks again. "Okay," she begins. "We're going to pull out of the parking lot and take a right. Go to the stop sign at the end of the block and turn left."

"Okay." Starting the car, I double check to make sure my mirrors are adjusted to where they need to be before putting the car in reverse and starting my test. We're a few blocks away from the DMV, already having gone through three traffic lights and a four-way stop before she has me signaling to turn on a residential road up ahead before the chills start to run down my spine again. Checking my rearview mirror, I see an older pickup behind us and realize that it's been following us through the last four turns Lydia has had me make.

"Go ahead and stop here."

"In the middle of the road?" Looking in my mirror again as I apply the brakes, I see the truck has pulled into a driveway three houses back, so I assume it wasn't really following me. They must have just been on their way home.

"Yes. This is a perfect spot for the last part of your test."

I'm not sure what she means by that but she's in charge here, so I'll do what she's requesting. As soon as the car comes to a complete stop, I turn my head to Lydia to await further instruction.

"You've done great so far," she says as she writes some more notes on her clipboard. "Now, we're going to do a three-point turnabout. Do you know what that is?"

"I do," I answer, remembering the day that Landon had me practice those out on a county road. It was so frustrating then because I kept running off the road, but he was so patient with me, even when I was getting upset about it.

"Have you done one before?"

Giggle at the fact that I've technically done about five hundred of them over the past month, I answer simply, "Yes."

"Good." She unfastens her seatbelt and I furrow my brows in confusion at her. "I'm going to get out of the car to watch you do this. You only get one shot so here's how it's gonna go." She opens her door and places one booted foot on the ground outside. "You have to complete the turn in no more than three points. If you touch the grass on either side of the street at any point, it's an automatic fail. Once you're turned around, stop and put the car in park and I'll get back in. After this, we're done."

"Got it."

"Okay. Take your time, Emilee. Start whenever you're ready."

I nod once at her and watch as she steps the rest of the way out of the car. Once the door is closed and she's taken a few steps away from the car, I put both hands on the steering wheel. Putting the car in drive, I turn the wheel as far to the left as it will go and lightly apply the gas. "That's one," I say to myself. Stopping where I hope is just before the grass, I put the car in reverse and turn the wheel as far as it'll go to the right and press the gas pedal again, making sure to keep an eye on my side mirror. I stop again before touching the grass, hopefully. "That's two." Finally, I put the car back in drive and turn the wheel all the way to the left before pressing the gas for the third point. As soon as I'm straightened out, I apply the break and come to a complete stop before putting the car back in park.

With a wide toothy smile, Lydia steps back into the car and fastens her seatbelt. "Great job!" she exclaims. "Okay, let's go back to the DMV."

I allow her to direct me back through town until we're pulling into the parking lot.

"I hope you're ready to have your picture taken today," she says as she steps out of the car. "Follow me."

My smile is so wide that it's hurting my cheeks, but I can't make myself stop. I passed. I follow her back inside and directly up to the counter. It takes several minutes for her to put the information in the computer before she directs me to stand in front of a screen for my photo. I'm probably the only one in the entire state that actually smiled for my driver's license photo, but I just can't help myself.

The card prints out instantly and she hands it to me in exchange for the permit. I watch as she feeds the permit through a shredder. "You're all done."

"Thank you," I say, pinching my new license between two fingers. Turning around, I see Landon standing from his chair. I'm sure he can tell by having been watching that I passed. Smiling, he saunters toward me with his arms held out to his sides. I skip the few feet between us and jump into his waiting arms where, of course, he catches me in a tight hug and spins me around twice.

"Congratulations!" he exclaims as he sets me back on my feet. "I knew you could do it." Cupping my cheeks, he kisses me softly on the lips. This day can't possibly get any better. "I hope you're ready to chauffeur me around the rest of the day. To the hardware store driver."

Giggling, I grab his hand and drag him toward the door. I'm more than happy to spend the day driving him around.

Chapter
TWENTY-FIVE

EMILEE

"SO, HOW LONG HAS Melodee worked for you?" I ask Landon as we pull out onto the highway leading to Independence. I spent the morning at his office hanging pictures in the conference room and reception area and got a bad vibe from his assistant. She seemed to have had an attitude toward me from the moment she saw us step off the elevator.

"She's been with me since I opened the company four years ago."

"She's kind of a bully."

His eyes narrow and the muscles in his jaw tick. I can see that he's getting upset and I hate that I'm the cause of it. "Did she say something to you?"

"Not really." He glances in my direction before turning his gaze back to the road. "I mean, she did but I just brushed it off."

"Emi?" Reaching across the console, he takes my hand in his and twines our fingers together. "What happened?"

"She just really gave me the creeps. You know? She was watching me the entire time I was hanging pictures. She kept saying little things like I'm not good enough for you and I should run back to daddy."

"Run back to daddy?"

"That's what she said." I don't release his hand before turning my focus back out the passenger window. He squeezes my hand – not in anger, more like he's reassuring me that he's still there.

"What the fuck is that supposed to mean?"

"I don't know." I turn back to face him. "It was weird. I'm choosing not to let it bother me though."

"Okay." His grip on my hand loosens and he runs his thumb along my knuckles softly. "If you're sure. I can say something to her if you want me to."

"No. I'm sure it's nothing against me. But I do think she has a little bit of a crush on you."

He coughs out a laugh. "What?"

"I think she's just angry that I was there with you. I think she likes you."

"I don't believe that. She's worked for me for four years."

"I know. But still." I leave it at that. I'm not going to argue with him about the inner workings of the female brain. I'll stand behind what I said. She's jealous and her little green monster wears anger on its sleeve. He might not see it, and that's okay, but I know it's there and I don't feel threatened by it.

"You know I don't think of her that way, right?"

Tilting my head to the side, I look at Landon's profile. He's relaxed but I can still see the bit of worry behind his eyes. Still, I believe him. "I know."

"Seriously, Kitten. She works for me. There's never been anything more than that."

"I believe you, Landon." I know it hasn't been long since we've been together, but I really do believe him. If he says there's nothing going on with his assistant and never has been, I have no reason not to believe him. He's never done anything to me to make me trust him any less.

Lifting my hand, he kisses the back of it before lowering it back to his lap.

"Like I said, she's a bully. That's something that I can deal with. I'm used to being bullied," I admit.

"I don't know if that makes me feel any better," he says with a grimace.

"I know, but it's the truth. I can't do anything to change my past though. All I can do at this point is learn from it. And what I've learned about bullies is that they usually have a reason for lashing out. It might not even be meant directly toward me. They might have something else going on in their lives that they can't deal with on their own and they just lash out at whoever seems an easier target."

"You're amazing, you know that?"

That makes me smile and I can feel the blush burning my cheeks. "Thanks." I look away from him for several seconds as I watch a field full of birds out the passenger window. I have no idea what kind of birds they are but they're white. There are so many of them that it looks like a section of snow-covered land right in the middle of the field. I should have brought my camera. If I had, then

I would make Landon pull over just so I could get a picture of them.

"There was one boy in high school that used to pick on me all the time," I begin. "He moved into town when we were in second grade, so I'd known him already for most of my life. He only had a few friends that I knew he hung out with outside of school. I never saw his mother, so I don't know if she was around. But his father was a drunk and was never home. It was just him and his two older sisters most of the time when he wasn't hanging out around town causing trouble with his best friend."

Landon doesn't interrupt me or take his eyes off the road, but I know he's listening. His fingers tighten occasionally around my own as I talk, his thumb running aimlessly back and forth against my hand.

"It was typical mean things most of the time. He'd knock the books out of my arms while I was walking down the hallway between classes. He'd bump into me from behind and knock me down. Then it started to get worse as time went on. He started ripping art projects out of my hands and slamming them on the ground to break them. He'd break into my locker and steal things out of it. He even broke the lens to my camera once, but the photography teacher got involved in that one since the camera technically belonged to the school."

"Did it ever stop?" Landon asks me.

"Not really. I chose to ignore it most of the time. I mean, I had enough going on at home after my mom hooked up with Charlie. Having a bully at school was nothing compared to what I went through at home."

"Damn."

"Yeah." I take a few calming breaths before continuing. "I was home alone one afternoon after school. My mom and Charlie were both at work, so it was nice to be able to just go home and close myself up in my room to do homework without worrying about anything else. But then my phone rang. And it was him. And he sounded terrified. He was crying into the phone and struggling to breathe between words. It freaked me out so bad that I ran as fast as I could to his house because I thought something was terribly wrong with him. And even though he had been the absolute worst toward me at school, I would have never forgiven myself if something was wrong with him and I didn't try to help him. I mean, he reached out to me of all people."

When I don't continue Landon speaks, "What happened?"

"He was shooting targets in his backyard with a pellet rifle. It was so stupid really. He said he'd been shooting targets for a few hours and got bored so when he saw a rabbit running across his backyard, he took aim and shot. He didn't think he'd actually hit the poor thing, but he did. He killed it."

"Fuck."

"I don't think I'd ever seen him show any emotion of a single thing the entire time I'd known him. But when I got to his house, he was crouched down on the ground, cradling this poor defenseless bunny in his arms. He was so broken over the fact that he'd killed something, and it was so stupid. But there was more to it than that, you know? It was like, for the first time, he was no longer the bully at school that had been picking on me for years. He was just another boy, and he was lost. And I needed to help him to find his way back."

"What did you do?" He squeezes my hand again in reassurance.

"I sat with him for almost an hour and let him cry. Then we found a shoebox and a shovel, and we buried the rabbit. We found a stone in the alley behind his house and used it to mark the grave and said a few stupid words over it, made up stories about how wonderful of a life it had led and the family it was leaving behind. Then we just started talking about everything and nothing until I knew he was going to be okay. Turns out, his father and Charlie were best friends. He knew what was going on at my house because it was the same at his. Only, his mother had left years before because she was tired of putting up with it. That left him and his two older sisters to deal with everything firsthand. He was no different than me, he just didn't know how to deal with it. We didn't become best friends or anything, but he never picked on me again after that."

"What ever happened to him?"

"He dropped out of school senior year. He moved away from home, and no one has heard from him since. His father died in a drunk driving accident not long after my mother passed away, but I didn't see him at the funeral. Both of his sisters still live in Independence and used to come to the diner occasionally with their own families. I used to ask them occasionally about their brother and they say he's doing great, but I don't know much more beyond that."

"He got away though. Good for him."

"He did. And I can only hope that he's made something of his life. But I learned so much from my interactions with him. So, you see? Not all bullies are mean just to be mean. He was cruel to me, but it was his way of dealing with everything else going on in his life."

"You're amazing. You know that?"

"I know." I giggle as I stare at the Independence Day decorations through the front windshield. Decorations that I've seen a million times since they never change and are never taken down. A chill runs down my spine as we drive down Main Street toward the diner. A town that I had hoped to get away from for so long, and hopefully this will be the last time that I ever step foot here.

Landon finds a parking space in front of the diner and puts the car in park. I stop him as he reaches for the button to turn off the car. "I'll only be a minute if you want to wait here."

"Are you sure?" He looks at me skeptically, his brows furrowed in concern.

"Yeah. I don't plan on being here for long. I just wanted to talk to Ralph and get my last check from him. I owe him an explanation at least."

"Okay, Kitten." His hand reaches around to cradle the back of my head before pulling me toward him. He kisses me hard and possessively before releasing me and resting his forehead against mine. "I'll be right here when you get back. We'll head back to the city and neither one of us will ever have to see this town again. We can finally put it in our rearview mirror and never look back."

"Sounds great to me."

Walking up to the door of the diner, I can see through the windows that it's practically empty. It's still early enough in the afternoon that the dinner rush hasn't started yet, the perfect time to come talk to Ralph. Stepping inside, I see Amber at the end of the counter wrapping silverware with another waitress that I've never seen before. She's probably new. Neither of them looks up at me as I walk by toward the entrance to the kitchen where Ralph is washing up the lunch dishes.

"Hey, Ralph," I call out as I push through the swinging door.

He spins around at the sound of my voice, a smile immediately spreading across his pale, time-worn features. "Emi?" He drops his last dish into the sink full of soapy water and yanks the towel away from his shoulder to dry his hands. "God, you look so different."

"That's good, I hope."

"I don't think I've ever seen you without your sweater on."

"A lot has changed since I've been gone."

"Well," he starts as he steps closer. Stopping only a few inches away, he places a hand on my shoulder and for the first time, I don't flinch away from a touch that isn't Landon's. "Change looks good on you, kid."

"Thank you. I'm sorry I left the way I did."

"Don't be. We managed here without you. Besides, you needed to get away. I never expected you to stay here forever."

"I just feel like I owe you an explanation." I lower my gaze to the floor as guilt washes over me. Ralph has never been anything but nice to me, and even though he says I don't owe him anything, I still feel guilty for just disappearing on him like I did.

"Nope. I may not say much to you girls when you're here to work. But I could see the life draining out of you ever since you lost your mama. Little by little, day after day. There wasn't much left of you to keep going here. You needed a way out, and I'm just glad you found it."

"Thank you, Ralph."

"Don't mention it, kid. Here." He steps away and walks toward the refrigerator in the back corner of the kitchen. Removing a magnet, he grabs a slip of paper that was being held against the cool metal. "This is for you." Walking back toward me, he holds the paper out for me to take from his hand.

Unfolding the paper, I see it's my check. It isn't much, not that I expected it to be, but that doesn't bother me. Folding it up, I place it into my back pocket and nod my head. "I'll get out of your way."

"Don't take this the wrong way, kid." Lifting my gaze, I wait for him to continue. "You're better than anything this town could ever offer you. I hope to never see you again." He smiles and the wrinkles around his eyes deepen.

Giggle softly, I throw my arms around his shoulders and squeeze. He pats my back awkwardly and it makes me laugh harder. "Bye, Ralph."

Pushing my way back through the swinging doors, I see Amber leaning against the counter with her arms crossed beneath her breasts. She has a scowl on her face as she watches me step toward the counter. "Nice to see you. Thanks for keeping in touch," she says sarcastically.

"Hi, Amber."

"That's all you have to say to me." She reaches out for me, regardless of all the times I've ever flinched when she's done the same thing. She pulls me into a tight hug, and I don't hesitate to hug her back. We may not have been best buddies when I last saw her, but we do have a history of being friends. It's the least I can do considering I will probably never see her again. "Ralph, I'm taking a break!" She calls as she turns me around and places a hand across my shoulders. She walks and I follow along beside her.

"How are things?" I ask as we walk toward the back hallway.

"They haven't been too bad. I've picked up more hours since you took off without word. Now we have Alicia working your old shifts and my hours got cut again. But seriously, you could have kept in touch."

"Amber, I haven't had a phone in years. I don't even know your number."

"Sure, whatever." She pushes the door open to the alley and I don't question it. I blindly follow her through the door even though what I really want to do is get back in Landon's car and drive away from here forever. "I'm just glad you're back."

"What?" She removes her hand from around my shoulders and I look up at her as she takes a step away from me. "I'm not back, Amber."

"You are. You just don't realize it yet."

"About time you came home." The voice behind me sends a chill down my back. Nervous goosebumps break out over my entire body, and I turn slowly hoping beyond hope that my mind is just playing tricks on me. But I know even before I see his face that it's not a trick. I'd know that voice anywhere. It's the same voice that's haunted my nightmares for years.

"Charlie," I gasp when my eyes meet his. My stomach plummets to my feet as his features morph into a look of pure hatred and I know that I'm not getting away from him. He moves so fast that I don't even see it coming but when the back of his hand lands against my cheek, I'm thrown to the side and go down hard on the pavement, my head bouncing against the hard surface hard enough that I see stars before it all goes black.

Chapter
Twenty-Six

LANDON

I SHOULD HAVE GONE INSIDE with her. I feel like I've been sitting here chewing on my thumb nail nervously for an hour already. Looking down at the clock on the dash, I see it's only been twenty minutes. I don't understand why I'm so on edge. She just went in to talk to Ralph, the owner of Freedom Diner, to get her last paycheck.

I resign myself to giving her a few more minutes before I go in looking for her. Reaching out, I turn on the radio to a soft rock station and lean my head back against the seat.

A car pulls up and parks beside me and I watch as a family of four gets out and walks into the diner. They sit at a table by the front window and a waitress that I haven't seen before walks over with glasses of water and menus. They've obviously been to the diner before since they order right away without looking over the menu first and the waitress walks over to the order window and hands the ticket directly to Ralph. Still, Emi doesn't come back out of the kitchen.

I should have paid more attention. If she came out of the kitchen already then, I must have missed her, but where else would she have gone? "Maybe she's in the bathroom," I say to myself. Several minutes later, I'm tapping my fingers on the steering wheel impatiently when Ralph sets the orders on the counter and Emi still hasn't emerged from wherever she's hiding. Pressing the button, I turn off the car and throw my door open to get out.

Pushing my way into the diner, I walk past the counter where the new waitress is standing and watching me with an expression of surprise. I step around the end of the counter and push open the swinging door to the kitchen where Ralph is standing at the sink washing a large boiling pot. "Where is Emi?"

He turns around after dropping the pot back into the water and dries his hands on the towel that was hanging over his shoulder. His brows furrow in confusion as he tilts his head. "She left already. Did she not come back outside?"

"How long ago did she finish talking to you?"

He looks at the clock hanging over the refrigerator on the opposite side of the kitchen. "Probably thirty minutes ago."

What the fuck?

"Well, where did she go?" My skin crawls with suspicion. Something is going on here and I'd bet everything I have that her stepfather is involved somehow. I'll be damned if I'm going to let him hurt her again.

Tossing the towel onto the counter beside the sink, Ralph walks over to the swinging door and pushes his way into the dining room. I step out behind him as he places his hands on his hips and looks around the area. "Alicia, where's Amber? She should have been back from her break minutes ago."

"She hasn't come back yet," the waitress I now know as Alicia says.

"Did Emi go with her?" I ask.

"Emi?" She looks at me with a confused expression. I guess she's the only person in this small town that doesn't know who Emi is. "Oh her. Yes. They walked out the back door together."

"She's probably in the alley then." Ralph exclaims as he turns back to look at me. "They may have lost track of time talking."

My shoulders lower slightly from around my ears as I realize I may have been overreacting. I nod my head at Ralph as he pushes back into the kitchen before turning toward the back exit. Only, as I approach the back door, a feeling of unease settles over me. It just doesn't feel right.

Opening the door, I step out into the alley to find it completely deserted. There's no trace of anyone having been back here within the last half hour. I don't understand where she could be. Why would she leave with Amber and not tell me? Walking to the end of the alley, I look around the side of the building to see if she's standing there talking to her, but I don't see anyone.

Pulling my phone from my back pocket, I call her. I don't want to come across as over possessive, she has the right to catch up with a former co-worker and it would be wrong of me to stop her. But I just can't see her going somewhere with her without reaching out to me first. Walking back toward the back entrance of the diner, I listen to the phone ringing in my ear. Only, it's echoing strangely. The phone goes to Emi's voicemail, and I immediately hang up and call back. It echoes again and I stop walking. Pulling the phone from my ear, I listen closely to the empty space surrounding me, thinking I'm losing my mind. Only I'm not. Stepping closer to the dumpster, I lean over the edge and hear the phone ringing clear as day inside the metal container.

What the fuck is going on here?

Sitting right there, on top of a black trash bag, is Emi's phone. It sits face up within arm's reach as if just tossed haphazardly into the dumpster in passing. Reaching my arm over top of the thick metal, I grab the phone in my fist tight enough that I'm afraid I may crack the screen.

Turning back toward the diner, I look closer at my surroundings thinking I may be missing something. It doesn't appear that there is regular traffic through the alley, other than the occasional garbage truck to empty the dumpster. My eyes are drawn to an oil stain in the center of the alley, standing out brightly in its rainbow reflection against the sun. Kneeling next to the stain, I run my finger through the multi-colored puddle and feel the warmth radiating from it. It's warm enough to still be somewhat fresh and too shimmery to have been sitting long enough to soak into the asphalt. But it's the other spots I notice not far from when I'm kneeling that catch my attention. Standing and walking closer, I kneel again and rub a finger through the dark stain.

Blood.

The backdoor of the diner swings open hard enough to bounce off the wall inside and part of me hopes that it leaves a hole in the drywall. My steps echo through the hallway as I storm back into the dining room and through the swinging door to the kitchen. The way Ralph's eyes widen at my appearance, I wouldn't be surprised if there were smoke coming out of my ears. I'm absolutely fuming at the thought of where Emi might be right now – who may be putting their hands on her.

Guilt eats away at me knowing that I never should have brought her back here. I promised to keep her safe from her stepfather and get her away from this fucking town. And the first time coming back, for a paycheck that probably won't even buy her a decent dinner, and this is what happens.

"She's gone," I breathe out between my teeth. "Her phone was in the fucking dumpster."

"What?" he asks as he steps closer to me.

"We need to call the police."

"How do you know she didn't leave with Amber on her own? Not saying anything against you, but I don't know you. Are you sure she wouldn't find a way to leave you?"

"Are you serious right now?" I growl, puffing my chest to make me appear bigger, more aggressive, against his accusations.

"I'm just saying. Let me try to call Amber and see what's going on."

He steps away as he pulls a cell phone from his back pocket. I watch as he holds it to his ear for several seconds before pulling it away and putting it back in his pocket. "No answer."

"Of course not. Look, you need to call the police. I'm pretty sure there was a car back there waiting for them when they walked into the alley. And I found blood on the asphalt. And it looked fresh." Holding my hand up, I let him see the blood still staining the tip of my finger.

He doesn't ask any more questions before pulling his phone back out and calling the Sheriff's office to get a deputy to the diner. "Why didn't you lead with that?"

"You're something else. You know that? You're the one being all combative with me thinking I've done something that she needs to get away from." The volume of my voice is increasing as I continue. "If you really gave a shit about her, you would have seen that she's healthier now than she ever was while she was here working for you. Getting her out of this town was the best thing I could have ever done for her." Threading my fingers through my hair, I pull against the strands and relish in the pain in my scalp. "I should have never brought her back here."

Ralph and I are practically in a face-off when the police finally arrive thirty minutes later. For such a small town, their response time is certainly lacking. If this would have happened in the city, they would have made it here within five minutes, I have no doubt about that.

I give the officer my information, as do Ralph and Alicia. He had Alicia close the diner after the one family that was eating here before paid and left. It seems like it was a slow day anyway, so I don't think it's going to hurt him to be closed the rest of the day. This is more important than cooking and serving up the daily meatloaf special anyway. Now, I'm sitting in a booth in the middle of the dining room while Ralph answers questions. I have the perfect location to be able to hear everything that's said.

"She'd been gone for a while," Ralph tells Officer Santos. I keep my gaze focused on my hands fisted together on the table, so they don't know I'm listening. "She walked out during her shift just almost two months ago and didn't come back. I knew she had quit, expected it actually. She hadn't been happy here since her mother passed away a few years ago."

"Do you know where she went?" Santos asks him.

"Not specifically. I assume she left with Mister Strong over there." He points at me with his thumb over his shoulder. "She came back in today to pick up her last check. We talked for a few minutes. She said everything was good with her and she was happy.

231

Then she walked out of the kitchen. I assumed she was going to be leaving with Mister Strong again."

"Thank you, Ralph."

I hadn't heard his conversation with Alicia, but I don't expect that I missed anything. She seems a little flakey honestly. I doubt she had anything to say to them that would help with the investigation.

I sense the officer approaching my table before I look up and see him. He sits across from me, placing his notepad on the table in front of him. "Mister Strong?" He addresses me as he clicks the end of the pen before placing the tip on his paper.

"Officer Santos?" I look up as he tilts his head to the side curiously.

"Do I know you?" His brows furrow in question and I bite back a chuckle.

"You should," I admit. "We went to school together since third grade." About the time I moved in with my grandparents after my mom and dad died. I'm not surprised he doesn't remember me though. Santos was one of the popular guys once we got to high school. Captain of the football team and everything. While he was mister goody two shoes, I was busy causing trouble and chasing girls. I'm not surprised that he followed in his old man's footsteps though, joining the police force probably right out of school.

"Landon?" He sits back in the booth, an almost shocked expression on his face. "Holy shit, dude." He laughs loudly and my eyes narrow at him in response. This isn't the time to reminisce. "Didn't you open that big design firm in the city?"

"That's me." My fingers begin tapping against the Formica tabletop impatiently.

"I'll be damned." Leaning forward, he picks up his pen again and prepares to take notes on our conversation. "So, you want to tell me what's going on?"

I tell him about how Emi and I met two months ago here in the diner. I don't leave anything out – telling him about how I ended up getting her to my apartment and seeing her bruises the next day. I tell him about her stepfather a little louder than needed and notice Ralph standing against the counter with a guilty look on his face having obviously heard everything. Then I tell him about today, "I looked in the alley for her since that's where she went with Amber. I found her phone in the dumpster, warm oil leaked on the asphalt obviously recently, and found blood spots not far from it. I came back inside and told Ralph to call you and here we are."

"You could be a detective," he laughs. "You're quite observant."

"Not really. But I know when something looks suspicious. Has anyone looked into her stepfather yet? Or found Amber?"

"We have officers going over to Charlie's house and we're trying to get a trace on Amber's phone. If she's still with either of them, we'll find her." That's the problem, isn't it? What if she's no longer with them? What if they already hurt her and dumped her off somewhere?

I nod my head once and he stands and walks across the diner where his partner stands with his hands on his belt.

"I had no idea," Ralph admits as he walks over to my table.

"You never wondered why she was wearing a sweater?" He looks guilty as he rests his elbows on the table and lowers his gaze. I'll admit, I should probably shut up. He feels guilty enough without me rubbing it in. "She wore the sweater to cover the bruises on her arms. She would grab something to eat here any chance she got because she was weak with hunger. It was the only thing she would eat all day."

"I swear to God I had no idea."

"I made her go to a doctor to get checked out. She was malnourished and had lost so much weight you could see her bones. She was covered with bruises all over her body from the abuse she was suffering at home. She had cuts all over her upper arms where Charlie attacked her with a steak knife." My head shakes slowly side to side in disgust. She told me so many times that no one ever noticed her. She thought she was invisible and I'm beginning to believe her now. "She just wanted one person to see her and help her. Everyone in this town turned their backs on her when she needed them the most."

"I thought she was just depressed because her mom had died."

"How long ago did her mom die, Ralph?" I slump against the peeling vinyl seat and hang my head. "You let her suffer with that loss for how many years without doing anything to help her out of it?"

"Couple years ago."

"A couple years." My voice trails off in disappointment. "Two months, Ralph." He looks up at me, his brows lifting in question. "I've known her two months and I've seen more of her than anyone in this town has in the twenty years she's been alive. She's been here her whole fucking life and not a damn one of you ever noticed her."

"I'm sorry."

"Don't you dare waste your apology on me, Ralph. I'm not the one you owe an apology to."

"You're right."

Chapter
TWENTY-SEVEN

EMILEE

IN MY DREAM, I'M on a boat being jostled around by the open waves – thrown to the deck to land on my side with my knees drawn close to my chest for protection. The waves continue to get rougher and rougher as I try desperately to ride them out without being tossed overboard. My shoulder and hip are slammed ruthlessly into the deck and I'm afraid if I don't get control of the boat, it'll capsize, and I'll be stranded in the middle of the ocean as shark food. Rolling to my back, I go to sit up and try to get to my feet. I just need to get control of the boat and steer us back toward land before this storm gets any worse and I'm lost to the sea for good.

Sitting up, my forehead bangs against an unforgiving surface and I lay back down in confusion. Lifting my hand, I place the tips of my fingers against the pain on my head and realize that this isn't part of my dream. There was nothing there for me to hit my head on.

Where am I?

Opening my eyes, I struggle to focus in the dark, but I can't see anything. The ground beneath me is vibrating and I'm surrounded by a deep ear-splitting hum that I can't place. Lifting a hand in front of my face, I notice that both hands raise at the same time, and I realize they're connected together. By what, I don't know. Trying to kick my legs, I realize they are connected similarly, and I have to take deep breaths to keep myself from panicking.

What the fuck is going on?

Where was I before I woke up here?

What was I doing earlier today?

I wrack my brain, my heart rate increasing and beating a staccato rhythm against my ribs.

Calm down, Emi.

First things first, I need to figure out where I am. I'm tossed around again, similar to how I was being tossed around the deck of the boat. Landing on my side, my hands press against the floor to steady my movement and I feel carpet. I know there's a hard surface not far above my head, I can't straighten out my legs without pressing against another surface of some sort.

Where is Landon?

"Shit!" I exclaim into the dark. I remember Landon taking me to the diner to speak with Ralph. Amber stopped me as I was getting ready to leave and wanted to talk while she took a break. But how did I end up here? If I had to guess, I'd say I'm in the trunk of a car. We're obviously moving with the way I'm being tossed around and the thunderous noise I hear coming from beneath me. Why would Amber tie me up and put me in the trunk of her car?

There are voices coming from somewhere in the distance and I struggle to make them out.

"...do with her?"

"Don't yell at me."

"Can't go to my house."

"…my cousin's house."

There are two voices, one male and one female. I remember Amber but I can't tell who else is with her. Drawing in a deep breath, I cough roughly against the fumes surrounding me. Rolling to my right side, I reach my bound hands out a few inches in front of me and feel where the carpet curves up on what I can only hope is the back seat of whatever car I'm in. Running my hands along the surface as far as I can reach, I feel for a break – something that I can push against in hopes that it moves.

It takes me several minutes of moving my hands, twisting my body closer to the surface, and praying to whatever deity might be watching over me right now before I feel a slight movement. It doesn't move far, halting as if there's something on the other side of it blocking it from opening. But it's just enough to let a little light into the trunk, illuminating my surroundings enough to see the duct tape wrapped tightly around my wrists. Twisting my hands side to side, I try to loosen the tap enough to slip out of it but it's no use. The tape was wrapped several times around, nearly cutting the circulation off in my fingers.

The car leans dangerously to one side as whoever is driving takes a turn way too fast, and I slide across the carpet. My head hits the side hard enough that it sets off a light show behind my eyes. The blinding flash of pain radiating through my neck and shoulders causing me to squeeze my eyes shut tightly against it.

"Slow down before you get us both killed." I hear Amber's voice clearly now with the small gap I was able to make in the seat.

"Shut the fuck up, Amber." Oh, God. I know that voice. A shiver runs down my spine as the memory of seeing Charlie in the alley being Freedom Diner comes rushing back to me. He was there, waiting for Amber in the alley. Her mother's car was sitting in the alley behind him when I turned to face him. That must be the car that I'm in now.

"Hello?" I hear Amber question. She must have had her phone on silent, I didn't hear a ring. Or I was just stuck in my head – because that's totally a possibility. "Yes, Melodee. We're on our way." Melodee? "I don't know. We left in a hurry and now it's raining pretty hard." The car swerves again and I'm thrown the other way. My ankle twists sharply as my feet hit the surface on the driver's side of the car and I bite my lip hard to keep from screaming out in pain. "Well, if this dumbass will drive a little slower, we might make it to you in one piece."

"We're fine, Amber. I said to shut the fuck up!" Charlie yells at her. "Jesus, I should have just left your ass at the diner."

"I'll call you when we're closer." It's quiet for a few seconds so I assume Amber hung up the phone. "You can lose the attitude toward me, Charlie. I got you your punching bag back so lay the hell off."

"Oh, I'm not keeping her," he chuckles, an evil sound that makes the fine hairs on the back of my neck stand on end. "I have no intention of keeping her this time. I should have taken care of her when I killed her mother."

My breath seizes in my chest, a lump forming so tight I can barely swallow around it.

Oh. My. God.

"Well, why didn't you then?" Amber asks him and I twist closer to the gap in the seat hoping to hear him better as he continues.

"I thought she'd be useful. That mother of hers was worthless as a one-legged man in an ass-kicking competition." He barks out a cynical laugh and my stomach twists in agony. "But the little bitch couldn't even stick around to keep my house picked up. She had to run off with that rich boyfriend of hers. Then he went and fired me."

What?

Landon never said anything about Charlie working for him. I feel a tear break through my lashes, trailing over my nose before dripping to the carpet. All this time, I knew my mother had been getting better. The doctor said the treatments were working. But Charlie killed her. That bastard fucking killed her and now he's going to kill me too.

"Charlie, watch out!" I hear Amber scream before I tossed around again. First my feet and my busted ankle slamming against the one side, before I'm thrown immediately the other way and my head crashes against the passenger side before I can get my hands up to soften the blow.

"God dammit!" He yells before the world tilts, and I'm thrown around roughly like a ragdoll in a washing machine.

The noise surrounding me are deafening – crunching metal and breaking glass mingled with the screams of both Charlie and Amber from the front of the car. The high-pitched wailing sound that I assume is Amber stops abruptly as I continue to be thrown around. My arms are shooting out in every direction, searching for something to grab on to and slow my tumble. A sharp pain radiates through my elbow, and I can't bite back the scream anymore that barrels through my chest. My head lands heavily against the hard metal surface of the trunk as the tumbling stops.

The air is deadly still as the silence creeps in around me. I'm trapped in what I can only imagine is the mangled remains of Mrs.

Dickson's car. I have no idea where I am. I don't know if Charlie and Amber survived the accident.

"I love you, Landon. I'm sorry." I whisper into the deathly stillness around me. "My life might be ending, but my love for you will live on forever."

The final thought going through my head before I allow the darkness to take me is that Charlie is going to get his wish. He finally killed me.

Chapter
TWENTY-EIGHT

LANDON

"IT'S BEEN TWO FUCKING DAYS, Santos!" I exclaim as I burst into the diner behind the officer.

"I know, Landon. I'm doing everything I can."

"Obviously, it isn't enough. Have you even found Amber? Have you found Charlie? Do we know if he was involved or not?"

"Look," he starts as he sits in the booth by the window. "I asked you to meet me here as a courtesy. I'm doing everything I can, Landon. I know you're scared but don't take it out on me. Okay?"

"You're right." Blowing out a frustrated breath, I thread my fingers into my hair and rest my elbows against the Formica tabletop. "I'm going out of my mind, Santos."

"I know." He looks up and I see Ralph approach our table from the corner of my eye. "Ralph? Why don't you join us." He moves over in the booth and makes room for Ralph to sit, his rounded belly pressing against the side of the table in the cramped booth.

"Here's some waters, guys." Alicia places a glass in front of each of us. "Can I get y'all anything else while you're here?"

"No, thank you," Santos answers without looking up at her.

I don't reach for my water. I know it won't do anything to extinguish the fire raging in my blood. The pain that I've been dealing with since Emi was taken from me. The soul crushing guilt of knowing that I didn't do enough to protect her.

"So," Santos begins as he pulls a small notepad from his breast pocket. I lower my gaze to the tabletop and pull my lips between my teeth. "We talked to Amber's mother. Apparently, Amber took her car that morning before coming in to work. She says she doesn't usually drive to work since she lives only a few blocks away but didn't think anything of it until she never brought it back. We got the description of the car and put out a BOLO including the tag number. No hits back on it yet."

Moving my hands to the tabletop, I fist them together nervously as I wait for him to continue.

"We've had an officer watching Charlie's house for the past two days and he hasn't turned up either. We have no reason to believe, based on what you were able to tell me about Emilee's past with him, that he's not involved."

Lifting my gaze, I watch as he calmly takes a sip of his water. It honestly grinds my gears how calm he can be right now. Ralph and I both are focused on him, waiting for something useful or some good news for once. Pain radiates through my jaw as I clench my teeth together hard enough that I'm afraid they may crack.

"We have a warrant issued for the arrest of both Charlie Tillman and Amber Dickson. But here's where it gets more interesting." He taps a finger against the table, and it takes all the self-restraint I can muster not to reach out and snap the digit off his hand. "We weren't able to find a working cell number for Charlie, but we did get Amber's from her mother. We were able to pull cell phone records. She had several calls to and from a number for a Melodee Carson on the day that Emilee was abducted."

"What the fuck?" I gasp as he mentions the name of my assistant. My recently volatile assistant. "What does Melodee have to do with this?"

"That's what I wanted to know," Santos continues. "I've known Amber my whole life. As I'm sure you have as well since she grew up here too. But I've never heard of Melodee Carson. So, I went back to her house and asked her mother. Turns out," he takes another sip of water and I hold my breath as I wait for his explanation. "Melodee is Amber's cousin."

"What?" My hands slap hard against the table causing the water glasses to shake dangerously. Ralph reaches out and sets a hand across his glass and mine, keeping them from tipping over.

"We had a detective in the city pick her up for us. We're holding her as an accessory at the station right now."

"Has she said anything? Does she know where Emi is?" I ask desperately.

"She doesn't," he says regretfully, his brows furrowed slightly. "She sang like a canary though when we started talking charges. Apparently, she knows that Emilee is Charlie's stepdaughter. She says that Charlie and Amber have been seeing each other for a few weeks now and that Charlie was seeking revenge for not only Emilee leaving town but for shacking up with you. He has a vendetta against you for him losing his job."

"God dammit!" I exclaim. I knew when I told Rob to let him go that he was going to cause trouble. But never in a million years did I think he would go to this extreme.

"That's not all," he interrupts my self-recrimination. "Apparently, they were on their way to her house but never made it there. She had talked to Amber at one point during the storm that came in that night. She said they were on their way, and she would call again when they got closer, but she never did."

All I can picture is my Kitten lying in a ditch somewhere between here and Melodee's house. She's been gone for two whole days already, there's no telling what shape she'll be in if and when they find her. If she's even alive.

No.

I can't let myself think that way. She has to be alive. I won't accept anything less at this point. I'll never be able to live with myself if my negligence caused her to lose her life. I won't be able to continue without her. There is no plane of existence where life is worth living if she isn't in it.

"We have patrols out mapping every route between here and Melodee Carson's house. We'll find her, Landon. You have to believe that."

I don't respond, just nod my head slowly in agreement.

"She's too stubborn to give up," Ralph says as he places a hand across my forearm. "We have to have faith in her ability to survive. She has to know we're looking for her."

"Keep your phone on you, Landon." Santos finishes his water and sets the glass down on the table. I watch him as he places his notepad back in the breast pocket of his shirt before standing. "I'll call you as soon as I have anything else. We'll find her." He places a hand on Ralph's shoulder then walks toward the door.

"She's the strongest person I know," I say. "But I can't get over the fact that this never should have happened. I never should have brought her back here. I should have had her press charges when she first told me about the abuse that Charlie inflicted on her. There are so many things that I've done wrong in this scenario, and I don't know if I'll ever be able to forgive myself."

"You're going to have to," he says harshly, and I lift my gaze to look into his bloodshot eyes, my brows lifting toward my hairline. "She doesn't need your guilt right now and it won't help her to heal from any of this. She's going to need your strength. As much as you're able to give her."

"You're right."

"Now," he starts as he slips from the booth. "Get out of here. You look like shit."

"That happens when you don't sleep for two days."

He places a hand on my shoulder as I stand facing him. "That needs to change. You need to be at full strength when they find her."

"I'll try."

He nods before walking back to the kitchen. Efficiently dismissed, I walk out of the diner and toward my car. I haven't been able to sleep. I haven't been able to eat. Fatigue is washing over me even as I stand here on the hot sidewalk outside of the diner. But I refuse to give up when I know Emi is out there waiting for me to find her and bring her home.

SITTING ON THE EDGE of the bed in the guest room, where Emi has her mini office set up, my stomach growls angrily. I haven't been able to eat anything since she was taken from me – I honestly don't know if I'll be able to keep anything down. I know Ralph says I need to keep my strength up for when she's found, but I can't bring myself to live if she isn't here living with me. It's not that I couldn't live without her – it's that I'm not willing to try.

I've never felt as lost and helpless as I do now. Just knowing that she's out there somewhere, possibly suffering, is enough to bring me to my knees. My entire life has flipped upside down in the course of the past forty-eight hours. Just knowing that Melodee – a woman that I've trusted for the past four years – was involved in Emi's disappearance fills my mind with fury. My skin is practically crawling with the massive amount of anger, and pure unadulterated rage that I have scratching to break free. There isn't a part of this city that would survive the absolute wrath that I'm itching to release on it. I'd burn the entire world down to find her, to keep her safe. To never let her out of my sight again.

I know I need to get some sleep. I can't sleep in my bed though – it still smells like her. Stepping out into the hallway, I shuffle my bare feet along the hard wood floor to the living room. My eyes catch on to the pictures hanging on the walls as I wander through my apartment. There isn't an inch of space that Emi hasn't touched. Her photographs are hanging on every wall.

Sitting on the center cushion on the sofa, I plant my feet on the coffee table and stare at the three pictures hanging over the mantel. The pictures that my grandmother bought at the Independence library. More reminders of the fucking town that nearly destroyed Emi before I whisked her away from it. The town that took her from me again, knowing that I shouldn't have ever taken her back there.

My ties to Independence were cut the day I got the call from Rachel that my grandmother's house had been sold. There was no reason for Emi to ever go back to that town, even for a measly paycheck from the diner. But that doesn't matter, does it? Charlie was seeking revenge for me having him fired. He would have still found a way to get to Emi, even without me going back to that town. Especially since Melodee was keeping her cousin informed.

Fuck!

It never mattered what I did. I couldn't have kept her safe. How could I have been so blind and stupid?

Laying my head back, I close my eyes. I'll just rest here for a few minutes, regain a little bit of my strength. It doesn't take long for me to slip into a fitful sleep filled with dreams of my Kitten.

In my dream, I see Emi standing in the middle of a field. The closer I get to her, the more I can see how battered and bruised she is, her hair matted to the side of her head as if covered in blood. Her arms hang limply to her sides, her face angled to the ground and her shoulder slumped in defeat as if she's lost the will to continue. I walk toward her slowly so as not to frighten her despite how my body vibrates with the need to rush to her and pull her against my chest. She lifts her head as I get closer and reaches out to me with one shaky hand. A single tear slides down her cheek, glistening in the soft morning light.

I begin to move faster, desperate to get to her and know that she's okay but the faster my feet crunch through the grass, the further away she gets from me. She holds her arm out toward me, begging me to reach out and take her hand, but I can't reach it. "Hurry, Landon," she begs as her image begins to fade against the sun rising higher and higher behind her. "I need you to find me before it's too late." Finally, I reach the middle of the field where she was standing not two seconds prior just as she fades completely. My arms reach out to circle around her waist just as she disappears, leaving my arms and my heart empty and aching.

I jolt awake suddenly, gasping for breath. Morning light is shining through the floor to ceiling windows in the living room, illuminating the room with a blinding light reflecting off the three pictures hanging over the mantel. Wiping my hands beneath my eyes, I'm surprised to find the moisture collecting on my cheeks. It's a new day and I'm angry with myself for sleeping as long as I did.

It's the beginning of the third day since Emi was taken from me. I know the statistics in missing persons cases enough to know what this means. I've read enough true crime in my life to know the chances of her still being alive after the first twenty-four hours are slim. Forty-eight is pushing it.

"Where are you, Kitten?" I whisper into the empty room, my eyes focusing on those three photographs again. "I need you to be okay."

Chapter
TWENTY-NINE

LANDON

INDEPENDENCE IS NOT A large town, it doesn't have a large police department. I don't know how many patrols they have out searching the roads between town and Melodee's house. Santos didn't say if they've joined up with the county sheriff's department or not and I haven't heard any updates on their search. I'm not going to sit around here any longer waiting for a phone call that never comes telling me whether or not she's been found. Whether or not she's still alive.

I believe with all my heart that she is still alive. I'd like to think that our souls are connected in such a way that I would feel if that weren't the case. Right now, I feel empty – like there's a part of me that is just missing. A hole in my chest where Emi should reside. But it only feels empty right now, not dead. I never believed in soulmates before, but with Emi I've become a believer.

Our souls have reached out to each other before. I honestly feel like her soul is crying out for me now – screaming for me to find her.

My mind made up, I grab my keys off the table by the door and rush to the elevator. As soon as I'm in my car, I plug my phone in to the charger. I should have charged it before passing out last night, but I wasn't thinking and it's almost dead. The last thing I want is for it to die without me realizing it and I miss the phone call that I'm desperate to receive.

The sun is high in the afternoon sky, and I've pulled into Melodee's driveway four times already. There are no more roads that lead to this address from Independence, and I've seen nothing that could possibly lead me to Emi's location. I've passed by about twenty patrol cars driving up and down the roads looking for the same thing as me. My heart sinks every time I pass by another one that doesn't stop, knowing that they still haven't seen any evidence that leads them to finding my Kitten. There have been no skid marks on the pavement, no broken guard rails on the roadsides. Nothing to indicate that they ran off the road during the storm.

"I've got to be missing something," I say to myself. I think back to one of the books I read not long ago, another true crime story by Julie Adams, about a girl that was abducted. They had tied this girl up and put her in the back seat of their car. When she regained consciousness, she fought back and tried to escape. They were speeding down a county highway in the middle of the night when she climbed over the back seat and grabbed the steering wheel. The driver lost control and the car flipped several times, flipping over a guard rail before rolling down the hillside and stopping against a row of trees. It took longer to find the car because there was no damage to the guardrail to indicate that anything had happened there. The search party and police had driven past it several times before finally finding the car while searching on foot.

The hillsides on these mountain roads are frighteningly steep. I can't imagine that anyone would survive if their car had rolled over the embankment.

"No. I can't think that way."

Surely, if the car had lost control during the storm, there would be skid marks on the pavement. Even if it is possible – regardless of how low of a probability – for the car to have flipped over a guardrail, I would still expect to see skid marks or something indicating a possible accident. "I just need a sign, baby. Give me a sign of where to look so I can find you."

Five hours I spend driving between Melodee's house and Independence taking every possible road leading between the two. Knowing that was the direction they were headed, I can't think of where else to look. They could be anywhere right now since they never made it to Melodee's house.

The sun is just over the horizon when I finally have to stop for gas. It'll be starting to set in the next hour, bringing with it a desperation to find something to lead me to Emi. My heart beats an erratic rhythm in my chest as I think about her being out there for another day, desperate for someone to rescue her. This useless muscle in my chest no longer beats to keep me alive, but for her. As long as my heart is beating, I have to believe there's a chance she'll keep living, keep fighting to get back to me. It doesn't belong to me anymore, but to her. She didn't take my heart from me though, I gave it to her willingly.

With a full tank of gas, I get back on the highway to make another pass on the roads that I've already been over numerous times today. As soon as I pull out on the highway, my phone rings in the console next to me. Looking at the dash, I see a number I don't recognize but answer it anyway. "Hello?" I answer pressing the button on my steering wheel.

"Is this Landon Strong?" the voice on the other end asks.

"Yes? Who's this?"

"This is Officer Brandon," he responds, and I swallow thickly around the lump forming in my throat. "Officer Santos told me to call you."

"Did you find her?" My foot comes off the accelerator, my voice thick with emotion as I wait for him to tell me that she's alive.

"I believe so, sir. We got a call from a group of hikers on the mountainside. They found a car at the bottom of a ravine, but we haven't gotten down to it yet. We have fire and rescue on their way here now to climb down and assess. Their ETA is about five minutes."

"Tell me where you're at. I'm on my way."

"I don't think that's a good idea, sir. I'll call you when I know more."

"Tell me where you're at!" I demand into the phone, my patience hanging on by a thread.

He doesn't respond but I can hear muffled voices in the background.

"Dammit, please. I'm going out of my mind here. I have to be there."

"Landon? It's Officer Santos." Pulling my lips between my teeth, I wait for him to continue. "I really don't think it's a good idea for you to be here. We don't know what we're going to find when we get down to that car."

"Is it her?" I know I don't want to hear it, but I still have to know.

"It's the right car."

My breath wheezes out of me between clenched teeth. "Where?"

He's silent for several seconds before finally telling me the location. I know he doesn't want me there causing a scene, but regardless of her condition when they pull her up that ravine, I have to be there.

"I'm on my way." I don't wait for another response from him before disconnecting the call. Pressing my foot down on the gas, I speed along the highway to the location I've already been past several times today.

What should have taken me fifteen minutes only takes eight and I'm slowing down as I approach the flashing lights of the emergency vehicles. There are ambulances, fire trucks, and police and sheriff's cars parked all along the road, stopping traffic from both directions. Pulling over on the side of the road, I turn off the engine and throw my door open.

My legs are heavy as if my shoes are filled with concrete as I approach the officers standing on the side of the road. "Sir, you can't come over here. Just go back to your car," one of the county officers says as he presses a hand to my chest to stop me.

"He's okay." Officer Santos walks over to where I'm glaring at the county cop. "He can stay with me." He reaches out and places a hand on the back of my shoulder, leading me around the county officer and closer to where the other officers are congregated.

I blink my eyes slowly to clear my blurry vision before looking around at my surroundings. There are no skid marks on the road, which I already knew because I'd been here so many times already today. The guard rail is intact, nothing has busted through it. There's not even a dent in the metal. There's absolutely nothing to indicate an accident of any kind. Leaning to the side, I'm able to look around the large fire truck blocking the road headed north and realize we're only another mile or two away from Melodee's house.

"Hey," Santos reaches out for my arm as I lean further to the side to get a good look at everything going on. "Don't feel bad, we missed it too. I can't tell you how many times I've been down this road in the last couple days."

Standing up straighter, I look at him in confusion.

"It was storming the night they were headed through here. The roads were wet. We don't know what happened to make them lose control. Could have been a deer or a bear for all I know. But…" He grabs my upper arm and pulls me back toward the side of the road. "Look here." He points and I follow the direction of his finger with my eyes. "Looks like they hit the grass just before the guard rail. The car is old enough, it doesn't have antilock brakes, but the lack of skid marks indicate they never hit the brakes at all."

Following the tire tracks in the grass with my eyes, I can see where it would have tilted enough to have flipped over the side of the ravine. Especially if it was still going at full speed. My eyes close of their own accord, my head shaking slowly side to side.

She has to be alive.

"Coming up!" I hear shouted from the group of fire and rescue workers standing over the guard rail.

"Landon, wait!" Santos shouts behind me as I break away from him and run closer to where I see a rope being lifted up the ravine.

"No!" I fall to my knees at the sight of the basket being lifted over the guard rail, barely feeling the bite of the pavement against my knees. I don't know who it is, could be Amber of Charlie for all I know, but just the fact that they're covered by a sheet tells me they didn't make it.

"Looks like she was thrown from the car," the man climbing up beneath the basket says. "She was about twenty feet away from where the car stopped against the trees. There's another body inside, they're trying to get him out now."

"Wait here," Santos calls out to me as he walks past.

I watch through blurry eyes as he walks over to the basket. They pull it over the metal railing before lifting it to a gurney and strapping the contraption onto the thin mattress. Not able to take my eyes away from the basket, knowing it's wrong in so many ways but hoping beyond hope that it's Amber lying lifeless in the basket, I wait for Santos to confirm.

I watch with bated breath as he lifts the corner of the blanket, exposing the identity of the woman lying within. He stands with his back to me, blocking my view of the basket, and I watch as his shoulders fall. Whether with relief or disappointment, I don't know. He nods to one of the rescue workers and they load the gurney up into the back of one of the ambulances.

My eyes staying focused on Santos, I watch as he turns to walk back toward me. "It's Amber." His head shakes as he kneels to the ground in front of me. "She was pretty banged up, but I'd recognize that shock of red hair anywhere."

Finally releasing the breath that I'd been holding, I sag in relief. I know we aren't out of the woods yet but at least she hasn't been pulled up with a sheet over her yet. I nod my head slowly before standing back to my feet and drawing in another deep breath.

"Coming up!" I hear called out again, and this time I turn my back. I know they were working to get a man out of the car and I'm sure it's Charlie.

"This the man?" Santos asks as he walks past me toward the back of the second waiting ambulance.

"Yes," one of the rescue crew answers. "The car's pretty banged up. Looks like it rolled quite a few times before coming to a stop against a row of trees. Let's get this guy loaded up and send another basket down."

"Have you found anyone else in the car?" Santos asks, his voice deeper than before.

"Not yet. The trunk is smashed in pretty good so I'm not sure if we'll be able to get it open or if we'll have to climb through the seats, but we're not leaving from down there until every inch of that car is searched."

"Thank you."

Turning around, I watch as Santos walks up to the basket to lift the corner.

"Charlie Tillman," he announces loud enough for me to hear.

A wave of nausea washes over me and I run to the side of the road, leaning over the guard rail as far as I can. I dry heave for several minutes before I feel a sturdy hand press against my upper back. I haven't eaten in almost three days now, there's nothing in my stomach to throw up. But that doesn't stop my body from convulsing uncontrollably, pain shooting through my ribs and lower abdomen.

Opening my eyes, I can see the ruined remains of the car below. It doesn't even look like a car from this angle anymore as much as a crumpled-up ball of metal. I just don't see how anyone could have survived it. My stomach lurches again bringing me to my knees, my hands fisting against the cold metal of the guard rail, the edges cutting into my fingers, but I hardly notice the pain.

"We need a back board!" someone yells from down below. "Hurry!"

My pulse beats rapidly against my chest, my eyes springing open to watch the scene happening below. I see a man running toward the car along the tree line, a back board hanging from his hand on the side. What I see next is the single most amazing miracle I've ever witnessed. Despite the condition of the metal wrapped around her small, frail body, they pull her from the wreckage strapped to the backboard. When they place her in the basket to be lifted up the ravine, they don't place a sheet over her.

Time moves so slowly as they place the basket on the gurney, it could have been a few minutes or several hours. Time is meaningless now as I watch the other half of my soul as they load her into the back of the ambulance.

"Go," Santos presses a hand against my back. I notice I'm standing right outside the back of the ambulance and don't even remember moving. "Go with her. I'll take care of your car."

I don't respond before I'm climbing into the back of the ambulance with my Kitten. She's battered and bruised, her hair matted to the side of her head with dried blood. Her eyes are swollen shut and there's a bruise marring one entire side of her face. Looking down at her body, I see both her hands are bound together by duct tape in front of her, one arm angled oddly and I'm sure it's broken. Her feet are bound together the same way and one of her ankles is twisted in an unnatural position.

I watch as the paramedic places an IV in her arm and hangs a bag of saline off a hook in the ceiling of the ambulance. He works around her swiftly as the vehicle begins to move, the sirens echoing loudly in the back of the ambulance are nearly deafening. I don't know how he can possibly work with all the noise and the way the movement causes him to sway on his feet, but I have more respect for him now than I have for anyone in the past. He's doing everything that needs to be done to keep her alive and I refuse to do or say anything to stop him from continuing his work.

She's alive.

I don't know how it's possible after seeing the state of the car she was in. But she's alive and that's all that matters.

Chapter THIRTY

LANDON

"DO YOU THINK SHE'LL wake up soon?" Ralph asks as he pulls a plastic chair to the side of Emi's bed.

"They started weaning her off the medication this morning. She'll probably wake up sometime tomorrow." Six days I've been sitting vigil at her bedside, keeping an eye on her as she sleeps peacefully and heals from her injuries. It's been nine days since I've gazed lovingly into her beautiful azure blue eyes.

It's honestly a miracle that she's still alive today. There was definitely an angel watching over her while she was trapped in the trunk of that car. Santos stopped by after she was moved to a private room and told me that the fire and rescue team that pulled her out explained the situation to him. They had told him there was a perfect hole that Emi had fallen into in the trunk. When the car rolled, it balled up the body of the car like a soda can, but that perfect little pocket of space that Emi was in had been left practically untouched.

She should have been crushed.

Her injuries should have been worse than they are. As it is, she came out severely dehydrated with a few broken ribs, a dislocated shoulder, fractured elbow, sprained ankle, and severe concussion. She'll be in some pain, and she has a long road of recovery ahead of her, but she's alive. They've kept her in a medically induced coma for the last six days to give her body time to heal. Once the drugs start to work out of her system, she should wake up. All the doctors were expecting to have worse news when they did the CT scan and MRI, but they didn't find anything. Of course, we'll have to see what state she's in mentally when she does wake up. I expect her to come out rough, but I have all intentions of being here with her when that happens.

"Have you been eating?" Ralph asks.

I look up at him and see his hand resting on Emi's arm. "I have. Not much, but enough that I don't lose my strength. I can't bring myself to be away from her for very long at a time."

"Just keep taking care of yourself. You can't take care of her if you aren't at you best for her."

"I know. This chair folds out into a single bed and the nursing staff have been nice enough to allow me to stay here with Emi. Steve, the doorman at my apartment, came by the other day and brought me some things from my apartment. I thought he was gonna lose it when he saw her lying here hooked up to all these monitors. They've gotten pretty close to each other in the last month or so."

"She needs more friends she can rely on. I hate that I never noticed before how lonely she was or what kind of shape her home life was in."

"Don't beat yourself up over it. There's only so much you can witness from that diner kitchen."

"That's no excuse." He moves his hand to his lap and lowers his gaze. I can see the guilt washing over him as he takes a deep breath before continuing. "I've given my entire life to that diner. I should at least pay attention to the people that work for me." He lifts his gaze and his eyes lock with mine. His are glistening with unshed tears. "I'm glad she has you now."

"Me too." Reaching up, I place my hand on her thigh – one of the few places on her body that isn't covered with bruises.

Ralph stands and moves the chair away from the bed, leaving it on the wall where he had grabbed it from earlier. "Take care of her."

"I will." I watch as he walks toward the door.

He stops with his hand on the door handle and says, "Don't take this the wrong way, but I hope I don't see either one of you back in my diner for a long time."

Chuckling, I shake my head side to side. "Don't worry. I have no intention of going back to Independence for a good long time. Maybe never to be honest."

Throwing his head back, he laughs loudly as he opens the door. "I'll hold you to that," he calls out over his shoulder as he walks out.

"You hear that, Kitten?" I ask Emi, even though I know she won't answer me yet. I don't know if she can hear me or not, but I don't want her to think she's going through any of this alone. If there's a chance she can hear me, I want her to know that I'm right here with her. "Ralph says we're not allowed to go back to Independence any time soon." Lifting a hand, I run the backs of my fingers over her cheek. The bruising on her face is lighter in color than it was six days ago, now faded from a dark purple to a faded green color.

She's still hooked up to so many machines, monitoring her improvement from one day to the next as well as keeping her hydrated and nourished. She has an IV in the back of her left hand, her right arm is in a cast from her bicep to her fingers because of the fractured elbow. They inserted a breathing tube to help relieve the strain on her body, as well as a feeding tube through her nose. It looks more frightening than it is honestly. I was worried about all the machines and tubes when I first saw her after she was admitted. But the doctor explained to me that it was to allow her body to heal itself without the added stress of trying to take care of herself. I haven't left Emi's side for longer than to take care of my own basic needs over the last several days and I've grown used to the beeps and groanings of the machines.

"Knock, knock."

Looking up, I see the night nurse Jessica walk into the room. "Shift change already?" I ask as she steps into the room and closes the door behind her.

"Yep." She smiles sweetly as she walks to the side of Emi's bed. "Just coming by to check up on our girl."

I watch silently as Jessica plugs information from Emi's vitals into her tablet. Once she's done, she places the tablet down on the side table and begins gathering supplies. She fills a glass container with water and uses it to fill the biggest plastic syringe I've ever seen. Connecting the tip of the syringe to the end of Emi's feeding tube, she pushes the water through the tube, effectively flushing it and clearing it of any remnants of the liquid diet being forced into her for the day.

Standing from my position at Emi's side, I help Jessica to move the pillows. We work in tandem to rearrange Emi from laying flat on her back, to leaning slightly to the left. This takes the pressure off her back and puts it more on her left hip and side – the nurses explained to me the first night we were here that this constant change in position will prevent her from getting bed sores. I hold onto Emi to angle her in my direction while Jessica fluffs up a few pillows and wedges them in behind her.

"Get some sleep," Jessica says when she's finished cleaning up. "I'm guessing tomorrow is going to be a big day." She smiles before turning and walking toward the door.

I kiss Emi softly on the forehead. "Goodnight, Kitten," I whisper before turning to arrange the pull-out bed for myself. It's the hardest, most uncomfortable thing I've ever had to sleep on, but I wouldn't have it any other way. There's no way I'm leaving to sleep somewhere more comfortable when my Kitten is still stuck in this hospital bed.

I KNOW THE NURSES CAME into the room throughout the night. They always do. They come in every two or three hours to check vitals and make sure nothing has changed. I never thought I would get used to them coming and going throughout the night, but surprisingly, I slept all through the night. Maybe it's the knowledge that my Kitten will be waking up soon that allowed me enough peace to rest. Or maybe it's my body knowing that I need to be fully rested for what today will hopefully bring.

Thankful that I was able to get Emi into a private room, I make use of the facilities to take a quick shower and brush my teeth. Steve was more than happy to go into my apartment the other day, while on the phone with me at the same time of course, to gather some things for me so I don't have to leave the hospital. I'm just finishing rinsing my mouth out when there's a knock on the door. "Come in," I call out as I dry my mouth and hands on a towel.

"Good morning."

Stepping out of the bathroom, I see Officer Santos standing just inside the door to Emi's room with two cups of coffee in his hands. He's dressed in street clothes today, looking more casual than I've seen him since high school. "Is one of those for me?" I ask with a smile as I reach out a hand in his direction.

"Yep." He holds a cup out for me, and I take it gladly. "It's from a vending machine down the hall so don't get too excited about it. I'm sure it's shit."

"As long as it's caffeinated," I chuckle before taking a sip. I wince at the bitter taste before swallowing it down.

Santos laughs before taking a sip of his own bitter tasting coffee. "So," he starts as he walks over to the plastic chair on the other side of the room. "Any changes?" He rests his cup on his knee as he turns his gaze to Emi.

"Nothing yet." Walking closer to the bed, I put a hand on her shoulder and squeezed lightly – a soft, reassuring touch. I've done the same thing every time I approach the bed just to let her know I'm here. "They started weaning her off medication yesterday though. I'm hoping to see something today that shows she's coming back to me."

"She's a tough one," he says with a nod of his head. "There's no way she would have survived that accident otherwise. Not to mention everything else."

"She's been through so much." My head shakes slowly as I pull the chair closer to the side of her bed, ready to take up my vigil for the day. I helped the day nurse, Stephanie, turn her already to her other side so she's now facing more toward where Santos sits. They'll be coming back in a few hours to move her again so she's lying on her back.

"Well…" he starts as he stands and throws his coffee cup into the trash under the sink. "I just wanted to stop by and let you know that Melodee's trial starts today."

"They don't need Emilee to testify?" I furrow my brows in question as my head cocks to the side.

"No. We have enough evidence against her that it should get to that point. There's no reason to make her relive any of it if we don't have to. She's been through enough as it is."

"I agree." A wave of relief washes over me, knowing that she can put all this behind her when she gets out of here. Charlie and Amber are both dead.

"Besides, she's going to have enough to deal with."

"What do you mean?" I ask, genuinely curious.

"I think you know what I mean." He turns toward me and places his hands in the pockets of his jeans. "She's going to need more healing than just physical. There's years' worth of trauma that she's going to have to deal with. Are you ready for that?"

"I will be," I admit, determined to do whatever I have to do to get her through this. I know there's going to be possible PTSD associated with not only what happened recently, but over the last several years. I don't know why I didn't think of it before, and I internally chastise myself for not even bringing it up, but she's been dealing with Charlie for years. Then the death of her mother on top of it. She probably hasn't even had time to really mourn the loss of her mother because she was too busy just trying to survive every day.

"Okay. You've got my number if you need anything." He walks toward the door to leave but I don't follow him. "I'll keep you posted about the trial. This is a pretty high-profile case, so I expect it'll be televised if you want to watch. As much as it sucks, this is the most interesting thing to happen in our little community in quite a while."

"Yeah," I start as I thread my fingers through my hair. "I have no intention of watching it."

"I don't blame you." Chuckling, he opens the door. "I'll be in touch, Landon."

I watch him as he walks out the door before it closes behind him. Turning my attention back to my Kitten, I place my hand back on her shoulder softly. "Did you hear that, Kitten?" I say softly as my hand begins to move slowly up and down her arm.

I'm not paying much attention, so I almost miss it at first – a slight movement beneath my hand. Moving my hand back to her shoulder, I still my movements and wait for something else. It takes several minutes before I feel it again, a lump of emotion forming in my throat as I realize that I hadn't imagined it.

Pressing the nurse call button, I walk around to the other side of the bed and grab Emi's hand. "I'm here, baby. I'm here." I lean over and whisper lovingly into her ear, repeating the same thing over and over again. "I'm here. I'm here. It's okay, I'm here. You're safe, Kitten. I'm here."

266

Nurse Stephanie walks into the room right as the machine at the head of the bed starts squealing loudly. I lift my gaze in alarm and watch the nurse approach the bed. She reaches up where her name tag hangs from her scrub jacket and presses a button. I hadn't realized she had a small black object hooked behind her name tag until now – similar in appearance to a pager, which is something that I haven't seen in years.

"What's going on?" I ask, my own heartrate increasing in concern at the sound of the alarms and beeps going on around me.

Stephanie looks up at me and smiles as she pulls the pillows from behind Emi, allowing her to lay flat on her back again. "She's waking up and she's fighting the breathing tube."

I'm confused why she's smiling at her fighting her breathing tube, that doesn't seem like something that she should be happy about. "Fighting her breathing tube?" Leaning over the bed, I place my hands on Emi's cheeks. "Emi, baby. It's okay." I don't know what to say to get her to stop fighting the breathing tube – it's helping her to breathe right now and I'm terrified that if she fights it, she'll stop breathing. I don't know anything about these machines other than the fact that they are helping her to stay alive and heal.

"It's completely normal. I paged the doctor to see about getting it removed. He should be here any minute." So that's what the button was that she pushed. "Just keep doing what you're doing. Keep her calm until the doctor gets here."

"Kitten." I kiss her forehead lightly and swallow around the lump in my throat. "It's okay, Kitten. I'm here. I'm here waiting for you to come back to me. I miss you so much, baby."

It's like my heart has waited until this very moment to start beating properly again. My eyes are burning as my vision begins to blur and I breathe out a sigh of relief when Emi stops fighting and her heart rate begins to slow down again. Then she does something that I've been waiting for her to do for the last seven days since we found her.

She opens her eyes.

Chapter
THIRTY-ONE

EMILEE

THE PAIN IS ALMOST UNBEARABLE as I press the button on the railing of my hospital bed to sit up straighter. I'm tired of lying here for most of the day, only getting out of bed for short trips to the bathroom – now that I finally convinced them to remove the dreaded catheter – and never by myself. I feel like an invalid. But with as bad as the pain is now, I'm thankful that they knocked me out for so long. I can't imagine how much pain I would have been in a week ago if I hadn't been made to sleep through the whole thing.

Thankfully, I've been able to eat real food since this morning. They finally removed the tube going up my nose after I threatened to yank it out myself. Landon didn't appreciate that and threatened to tie me to the bed if I didn't behave. Any other time and I would have thought that a good idea, but I feel horrible for what he's had to go through for the last week, so I relented easily.

I did finally convince Landon to go down to the cafeteria to get himself something to eat, which is where he is currently. I've finally gained back enough strength since waking up two days ago that I can stay awake long enough to have a full conversation. I have so much that I need to talk to Landon about when he gets back. Not only what happened to me but what I heard – about my mother and Melodee. He hasn't given me any indication that he knows anything about Melodee, hasn't talked about my disappearance. I know it's going to be hard for him to talk about, but I need to get it off my chest.

Oh, sweet relief.

I'm just getting myself settled in a more comfortable sitting position when the door to my room opens. Landon stops mid-step as he enters the room, his gaze locking onto mine as a smile stretches across his handsome face. I'm sure my smile mirrors his as he finally begins to move closer to my bed.

"What's that?" I motion to the pink bear I see clutched in his right hand.

"For you." He reaches his arm out toward me and I gasp at the adorable bear he is holding. "I've been here for over a week and today was the first time I took the time to look in the gift shop." He shrugs and I watch as a light blush tints his cheeks pink. I don't think I've ever seen this side of Landon before. A shy and embarrassed Landon is also a sexy Landon.

"It's adorable. Thank you." Grabbing the bear, I clutch it tightly to my chest. My heart swells just a few more sizes with love for this man. "Did you get something to eat?"

"I did." I keep an eye on him as he moves around the room nervously before finally sitting in the hard plastic chair to the side of my bed. I know he's had a long week and probably hasn't done much to take care of himself. He says he's been here since I was admitted, and that Steve brought him some clothes from the apartment. But he still has dark circles under his eyes, so I know he hasn't been sleeping well. I'm anxious to get back home – not only so I can get on with my own life, but so Landon will start taking better care of himself again. I hate that he's had to give up so much of his time to be here with me.

Moving the bear to my lap, I lower my gaze and struggle to find a way to start this conversation. As always, he's so in tune with me that he knows when something is bothering me. "What's wrong, Kitten?" He stands and places a hand on my shoulder.

"I'm sorry, Landon." I start, not looking up at him but keeping my eyes on the bear. "I'm sorry for everything that I've put you through over the last week."

"Hey," he interrupts me. "None of this was your fault. I'm only sorry that I wasn't there with you to stop all this from happening." He bends forward and presses his forehead against mine softly. "I should have never let you go in there by yourself. None of this would have happened if I had been there to protect you. I promised to keep you safe, and I failed you." Lifting his head, he cups my cheek with one hand. "I should be the one to be apologizing to you."

"I don't think that would have made a difference." I lift a hand and place it over his on my cheek. His brows furrow in confusion at my words. "Charlie wanted revenge. He would have found a way to get to me no matter what."

He closes his eyes and nods his head slowly.

271

"I never knew he worked for you." I say softly.

"I only realized it was him a couple weeks ago," he admits. "I have a foreman, Rob, that hires and manages his own crew. Charlie was one of our construction workers, but he'd been causing problems on the job site for a few weeks. Rob and I had a meeting and I told him to keep the documentation and let him go. It wasn't until that meeting that I even put two and two together that he might have been your stepfather." He cocks his head to the side before speaking again. "How did you know?"

"I heard part of their conversation while I was in the trunk of the car. I had pushed against the backseat enough to get it to open enough for me to hear what was going on. He said he was getting back at you for him being fired." I pause and take several deep breaths, gathering the strength to continue. "He said he killed my mother."

"Oh, baby. I'm so sorry."

"I knew she was getting better. Even her doctors said she was getting better. I never thought anything of it though. I just thought they had been telling me that to make me feel better. But Charlie was ranting that night about how he should have killed me when he killed my mother."

"Jesus, Emi. I don't even know what to say about that."

My eyes close as he smooths the hair away from my forehead. The touch alone is calming, and I can feel my heart rate slowing. "They were taking me to Melodee's house. I don't understand what she had to do with anything."

"Baby." He starts before pulling the chair closer to the bed and taking my hand is both of his. "I never knew. We only found out after the fact. But Melodee and Amber were cousins. She had been contacting Amber about you for several weeks."

"Oh. Well, that explains why Melodee was so hateful toward me." Just then, something he said hits me square in the chest like a fist. "Were?"

"What?"

"You said they were cousins."

His cheeks blow out and he squints his eyes before talking. "Kitten," he starts softly, cautiously as if approaching a wounded animal. "How much do you remember of the accident itself?"

"Not much. I remember Amber yelling something at Charlie. Then I woke up here."

"There was a storm that night." Keeping my hand held tightly in his, he sits back in his chair. "The roads were pretty slick. Charlie went off the road and hit a ravine. The car rolled almost fifty feet away from the road, down the embankment. Amber was thrown from the car. Both Amber and Charlie died in that accident, baby."

They're dead? Landon reaches up and swipes a tear from my cheek with his thumb before I even realize I'm crying. I don't know why I'm shedding a tear for the ones that abducted me and tied me up in the trunk of a car. "Wow." I don't know what else to say. I'm heartbroken that someone I used to think of as a friend is gone. But at the same time, I'm relieved that I don't have to worry about either one of them again.

"I thought I'd lost you, Kitten. I was there when they found the car. I watched them pull Amber and Charlie up the hill in a rescue basket." Looking up, I see a tear roll down his cheek.

"Stop." I pull my hand in his, dragging him closer and reaching out with my other hand to cup his cheek. "He didn't win. I'm still here." Closing his eyes, he nods his head. "He was going to kill me. You know?"

"What?" He looks up, a shocked expression in his wide gaze.

"He said he was going to kill me. They were taking me to Melodee's house to kill me." I watch, confused, as Landon leans away from me and pulls his cell phone out of his pocket. "What are you doing?"

"Calling Officer Santos," he says nonchalantly as he scrolls through the contacts on his phone.

"Who?"

He holds his phone against his ear as he looks up at me. "Officer Santos from Independence. He's been there since this started." He stands and walks away from me as he begins to talk on the phone. I can't hear even his side of the conversation since he's standing by the door and he's speaking quietly.

I sit patiently, my hands absently stroking the soft fur of the teddy bear in my lap. "What's going on, Landon?" I ask as he hangs up the phone and walks back toward me.

He sits in the chair again and takes my hand in his before kissing my knuckles softly. "Melodee is on trial right now for accessory to kidnapping. I told Santos about Charlie's plans and what you overheard in the car. He says there's a chance they'll also charge her with conspiracy to commit murder."

"She really did hate me. Didn't she?"

"I'm so sorry, Kitten."

"Oh good," we're interrupted by the doctor walking into the room without knocking. "You're awake."

"Yep," I reply enthusiastically. Landon sits back in his chair again, but he doesn't release my hand.

"So," the doctor begins with a smile. "Are you ready to get out of here?"

"Really?" I question at the same time Landon says, "Are you sure?"

The doctor chuckles softly and continues, "Absolutely. You're doing great considering your injuries. You've healed nicely and you're eating solid food. I don't see any reason why you can't continue to heal in your own bed."

"That would be amazing." I'm ready to get out of here. Even though I've only been aware of two days in the hospital, my body knows it's been here so much longer than that. And hospital food? Yuck!

My doctor takes several minutes to go over discharge instructions and aftercare. He writes me a prescription for pain medication that I probably won't even take but don't argue. Bottom line is that I'm to take it easy while my body continues to heal – I do still have two broken ribs after all. But the idea of going home, to Landon's apartment, is so enticing. Not to mention, I really need a proper shower and that's hard to get in the tiny shower stall this hospital bathroom has.

"Just a warning," the doctor starts before stepping toward the door. "The press is outside. We've kept them from coming into the hospital for the safety of our patients and staff. But once you're outside, you're fair game. You might want to call someone to come get you and take you home."

"No problem," Landon states with conviction and I wonder who he is going to call to come help us get out of here.

"It's been a pleasure to have you both here." Landon stands and takes my hand as the doctor walks toward the door. "But get the hell out of here and go home." We both watch as the doctor laughs.

"You hear him," Landon says. "Let's get you ready to go."

"Thank God. I'm so ready to go home." I admit. With the patience of a saint, Landon helps me to get dressed in the clothes he had hiding in a duffel bag this entire time. I hadn't even realized he had clothes here for me. Not that I should be surprised. He's so good at taking care of me. "I love you, Landon."

With one hand wrapped around my waist, holding me steady, he bends down and kisses me softly on the lips. It's not a deep kiss and I'm okay with that. This kiss is just as sweet and possessive as anything else. "I love you too, Kitten."

I watch, sitting on the edge of the bed after getting dressed and letting Landon put my shoes on, as Landon types out a text message on his phone. He stares at the screen for several seconds and I assume he got the response he wanted as he places the phone back in his back pocket.

It's not two minutes later that a nurse walks in pushing a wheelchair. "You ready?" she asks as she bends over the lock the wheels on the chair.

"I'm ready." I practically jump off the bed with excitement as I lower myself into the wheelchair.

"It'll be a couple minutes before our ride gets here." Landon says, picking up the duffel bag and throwing it over his shoulder. He grabs the teddy bear off the bed and hands it to me to hold.

"That's fine. I'll take you downstairs and wait with you in the lobby until your ride gets here. I've been instructed not to take you outside until they're here though. Damned press. They'll run after anything they think will give them ratings and views."

We're sitting in the lobby ten minutes later when a black SUV with dark tinted windows pulls up right outside the door. "Ride's here," Landon announces, and I'm instantly confused. I've never seen that SUV before and have no idea who it could possibly be.

I watch, transfixed by the sight before me, as three large men get out of the SUV. But it's the fourth one that steps out of the front passenger seat that jumps my heart into an erratic, excited rhythm.

I watch, my mouth opened in awe, as the three men stand facing the crowd of journalists that have gathered outside the hospital entrance. Their arms are spread out to their sides as if creating a barricade of sorts.

But it's Steve that my eyes are locked on as he walks right into the hospital and kneels down in front of my wheelchair. The bright welcoming smile that I've come to love, the deep dimple peeking out beneath his walrus mustache. My very own Tom Selleck look-alike and the only other person, besides Landon, that I'd ever consider a close friend. "Steve," I whisper, too shocked still to find my voice.

"Emi," His smile gets impossible larger and more vibrant. "Are you ready to go home?"

Still unable to talk around the lump in my throat, I just nod my head.

"May I?" Steve asks, looking up at Landon who is standing next to me silently.

"Of course," Landon answers, nodding his head and smiling back at Steve.

Without another word, Steve stands while placing one arm behind my shoulders and the other below my knees. He picks me up as if I weigh nothing and cradles me against his chest. "I can walk. You know?" I chastise as he walks with me toward the doors.

"I know." He squeezes me a little tighter against his chest and chuckles softly. He walks with me swiftly to the SUV where the back passenger door is already standing open and waiting for us. Leaning into the vehicle, he plants me softly into the backseat and helps me to buckle my seatbelt. Once I'm seated, everyone else climbs in around me – two of the huge men climb into the third row, one behind the driver's seat, Steve in the front passenger seat, and Landon beside me.

The drive to the apartment is quiet as I watch the city pass us by through the passenger window. My teddy bear is clutched tightly to my chest and Landon has a hand resting on my thigh as if to let me know he's still there.

This is my life now. I've gone from being the invisible small-town girl that didn't have a way of escaping, to being the one that has people that care about her.

Yeah. This is the life that I want to live from here on out.

Chapter
THIRTY-TWO

LANDON

I'VE HAD EMI ALL TO myself for a week. I know she's getting stir crazy and wants to get out of the apartment, but I've been hesitant to take her out anywhere.

When we left the hospital a week ago, the press was surrounding the hospital entrance. Melodee's trial has been dragging on, especially after we had more charges to put against her with the attempted murder of Emilee, and the press has since moved to standing outside of our apartment building. At this point, I'm going to need to take Emi away from here, to some private island somewhere, just to give her enough peace to finish healing.

She's doing better, her ribs are mostly healed, and the stitches have been removed from her head. She still has a cast on her arm and ankle, but they should be able to come off in the next couple of weeks. We did go in a couple days ago though and have the one on her ankle switched to a walking cast, so she isn't hobbling around anymore on crutches. The downside is, I don't have a good excuse to carry her around now. I'll admit, I really enjoyed having her at my mercy and being able to carry her from room to room inside the apartment. But I know she missed her independence.

"It looks like they're finally giving up," Emi calls out from the floor-to-ceiling windows in the living room.

Stepping up beside her and placing my hand on the small of her back, I look down to the street twelve stories below where the press vans are pulling away from the curb. "Thank God."

"I'm sorry they stuck around for so long. I know it's been a pain to get to and from the office the last couple of days."

Okay, so it was a pain to push my way through the press. Somehow, they found out who I was after they connected Charlie, Emi, and myself together. They found my firm and camped outside the building there too. "You don't have to apologize for that. It's not your fault that there are so many cockroaches out there looking for a story."

"I offered to give them a statement if it would have helped them to go away."

"No," I gently turn her around to face me and place my hands on her shoulders. "Santos said it was a bad idea. They've only been stalking us because the trial against Melodee is closed to the public and the press can't get in. But he's expecting a verdict to be read sometime in the next day or so. They'll have their story when it is, and they'll leave us alone."

"Well, it looks like most of them are leaving now. Maybe someone else did something stupid and they want to chase it for a while."

"Could we get so lucky?" I laugh. It will be nice, however, to be able to go back outside without being mobbed by the press. As much as I don't mind it when Emi aims a camera in my direction, I've grown tired of having all these strangers flashing their pictures of me as I'm going to and from work. Thankfully, the tenants in the building here have agreed to keeping all entrances locked day and night. We've had two people working the desk since Emi got home from the hospital just to help when needed and make sure no one sneaks in. It was Steve's suggestion and everyone else was instantly in agreement.

I should be jealous of the friendship between Emi and Steve, but I'm not. She already explained to me how she sees him as the grandfather that she never had, and I know Steve feels the same. He and his wife never had children together, but he's always treated everyone he meets as part of his family.

"So," Emi starts as she wraps her arms around my neck. "I was thinking maybe I could go sit with Steve while you go to work today."

"Absolutely not!" I argue.

She pulls back and tilts her head to the side. "What? Why not?"

Guilt washes over me and my brows pinch together nervously. "Emi." My eyes close as I cradle her face in my hands. "You're still healing. And there are still cockroaches crawling around outside the building."

"They're outside, Landon. I'll still be safely contained behind the glass with Steve."

"That won't stop them from taking pictures of you through the windows."

J.A. Smith

She blinks at me innocently and I have to bite my lips between my teeth to keep from laughing at her cuteness. "I'm not ashamed of what happened to me, Landon."

My brows furrow, now in confusion. "I never said you were."

"I won't give them a statement because you and Officer Santos convinced me it was a bad idea. But I'm not going to hide forever. I'm ready to get back to my life. I was thinking of camping out in the lobby and taking some pictures of Steve."

"Baby, I don't want you to have to hide either. I just want you to finish healing. And I want you to be safe."

"I am safe. Have you not noticed the size of the men you have working downstairs. I mean, my God. You'd think you were royalty or something with the amount of muscle you have watching over this place."

"That wasn't the intent. Actually, Steve hired most of the guys we have working here. Says it makes him feel better knowing the people living in this building are well protected if anything happens."

"My point exactly. I'm perfectly safe here, even if they can take pictures of me through the windows. Besides, I'm a photographer myself so who am I to tell someone they can't take a picture?"

I groan wordlessly but eventually relent. "Fine."

Emi reaches up and brushes her palm down the side of my face in a soothing gesture. I'll never understand the size of this woman's heart. I mean, she's the one that almost died and here she is soothing me. I place my hand over hers and hold it against my jaw.

"Landon," she starts before resting her forehead against my chest. "You don't need to worry about me all the time. I promise, I'm safe here and I'm not going outside."

"You've been through so much, Emi. And I'm not just talking about the last few weeks. I'm talking about even before I met you. You deserve so much more than the hand you've been dealt."

"We learn from our pasts, Landon. The good and the bad. We learn who to trust and who not to."

"You can trust me."

"I know I can," she admits. "I'm not saying my life is always Unicorn farts and rainbow sprinkles. But I have something now that I haven't had in a long time."

"What's that?" I ask her while running my hand down her back.

"Love," she breathes softly. "I have love. That's something I haven't had in a long time. Not since my mother died. That's something that helps me be able to face anything. Love makes the hard days seem bearable and the good days that much brighter. It kept me alive while I waited for you to find me. It gives me something to fight for every single day."

"You're right." Bending down, I kiss the top of Emi's head softly. "I do love you. And I trust you to stay safe. So, I'll deal with you downstairs with Steve today. I might not like the idea of those cockroaches stalking you, but I'll get over it."

"Thank you."

"You're welcome. But just know that I have no intention of working more than a few hours today. I don't have an assistant anymore, so I have a ton of emails I need to get through and meetings to schedule myself. Then I'm coming home."

"Okay."

"I'll see you in a few hours." She stands on her tiptoes and kisses me softly before walking me to the door. I haven't even gotten to work yet and I'm already ready to be back home. This is going to be a long few hours of work.

"ARE YOU WITH EMILEE right now?" Santos asks through the Bluetooth in my car.

"Not yet," I answer. "I'm on my way home from the office."

"How long until you get there?"

"I'm about five minutes out. Why? What's going on?" I don't know whether I need to be worried or not, but I press my foot down harder on the accelerator just in case something has happened that I don't know about.

"You should have plenty of time. When you get home, turn the TV on. Channel seven."

"What? Why?" I ask, feeling a little more relieved that it isn't something life threatening.

"The trial's over." He pauses and I want to reach through the phone and strangle him. "They're going to be airing the story on the news in about ten minutes. I think you'll be pleased with the outcome."

"Why don't you just tell me?"

"Nah." He chuckles. "I think you'll want to be there when Emilee hears it. You can call me afterward if you want to."

"Thank you for the heads up." I breathe a sigh of relief that this is almost over. Santos doesn't say anything more before disconnecting the call. I dictate a text to Emi to see if she's still in the lobby or already back at the apartment as I pull into the garage below the building. She texts back immediately that she just got upstairs so I take the elevator straight up to the twelfth floor.

As soon as I step off the elevator, Emi is standing in the doorway to the apartment looking innocent as ever. "Hey, you," she says as I step closer and wrap my hands around her small waist.

"Hi," I respond before bending down and placing a kiss on her soft lips. "How was the rest of your morning?"

"It was great. I got some really good photos of Steve and Adam. The photographers outside only took a couple pictures of me through the windows but then they left in a hurry just before noon."

"That's really good, Kitten. I can't wait to see the pictures that you took today." She smiles and tilts her head back, locking her brilliant blue eyes on mine. Bending closer, I kiss her and she opens her mouth immediately. She tries to deepen the kiss but I pull back – she isn't healed enough for anything more just yet. I know she's going to hate it, but I can't let her go any further.

"Landon," she gasps as I take a step back from her, watching her arms drop to her sides.

"Come on." Reaching out, I grab her hand and pull her toward the sofa.

"What are you doing?" Giggling, she follows behind me with an adorable skip to her step.

"There's something we need to see." Leading her the rest of the way to the sofa, I help her sit carefully so she doesn't hurt her ribs. "Santos called me this afternoon while I was on my way home."

"Oh."

"Yeah, oh." Laughing, I turn on the television and flip through the channels until I get to the right one. The news is already on, so I hope we haven't missed it already.

"Did he tell you what this is about?" she asks nervously, her bottom lip pulled tightly between her teeth.

"No. But he said we might be happy about it."

"So," the voice on the TV begins as I turn up the volume. "You can expect more rain in the coming days along with rising temperatures and humidity."

We both turn our attention to the television when the reporter begins her story while standing in front of the courthouse. Neither of us speak while we watch…

"…Melodee Carson has been charged and convicted of being an accessory before the fact to kidnapping. Her phone records indicate multiple texts and phone calls to Amber Dickson regarding the potential abduction of Emilee Jackson which did occur on Friday, May 13, 2022. She has been charged $50,000 in fines and sentenced to four years in state prison. Additionally, she has been convicted and charged with conspiracy to commit a homicide. There was sufficient evidence gathered at the defendant's address to indicate that a premeditated homicide was to take place upon arrival at said residence. In addition to the above-mentioned charges, she has also been charged $250,000 in fines and sentenced to an additional twenty-five years in state prison. The sentences are to be served consecutively with no possibility of parole in the first fifteen years…"

"Holy shit," Emi breathes as she collapses against the back of the sofa. "It's over."

"It's over," I say in agreement. A sense of calm that I hardly recognize washes over me – though I'm not entirely sure how I should feel about it. Pulling my knee up on the couch, I turn to face Emi and see a tear rolling down her cheek. Cupping her face in my palm, I wipe away the tear with my thumb. "Don't cry, Kitten."

"I can't believe it's really over." She inhales deeply and I carefully pull her into my lap and cradle her head against my chest, my chin resting on her head. "I'm sorry." She gasps. "I don't know why I'm crying."

"It's okay," I whisper as my hand trails circles along her back. "You've been through hell, baby. It's okay to just let it all out now. You've been strong for so long." Our bodies rock slowly side to side as I listen to her quietly sobbing against my chest. "You're the strongest woman I know. My fierce little kitten. You've had to be to put up with all the shit that you've had to put up with. But you don't have to be strong right now. I'll be strong enough for both of us. Me and you, baby. From here on out."

Epilogue

EMILEE

SIX MONTHS AGO, MELODEE was sentenced to twenty-five years in state prison for her involvement in my kidnapping and attempted murder. The press had left me alone after that, but that didn't stop me from giving a statement. Of course, we talked to Santos and got a lawyer before making a statement to the press. We wanted to make sure our bases were covered first. But I still wanted my side of the story to be told.

Ian Santos, who I'm surprised I didn't already know considering he's from the same town I grew up and spent most of my life in, has actually become a good friend of both Landon and myself. Turns out, he's a pretty cool guy. He and Landon are the same age but weren't close growing up since Santos was apparently more of a jock whereas Landon was a womanizer and troublemaker – I still have a hard time imagining that. It makes me wonder if things would have been different if I had gotten to know Santos a few years ago. Not that I would change anything with Landon. I've never been happier.

Landon finally hired a new assistant. He didn't want to, of course, but I convinced him that he needed to bite the bullet. Shaun, the man he hired last week, started at the beginning of the week. I stayed with him for two days training him as best I could before making my exit. I filled in the best I could while I was there, even though I've never worked a desk job before. I'm a quick learner so I picked it up pretty quickly, but it just wasn't what I wanted to do with my life.

I thought I wanted to go back to school and make a career of traveling and photography. Things have changed quite a bit though. Turns out, I'm pretty good at social media marketing. When I wasn't working at the office, keeping up with all the emails and phone calls that come through Landon's office, I was creating and maintaining a social media account for Strong Designs. All the pictures that I've taken of Landon's designs and completed buildings around the city are not only hanging all over his office, but they're all over the internet now too.

It might have taken me a while to learn all the different social media platforms available, but it turns out that it isn't much different than my photo editing software when it comes to creating creative content and posts. I've picked up a few other freelance marketing and photography gigs around the city and have done fairly well. And – get this – I'm an official business now.

As of this morning, I am the proud owner of Elegant Exposures. I get to make my own hours and currently work from home. We took the bed out of the guestroom and filled the space with more office furniture than I'll ever need. I get the best of both worlds – I get to go into businesses and take pictures of their products, their location, their happy customers, and post them on social media. I get creative freedom on the content and posts and even get free products from a few of my clients. They pay me well to help drive online sales and bring people into their shops. It's a lot of work, but I'm enjoying doing it.

Landon says he's going to design me a storefront to work out of at some point but I'm putting that off until I get big enough to have to hire employees. For now, I only have six clients, not including Strong Designs, but I'll get there eventually. I'm not in any hurry to expand my business since I'm just getting it started.

Landon is supposed to be coming home from work early this afternoon so we can go to Independence. I didn't think I would ever want to set foot back in that little timeless town, but I had no choice after Charlie died. It turns out, my mother's house was actually mine after she died. Of course, I had no desire to keep it – there were too many bad memories there – so Landon hired a crew to clean it out and do some repairs. He even bought a new porch swing to hang on the newly replaced porch. We contacted Rachel and had her take pictures of it and put it on the market for us. It sold faster than I thought it would to a young, newly married couple and I was happy to see it go.

We've made it a point to stop into the diner every time we've been to town just so we could have Ralph's famous meatloaf. Today, I'm going to take photos of the diner and start a social media page for Ralph. He hasn't asked me to, of course, but I'm going to do it anyway. I feel like it's something that I need to do considering the history I have at the diner. Freedom Diner has always been a big part of my life between my mom working there, and then myself when I got older. It'll always have a special place in my heart.

"I'm home, Kitten." I hear the front door open and close. "Where are you?"

"I'm in here!" I call out from my office where I'm editing the photos I took while I was out this morning.

"Mmm," Landon starts as he wraps an arm around my shoulder from behind and kisses the top of my head. "Those look really good, Kitten." The photos on my laptop are of a local florist that's run by a mother and daughter. It's a cute little shop set in the middle of downtown, a chic little cottage set in the middle of several large steel and glass buildings. It's hard to miss when you're driving through the city, the little pop of blue and purple vinyl siding is a stark contrast against the shiny silver and reflective glass buildings. I took several photos of the shop itself to edit and post in both color and black and white.

"Thank you." Closing out of the editing software, I make sure my work is saved and close the lid to the laptop. Landon steps back as I stand and I reach up and wrap my arms around his neck, pulling him down for a kiss. "Are you ready?"

"I am." Smiling, he brushes a stray hair away from my forehead. "Do you want to drive?"

"Sure." As much as I hated driving for longer trips before, I don't like being a passenger anymore after that day with Charlie and Amber. Even sitting in the front passenger seat, I get nervous now when I can feel the world around me moving and not being in control myself. My therapist says it's a form of PTSD because of the kidnapping and has given me some techniques to deal with it, but Landon still gives me the option of driving now. "We'll take my car."

"How did I know you were going to say that?" he asks with mock agitation at the idea of taking my car, I know he secretly enjoys it. He bought me the car, despite how much I tried to talk him out of it, two weeks after I got out of the hospital. It's a Mercedes GLE and it's fully loaded with all the extras and safety features. Compared to his car, mine might as well be a tank, but I love it.

He grabs my hand, twining our fingers together as he leads me through the apartment. He carries my camera bag slung over his shoulder and I grab my keys from the table by the door on the way out.

The drive to Independence is long and quiet. Neither of us say anything to the other, Landon keeps his head turned out the passenger window watching the scenery passing by. Both my hands stay on the wheel, my concentration staying on the road ahead of me.

Freedom Diner is mostly empty when we arrive, which is not surprising considering it's the middle of the afternoon and it won't have another rush of people until closer to dinner time. Stepping out of the car, Landon hands me the camera bag and I get straight to work taking photos of the outside of the dinner. The afternoon lighting is perfect against the faded, white-washed brick of the building. Through the window, I get a few candid shots of the unfamiliar waitresses standing at the counter rolling silverware, smiling innocently and laughing during a silent conversation between them.

Stepping through the door, I turn and watch as Landon follows silently behind me. Smiling to myself, I remember the first time I saw him walk through those same doors. This is very similar, almost déjà vu, as he steps inside wearing the broken suit he left wearing for work this morning. Lowering my gaze to the floor, I feel the heat in my cheeks at the memory of that first encounter. How I had been instantly attracted to him but thought he would never see me as anything other than invisible. He hadn't belonged here, despite having grown up here himself – but I didn't know that then. On that first day he'd wandered through those doors, I just thought he was a random stranger that was passing through town.

Lifting the view finder of my camera to my eye, I take a few pictures of Landon walking through the diner. These shots are for me. He smiles and winks at me when he turns his head and catches me taking his picture. He's gotten used to me focusing my photographic attention on him lately, not faulting my incessant need to capture every memory with him possible. I lost so many of my memories over the years, photographs chronicling my youth and those of my mother, and I have no interest in losing any more.

"Just have a seat anywhere," one of the waitresses announces, not looking up from her silverware rolling chore. "I'll be right with you."

Cocking his head to the side, Landon lifts a single brow in question as he raises a hand to lead me toward a booth against the wall. Turning, I look at the booth he motions toward, the same booth he sat in each time he'd come to the diner so long ago. The same booth I had joined him at for lunch twice. "Shall we?" he asks, placing a hand softly against my lower back and leading me to the cracked and peeling vinyl booth.

Keeping one eye on Landon, I see the waitress approach our table out of the corner of my eye. "What can I get you today?" she asks as she sets two glasses of water on the table.

"Meatloaf," Landon answers easily. "We'll both have the meatloaf."

"Great choice," she responds. It's an easy enough order, and probably often enough too, that she doesn't bother writing it down on her notepad. "I'll be back in a few minutes."

"Meatloaf?" I ask with a giggle.

"Hell yeah," he responds. "It's the best."

"Of course, it is."

"Best in town," he chuckles, the sound rumbling through his chest and sending a chill down my spine.

"Probably the entire county."

"Maybe you should do a feature on it for social media," he suggests and it's actually not a bad idea.

"Here you go," the waitress sets a plate down in front of each of us and I've already got my camera in hand to take a picture of the meal. I never thought I'd be one of those influencers that takes more photos of food than she eats, but then I have no intention of letting this delicacy go to waste.

"There have been a lot of memories made over this meatloaf, I think," Landon states as he cuts off a piece of his buttery meat with his fork. "My grandfather loved the meatloaf here. He used to bring me here when I was younger, without telling my grandmother of course."

Giggling softly, I cut off my own piece of the delectable meat and take a bite.

"When I pulled up to this diner almost a year ago, it was the only thing on my mind. As much as I didn't want to be back in this town, I couldn't pass up a chance to have this meatloaf again."

I watch as he chews another bite before swallowing. Looking over his shoulder, I see Ralph watching us from the window to the kitchen, a smile crinkling the tan skin around his eyes. Setting my fork down on the table, I move my gaze back to Landon and reach across the table to place my hand over his. The bell over the door dings indicating another hungry patron entering the small diner, but I don't take my eyes away from Landon.

"It wasn't the meatloaf that brought me back the next day." One corner of his mouth tips up in a half smile. "Or the day after that. It was you."

Remaining silent, I allow a single tear to slip down my cheek.

Lifting his free hand, Landon reaches across the table and swipes the tear away with his thumb. "I never realized how many great memories started here, in this timeless town or this tiny diner."

My lungs freeze, taking away my ability to breathe, as Landon stands and walks around the table to stand beside me. I watch, completely frozen, as he sinks down to his knee before taking one of my hands between both of his and squeezing tightly.

"What's one more memory, right? And what better place to make that memory than right here, where it all started."

I swallow around the lump in my throat and feel the warmth as more tears begin to run down my cheeks.

"I love you, Emi. So much. You may have thought you were invisible, but I've always seen you. You appeared like a beacon of hope, shining so brightly that your image is burned into my very soul. There's no part of me that will ever exist without you."

I continue to stare, motionless and barely breathing, as he reaches one hand into his pocket.

"Marry me, Emi. Build a life with me. Say you'll be mine forever."

My voice has evaded me, the tight lump in my throat blocking my ability to make noise. Nodding my head quickly, I mouth the word *yes* soundlessly. Only then do I move my gaze down to my hand to see Landon placing the most beautiful, antique, rose-gold engagement ring on my finger. It's a perfect fit.

Standing, Landon scoops me out of the booth, wrapping his arms tightly around my waist and lifting my feet off the floor. He spins me around twice while holding me against his chest before lowering me to the floor and crashing his mouth against mine. I open immediately, allowing him to direct and deepen the kiss to the sound of applause all around us.

When he breaks away, he spins me around to see where the clapping is coming from. Ralph has come out of the kitchen and is standing behind the counter with both waitresses, a huge smile spread across his face. It's only then that I see Office Santos sitting at the counter in uniform facing us.

"She said yes!" Landon exclaims.

"Oh, Landon," I gasp as I finally get a good look at the ring on my finger. "It's beautiful."

He grabs my left hand and kisses my knuckles softly. "It was my grandmother's." He rolls the ring back and forth on my finger with his thumb. "She gave this to me after my grandfather passed away. She told me to make sure that I gave it to the one person that puts my soul back together. The one that holds all the pieces of my heart. I never understood what she meant until I met you."

Lifting my free hand, I cup his cheek, relishing in the softness of his beard brushing against my palm. "I love you."

"Always and forever," he whispers in response.

Dear READER

I hope you enjoyed reading about Emilee as much as I enjoyed writing about her even though this wasn't the book that I had originally set out to write. If you've read any of my other books, you were probably hoping for a spin-off from the *Metro Love Stories*, which is exactly what I had started to write. But Emilee had other ideas. She spoke so loudly to me that I couldn't ignore her anymore.

Let me tell you a little bit about my writing process. Do you know the difference between a pantser and a plotter? A pantser doesn't outline their books. They literally just sit down and start to write and see where the story takes them. A plotter, however, outlines everything and follows it completely during the writing process. Plotters spend time with character development and world building. They know where the story starts, every little thing that happens along the way, and how the story ends. I'm a plotter, most of the time. I spend so much time outlining my stories from beginning to end that all I have to do is follow the outline and let the words put themselves together.

So, what does that mean about Emilee? Guys, I started writing a spin-off book from my *Metro Love Stories* series. I really did. It's completely outlined and ready to get to 'putting it together'. But one day, I sat down at my laptop, and I started writing. It started as an exercise in 'blind writing' and ended in a book. Emilee was born at the tips of my fingers with a story to tell. I was just her vessel to get it out to the world.

What does that mean going forward? Well, I have several books already being outlined as we speak (my brain doesn't stop thinking of more ideas). Will I do another pantser style book again? Honestly, probably not. This was the single most frustrating experience of my entire life. Did it take me a year to bring out another book? Yes. Yes, it did.

I'm excited to get started on the next book I have outlined and ready to go. If you haven't read the *Metro Love Stories* books, I'd recommend you do that. The next book is going to feature a character that made her appearance in Cypress' book, *The Story of Her Redemption.*

See you again soon!

About
THE AUTHOR

J.A. Smith is a new author living in Virginia with her husband, son, and two overactive Pomeranians. She has found a balance between working a full-time job with reading an obsessive amount of romance novels while writing her heart-shattering stories to share with the masses. Granted, this balance includes copious amounts of caffeine and aspirin.

Also by
J.A. SMITH

The Story of Her Life

J.A. SMITH

Julie is a young reporter looking for her big break in an effort to advance her career. In her search of the story that will get her front-page recognition, she may be biting off more than she can chew. Devan is a freelance photographer that takes pennies for his pictures just for a chance to see Julie again. When she gets too close to a story, can he be there in time to save her from the danger she uncovers? Will they realize together that even a phoenix has to burn in order to rise from the ashes?

The Story Of Her Life is a full-length standalone novel with no cliffhanger and a guaranteed HEA.

Trigger Warning: The Story Of Her Life includes rough and sometimes intense scenes. If such material offends you, please don't buy this book.

J.A. Smith

Her Story of Survival

J.A. SMITH

Marie has been hiding in plain sight for the last four years. But like a puzzle that has been put together and torn apart numerous times, she feels like there are pieces missing. But she's safe. She got out. She survived.

Matt has built something of himself and is proud to be the opposite of his father. He's a caring, humble business owner that still struggles with the darkness of his past. until a woman with pink hair wearing a bright yellow dress brings a burst of color into his life.

When Marie's past becomes her present, she relies on the strength of her friends and loved ones to see her through.

Trigger warning: Her Story of Survival includes rough and sometimes intense scenes including domestic abuse.

The Story of Her Redemption

J.A. SMITH

Cypress grew up as a nomad. Everything she knows of life, she learned inside the confines of an Airstream camper while traveling the country from one street fair to another. As an adult, Cypress left her gypsy life behind to plant her roots and open a boutique. But she has never been able to stop looking over her shoulder as her past continues to haunt her.

Chris is a missing-person detective that has dedicated his career to saving women from fates worse than Hell. When a bohemian gypsy flutters into his life, he learns that separating his work from his personal life isn't always as easy as one would like.

Parts of Cypress' past sneak out of the shadows when they're least expected. Pieces of her puzzle start to come together in ways neither one of them ever imagined. Will Chris be able to help Cypress find redemption from her past?

Trigger warning: The Story of Her Redemption includes rough and sometimes intense scenes including psychological and emotional abuse and voyeurism.

Printed in June 2023
by Rotomail Italia S.p.A., Vignate (MI) - Italy